Guardian of the Stones

VICTORIA OSBORNE-BROAD

Book two of the Jewels of the Rainbow trilogy

Guardian of the Stones
by Victoria Osborne-Broad
© Victoria Osborne-Broad 2019

Paperback ISBN: 978-1-9160616-0-6
Ebook ISBN: 978-1-9160616-1-3

First published in 2019
Publication support
TJ INK
tjink.co.uk
Printed and bound in Great Britain by
TJ International, Padstow, Cornwall

For David

Contents list

Chapter One

Monday 8th September 2014

The day that Seona's letter arrived changed Gerry's life. For weeks she'd been existing rather than living, and she assumed that would go on for ever. She'd lost everything that mattered to her, above all Justin, who'd bewitched and then deceived her. Now he was dead and she would never see him again. And she had to cope without her great-aunt Seona, her confidante and adviser, who had died after Gerry left home for Uni, three years earlier.

It was Monday morning and Gerry's day off. She was standing in the kitchen, holding a mug of coffee, when she heard the sound of tyres on the drive. Looking out of the window she saw the postman's red van stopping outside the house. He was a smiling, middle-aged man who wore shorts in all weathers. Most days he climbed out of his van, strode into the courtyard, pushed the post through the letterbox and was off, with a cheery wave if he saw Gerry, or Claudia, her landlady, at one of the kitchen windows. Today, however, he rang the bell. Gerry put down her mug and went to the door with a sudden, jolting memory of a small red car juddering to a stop where the post van was standing now. A memory of Monica Fraser, Justin's girlfriend, banging on the door to shock Gerry and Claudia with the news of Justin's violent death.

It must have been that memory which was making Gerry's heart thump as she opened the door. The postman was holding a yellow padded bag with a Scottish postmark. Gerry recognised her brother Bill's handwriting. That was odd, as it wasn't her birthday, and Bill rarely even emailed her. It was addressed to Ms. Gerralda Hamilton.

'Morning,' the postman said cheerfully. 'This one needs signing for.'

Gerry wrote her name with the little pointed plastic stick on the screen pad which the postman held out. She took the package and felt a distinct shock, as if it was alive, or charged with electricity.

'Thanks,' she replied, adding, 'it's only my family who call me Gerralda.'

But that wasn't true. She'd been called Gerralda in the past, by the Bees and the Makers. And Justin had called her Gerralda. No. She mustn't think about any of that.

Gerry watched the red van turn round and disappear up the lane. Then she slowly closed the kitchen door and, ignoring the half eaten piece of toast on a plate beside the kettle, walked through to the large conservatory, for once not even noticing the magnificent view across fields and slopes to Cornwall's north coast. She put the padded bag on the long table in the centre of the conservatory. Early autumn sunshine filled the room, creating an illusion of rainbow light round the bag.

Gerry fetched a pair of scissors and cut through the sticky brown tape which Bill had used to seal the package. Why should something from her brother be making her feel shaky? Once she'd got the tape off Gerry looked inside. She could see a large envelope and a letter. She took the letter out first and read it. After a paragraph of family news, Bill had written, "You remember the Fergusons, who bought Seona's house after she died? They came round in the spring with an envelope we must have missed when

2

we cleared the place. Said it had got wedged in the corner of a shelf in a dark cupboard in the spare room, something like that. It's got your name on it, and Ma kept it, thinking you'd be home in the summer, but you didn't come, so I'm sending it. I can't think how we didn't see it at the time, but here it is, and better late than never. Hope to see you soon."

A thump of guilt hit Gerry at the bit about not going home in the summer, but it was far outweighed by the wash of emotion as she put her hand on the envelope and slid it out of the padded bag into the light. The outside simply read "Gerralda Hamilton" in Seona's copperplate handwriting, which she hadn't seen for so long. It wasn't just a letter; there was something small, square and solid inside. Gerry wanted to read what her great-aunt had written before looking at whatever she'd sent, but could feel tears beginning even before she started reading the letter. To get a message from Seona now, when she'd been so miserable for so long, was unbelievably comforting, but it also brought back all the heartache Gerry had felt at Seona's death. Seona had died while Gerry was away at Uni in London and she hadn't even been able to say goodbye in person.

The letter looked to be disappointingly brief, and must have been written only days before Seona died, a few weeks after Gerry's eighteenth birthday. For that birthday, Seona had given her a gold chain with a Celtic design. Gerry hadn't taken the chain off since the day in June when she'd bought a blue stone from a Penzance market stall and been plunged into a world stranger than she could ever have imagined.

"My dearest Gerralda," the letter began, and again Gerry felt the push of tears under her eyelids as she read. The handwriting was still quite firm, but Gerry knew it so well that she could see a slight shake in places. The letter began, "I will do all that lies within my power to ensure that this will reach you at the right time. If I succeed then you will understand. If I do not, then please keep the enclosed until you should need it. I promise that you will know when that is. Take the greatest care of yourself, for my sake as well as your own." The letter ended, "My last thoughts will be of you. I would beg you to wear this at all times, and if that is sometimes not possible then keep it on the gold neck chain I gave you on your last birthday. Do this for my sake, and may the Goddess protect you."

This last was so unexpected that Gerry cried out, yet she felt that somehow she should have known. Seona, with her cats and her herbs and her spinning wheel, her understanding of the powers of the mind and her love of Celtic mythology, would of course have been familiar with the traditions of the Goddess. It was Gerry who'd been ignorant of them till this summer. She still knew next to nothing.

The letter ended simply, "Your loving Seona".

Hardly daring to breathe, Gerry slipped her hand back inside the envelope and drew out "the enclosed". It was wrapped in brown paper, and to Gerry's disbelieving fingers it felt warm and alive. She tore off the paper and found a small dark blue box with the name of an Oban jeweller on the lid. She pressed the catch gently and opened the box, almost afraid of what might be inside. It seemed to her that tiny beams of light danced around it: red, orange, yellow, green, blue, indigo and purple. Then as Gerry saw what it contained she cried aloud again in incredulous wonder.

Inside the box, resting on dark blue velvet, was a ring with four small square stones set in gold on a plain gold band. Gerry knew them: red garnet, yellow topaz, blue sapphire and purple amethyst. The Jewels of the Rainbow. The jewels on the Chalice of the Rainbow, which she'd tried not to think about since giving it to the museum back in the summer. She slipped the ring onto the middle finger of her right hand, and found it was a perfect fit. Gerry held her hand up in the sunlight and four miniature shafts of coloured light danced into being, one from each gemstone: red, yellow, blue and violet. They wrapped themselves around her finger like the ribbons on a maypole. Then they overlapped, red and yellow making orange, yellow and blue for green, and blue and violet for indigo. The colours of the rainbow.

The ring felt as comforting as if Seona herself had enfolded Gerry in a warm hug, and she basked in it, feeling a smile spreading across her face. After the wretchedness she'd been living in for all these weeks, it was balm beyond belief to feel that sense of support and reassurance which she'd missed so much. She didn't understand how Seona could possibly have sent these particular jewels, and right now she wasn't even going to try to make sense of it. All she knew was that she felt protected for the first time since leaving her home in Lochallaig for the college in London.

But Seona, always practical, wouldn't have let her great-niece indulge in self-content for long. Nor, Gerry found, would her gift. The sparkling beams settled down and the minute rainbow wove itself neatly round the band of the ring, an unobtrusive little stream of colours which Gerry somehow knew no-one else would be able to see. She could feel it nudging at her mind, and reluctantly began to drop the barriers she'd put up after Justin's death. Gerry wanted to shy away, knowing that what she had to confront would be painful, but the prodding was insistent and wouldn't let her ignore it. She covered the ring from sight with her left hand, but that made no difference. It was still pushing at her. She had a sudden memory of Seona's last cat, a silver tabby, pressing her head against Gerry's ankles when she wanted her dinner. Soft and pretty as the cat looked, she was absolutely determined and would let nothing prevent her having her own way. This little Rainbow Ring seemed to possess the same qualities.

Gerry picked up the padded bag and replaced Bill's and Seona's letters inside, along with the empty jeweller's box. She took them up to her room and began to get ready to go out. There was a task she had put off for too long. It was time she went back to Truro, to the Royal Cornwall Museum. She would take her ring to visit the source of its power.

Gerry tried not to look at the ring as she drove eastwards up the A30; it was hard enough to concentrate on the traffic. The comfort she felt from the ring seemed to lessen as she got nearer to Truro. Instead Gerry became as nervous as she'd been earlier when the postman handed over Bill's letter. This was stupid. The Kelegel a'n gammneves, the Chalice of the Rainbow, was safe in the museum. Seeing it again ought to give her, what was it they called it, "closure".

By the time Gerry walked up the cobbled street running through the centre of Truro and turned into River Street, the ring had become completely unresponsive. Gerry had to push herself as far the museum building, her every step dragging. Once she reached it, however, she found herself drawn up the path and the steps, as she'd once been pulled towards the Kelegel in its hiding place behind the stone in the fogou, the cave on the hilltop. Gerry didn't need to consult a floor plan or ask where they kept items from 6th or 7th century Cornwall. She knew where to go.

She approached the display cabinet which held the Kelegel confined behind the security glass on a shelf by itself. Back in the summer Gerry had gone through all the formalities required to hand over a piece of treasure to the museum, and had then tried to put it behind her. She was longing to see the Chalice again, yet wary too. Then as Gerry took in what she was looking at, she went cold. She had gifted the museum with a beautiful but inert piece of Cornish history. It had become an historical object and nothing more. Gerry had watched, helpless, on the day in the past when the Kelegel's powers were destroyed, and she had held the lifeless cup in her own hands afterwards. Furthermore, centuries beyond their own time, the Jewels of the Rainbow, the Tegennow a'n gammneves, would inevitably have lost all their powers. Gerry had already seen that they could do nothing in an age that was not theirs, that they had not lived through.

But the chalice in front of her now was alive. It was impossible, but Gerry knew she was not mistaken. Even under the artificial lighting she could feel the energy pulsing within the four great gemstones in their rich colours, a force that sunlight would release in full. It was so strong that she could hardly believe the sightseers wandering unconcerned around the other exhibits in the gallery were unaware of it. Gerry knew then that the stones had called her. Was this what Seona had meant when she wrote, "I will do all that lies within my power to ensure that this will reach you at the right time"? What was happening here?

In sudden panic, Gerry turned and ran, heedless of how the other visitors in the gallery were staring at her, till she stood panting on the doorstep of the granite-fronted building. Then as her gaze rested blankly on the people on the opposite pavement, what she saw there turned her fear and confusion to utter terror. It was hardly a conscious action to pull out her phone, hit a name and leave a message. Instinct drove her to the one person who might understand.

'Debs, it's Gerry. Please tell me what time you're finishing work today and where we can meet. I've got to talk to you.'

Gerry had started work at the Cornish Studies library in Redruth the day after giving away the chalice, and had never gone back to the Penzance branch. She hadn't kept in touch with anyone from the Penzance library, not even Debbie, her best friend. It had all been part of trying to put the events around the Chalice out of her mind. Debbie was the only person Gerry knew who wouldn't reproach her for ignoring her for weeks, then phoning out of the blue when she needed her.

The two young women sat by the sea front in Penzance, in the old Volvo estate car that Gerry had inherited from Seona. Until the ring arrived, the car had been the only thing of Seona's that Gerry owned, and she always felt a connection with her great-aunt when sitting in it. Along the front, the long line of cheerful flags which had flapped in the breeze high above the railings all through the summer had disappeared along with the holidaymakers. A few teenagers, outdoor jackets over their school uniforms, were leaning against the railings. The tide was in and the first strong wind of the autumn was whipping up waves across the bay. One girl leaned out, waiting for the slap of salt water across her face. When it came, she screamed with laughter and shook her wet hair at her friends.

Gerry had been desperate to talk to Debbie, but now she hardly knew where to begin. She touched her ring absently; it was being quietly inconspicuous.

'Let's go and sit on the wall,' Gerry suggested, hoping the fresh air would help. Debbie agreed, and they got out of the car and sat on the low stone wall which separated the upper pavement by the road from the lower one. The latter, Penzance's promenade, was much broader, running between the wall and the railings above the beach. As her friend was still silent, Debbie began instead.

'Gerry, I'm here because you said you wanted to talk. That's all right, but if you've changed your mind, I ought to be getting home.'

'I'm sorry.' Gerry looked absently at a seagull which was moving along the pavement, pausing to peck at a piece of litter blown against the wall. 'It's just – oh, it's harder to tell you than I thought it would be. Okay, I went to the museum today, up in Truro.'

'To see your chalice?' Debbie asked, then smiled at Gerry's expression. 'Don't look so surprised, I read about you in the "Cornishman". Unless you want to tell me another woman found some gold thing at Chapel Carn Brea the same time as you did? It had a name, didn't it – I remember you told me.'

'The Chalice of the Rainbow,' Gerry said. 'It had four big coloured gemstones round its sides, and it was made so that if the sunlight caught the stones at the right angle, you'd get the colours shining through and turning into a rainbow. It was like magic.'

It wasn't just "like", it actually was magic, but she could hardly explain that. Debbie wouldn't believe in magic.

'Yeah, I saw the picture in the paper,' Debbie said, 'but it just looked like a gold cup to me. But look, what's happened? You didn't phone me in a panic just to tell me you'd gone up to Truro.'

'No, though it was weird seeing the chalice there. I wanted to rip it out of the case and tell everyone it was mine.'

And then Gerry had felt the power coming out of it.

'You'll be lucky; it'd have burglar proof glass, I expect.' Debbie was as pragmatic as always. 'And then? That can't be all.'

The teenagers by the railings were laughing a lot. The sound carried over the pavement, and Gerry felt an odd longing for something she'd never had. Even in her schooldays, she'd never been that carefree. She'd always been too serious for her age.

'No, it wasn't all,' Gerry agreed. 'I came outside again

9

and there were people everywhere. And then – well, then I saw the Wasps.'

'Saw the wasps?' Debbie queried, surprised at this apparent change of subject. 'Did you get stung? Was that why you were in such a state when you rang me?'

Gerry wished it had been that simple. She shook her head.

'No, it's – well, you remember those men, the ones who came to your house with Justin? He called them the Wasps.'

It had been a typical joke of Justin's. The women who guarded the Chalice were the Bees, Gwenen in Cornish. Justin named his helpers the Wasps because bees can only sting once and then die, but wasps can sting repeatedly.

'I'm not likely to forget them, am I?' Debbie answered. 'Not after what happened. But that's weird. I thought I saw them in Penzance a few days ago, but they disappeared and I couldn't be sure.'

Gerry felt herself go cold again. She wanted to cry out, 'Why didn't you tell me?', but knew it was her own fault for not keeping in touch. Besides, Debbie could have no idea why it was quite impossible that the Wasps, Gohi in Cornish, should be back here.

Debbie was still speaking. 'It was scary seeing them again; I'd not seen them around since that day. Nor that Justin of yours either. I thought they'd gone back home. If they were from Eastern Europe, I mean.'

'No, I've not seen them either.' Gerry's heart was beginning to thump. She put her left hand across her ring again and felt a tiny touch of warmth. She tried to remember exactly how it had happened. 'I can't be totally certain it was them I saw in Truro. I was standing on the steps outside the front door of the museum.' She'd been trying to decide whether to go back in and look at the chalice again. After all, she'd gone all that way just to see it.

'The pavements were busy, you know what Truro's like, loads of people going in and out of the shops, coming over to the café or the bus stop. The Wasps were simply there in the crowd on the other side of the road.' Gerry's eyes had been drawn to them as her feet had been to the display case. 'They were looking at the museum; I don't know if they saw me or not. Then a bus pulled in at the stop by the entrance and hid them. By the time it moved off they'd vanished.'

Debbie's round face was puzzled. 'Gerry,' she said slowly, 'I can see it was a shock for you seeing them out of nowhere like that. I felt the same myself when I thought I saw them in Penzance. But you sounded scared out of your wits. I mean, I hope I never see them again. Or that Justin. He may look drop-dead gorgeous, at least if that's your type, but he's downright vicious.' She shivered. 'I still remember your broken rib. And that smile of his.'

Justin. Of course, Debbie didn't know. Gerry's throat went dry as she remembered. Her voice was husky as she said, 'Debs, Justin was killed. He died that same day.'

'Oh, Gerry.' Debbie reached out and took her friend's hand. 'I'm really sorry. What happened?'

Gerry looked at her helplessly, meaning to say she needn't feel sorry. Justin had been a selfish bastard, and cruel, as Debbie had reminded her. But he'd made her fall for him too deeply to forget him and move on.

'His body was found on a beach,' Gerry explained, 'on rocks at the foot of a cliff, with his head bashed in. They couldn't tell if he fell off, was pushed, or if he was already dead when he went over. But Justin made a lot of enemies. And Monica came and told me and Claudia all about it.'

'Monica?' Debbie looked surprised at the introduction of their spiteful fellow-worker into the conversation, then exclaimed, 'Hang on, didn't you tell me she was shagging

11

Justin too?'

'Yeah,' Gerry said. 'The police had called her in that morning to identify the body. Then she came storming up to Windhaven, marched in and actually accused Claudia of paying someone to kill Justin. Can you believe, she said Claudia was jealous of her. As if.'

Debbie was round-eyed. 'She said – what?? So what did your Claudia do?'

Gerry smiled. 'She was wonderful. Stood there totally calm, and just told Monica to get out and not come back.' And afterwards Claudia had gone to pieces, but that was private.

'But,' Gerry said, going back to the original question, 'that's why I panicked when I saw the Wasps. How could they come back without Justin? You see, they can't get here by themselves.'

'Why not? Are they illegal immigrants or something?'

If I told you, you wouldn't believe me. Gerry couldn't say so; that sentence just asked to be challenged. 'It's not that,' she said instead. 'The thing is, you know Justin was after the chalice and he was using the Wasps to help him; or he thought he was. But I was there when they saw it, and I tell you, they wanted it as much as Justin did. You haven't seen it with the gold dazzling in the sunlight, and the stones blazing with colour. Trust me, they'd kill for it.' *They were going to kill me when they found me watching them in the woods.* 'It's worth a bomb – pure gold, and those four huge jewels. And now,' she swallowed, 'now they're back here and without Justin to control them.'

Gerry had spoken so seriously that even if she didn't understand, Debbie didn't argue. This was the heart of what Gerry feared. There was just one thing more terrifying than the idea of the Wasps unfettered and on the loose, and that was her guess as to who might have sent them. She could think of only one person with the power to do it. Baranwen, Guardian of the Chalice. The clues ran in circles in Gerry's brain: the chalice

12

calling her from forty miles away, the pulsing of life within the stones, the Wasps at the museum. And Debbie had seen them in Penzance.

Gerry's fear was shifting to Debbie; she was beginning to look as scared as Gerry felt. With a catch in her voice, Debbie said, 'I don't want them after me again.'

That snapped Gerry out of her own dread. 'It won't be you they're after,' she said firmly. 'It would be me.' Then she added, 'And maybe Claudia.'

'Claudia?' This took Debbie completely by surprise. 'What's it got to do with Claudia? Though she was Justin's girlfriend, wasn't she?'

'That would depend on who killed him and why,' Gerry said. 'There's no way he died by accident.'

'Well, did you go to the police?' Debbie asked.

'No – what could I tell them?' Gerry replied. 'That I was sure it was murder, but I'd no idea who or why? Like they'd take me seriously.' Like she could tell them why she was so sure. 'Claudia's got troubles of her own right now,' she said, changing the subject. It was all getting too painful.

Debbie didn't try to push her back to the topic of Justin.

'So what's happened to Claudia, then?'

'She only told me about it the other day,' Gerry explained. 'I think she hoped it would sort itself out. It seemed a bit of a joke at first, but it's gone on and on and it stopped being funny a long time ago.' She gazed absently at the sea for a moment, then faced Debbie directly.

'You know Claudia owns an art gallery in Chapel Street?' Debbie nodded, her eyes fixed on Gerry's face. 'Well, apparently there's a man who's been going in there every morning and just watching her. He stays there for an hour or two. Seems it's been going on for weeks, but I mean, the gallery's open to the public, anyone can come in. She can't call the police, he's not breaking any law. She told me a few days ago; says it's driving her mad.' It had been the first crack in the wall of ice that Claudia had put around herself after Justin's death. 'She said it's like having a fly buzzing round you that you can't swat, but you can't concentrate on anything else. And she can't do a thing about it.'

Gerry remembered the look on Claudia's face. Since they'd heard about Justin's death and Gerry had seen Claudia's defences shatter, she'd felt oddly protective towards this woman who was, on the surface, so successful and sophisticated.

'If he was just, like, besotted with her she could deal with it,' Gerry said. 'The way she looks, she'll have had that before. Reading between the lines I'd say she feels it's more like he's staring at her in a "just you wait" kind of way.'

'Poor Claudia. Must be awful for her, going in each day and wondering when he's going to walk in.' Debbie was always quick to take the point. 'He's not following her home, is he?'

'Not that I know of.' The idea made Gerry's insides crawl. You wouldn't feel safe in your own home. Shit, you'd dread coming back at night. 'Deb, I wish you hadn't said that.'

'Sorry. But you've got to admit it's possible.' That was uncomfortable but horribly true. Then Debbie came out with a worse suggestion. 'You don't suppose they're connected, do you? I mean Claudia's stalker and these Wasps of yours? Have you ever seen the man?'

'No.' That idea was the most frightening of all the day's alarms. It could potentially bring the danger, whatever it was, right to the house. And there was danger, Gerry couldn't deceive herself about it; the whole day had been leading up to this. You'd dread coming home. In case something, no, someone, was waiting for you.

Chapter Two

Gerry's dreams had been ordinary for weeks. Disjointed, frustrating, illogical as dreams are, but no more so than normal. But the trip to the museum and the talk with Debbie had smashed the barricade she'd built between her daily life and the memories she'd been unable to face. So her dreams that night visited them all: a beach with jagged rocks below rearing cliffs, a broken body covered in blood. Baranwen the Guardian's terrible cry as the powers of the chalice were destroyed. The Kelegel locked in a glass case but throbbing with power; and the Gohi approaching the museum. They were distorted, as things always are in dreams, but close enough to the reality to wake her up in terror. Gerry switched on the bedside light and padded through to her bathroom to get a drink of water. It was three in the morning, but she was too scared to go back to sleep. She left the bedside light on, and sat on the bed, thinking. As the first panic receded, Gerry was left with the idea that there was something wrong about the Wasps as she'd seen them in Truro, standing on the pavement opposite the museum, and again in her dream just now. Then it came to her. It hadn't been so obvious when they'd been in the middle of a crowd on the busy shopping street of the city, but now she realised there had been only three of them. Talan, the neat, fair-haired craftsman, hadn't been there. Perhaps, being less bloodthirsty than the others, he'd simply tired of their actions.

Gerry was still too wound up to settle, and thought of going for a walk round the gardens in the hope that the fresh night air might calm her. She got as far as pulling on jeans and a sweater, then changed her mind. She sat down on the bed again without getting undressed, and closed her eyes, leaving her mind blank. And found herself somewhere she didn't expect to be, watching someone she didn't, at first, recognise.

It was a woman gathering plants by the edge of a stream. Her back was towards Gerry and she was kneeling down, seemingly oblivious to the damp grass staining the brown skirt of her gown. There was a soft woven basket lying on the ground nearby. As Gerry watched, the woman scrambled to her feet and moved towards it, one hand clutching a large bunch of leafy green stems.

As she turned, Gerry knew her. The braided hair with its reddish tinge and the plain gown had looked familiar, forewarning her, nudging memories of people and places. Then the woman saw the newcomer.

'Gerralda!' For a few seconds her face lit with a smile of pleased recognition, but this was immediately replaced by anger. Gerry was sorry; she'd preferred the spontaneous look of welcome.

'Meraud?'

Gerry checked her impulsive step forward. She could feel the damp through her slippers, and was glad of her warm clothes. At least Meraud hadn't accused her of dressing as a man, though the sweater and jeans were similar enough to tunic and hose. Then Gerry felt a slight throb from the gold chain about her neck, the one Seona had given her. That hadn't happened since the day the powers had been taken from the Jewels of the Rainbow.

'Meraud?' Gerry repeated, then added, 'I'm glad to see you again.'

Meraud had been the healer among the Gwenen, and had helped Gerry on her first visits to the past. Now, however, she looked at her visitor with pure hatred.

'And we all hoped never to see you again,' Meraud spat out. 'Since the day you brought those women to us to destroy the Tegennow a'n gammneves.'

It had been Baranwen, not Gerry, who'd brought the Makers of the Chalice to the Gwenen, and so caused her own downfall. It had been the very last thing Gerry had wanted. But if Meraud, who'd been kind to her, was this bitter, who else among the Bees would believe her?

'I thought I could never come back,' Gerry said. Lame as it was, it formed a beginning. 'I don't understand how I can be here now,' she went on, feeling her hands beginning to shake. 'I lost that gift when the Jewels lost their powers.'

Justin and Baranwen had each taken her back to the past for their own purposes. Then she had done it herself with the help of Seona's gold chain. But that had been lifeless since the day the chalice had lost its power. So if the Kelegel truly was restored, had the chain regained its own power too?

A slight breeze moved to ruffle the grasses and lift the water of the stream into ripples. Some small furry animal slipped from its hole in the bank into the water with the gentlest of splashes. Two willows grew by the edge here, trailing their soft branches in the stream. The breeze took a handful of the fading yellow leaves and shook them out to drift over the surface of the stream.

Gerry looked with diminishing hope at Meraud who stood unmoving, her plants forgotten in her hand.

'How can you expect me to believe anything you say?' the healer burst out at last. 'You gave us evasions and half-truths, then claimed to come from another time, of all things.' She shook her head. 'Are you here to bring us more disaster? If there is anything still left you can do to hurt us.'

Gerry gathered her courage, what little she could. 'Meraud, I can see you don't trust me,' she began. That was the understatement to beat all understatements. 'Please, though, can you at least tell me something? Have you seen anything of Baranwen, since?' Since that day.

Meraud looked surprised, which was a very slight improvement.

'She? No, she left,' she said. 'Disappeared the same evening. No-one has seen, heard from or even heard of her since.'

The Goddess help us all, Gerry thought. It looked as if her guess was right. Meraud, who was quick to sense distress, softened a trace more. She took a step in Gerry's direction.

'Why, what should that mean to you?' she asked in surprise. 'What do you fear?'

Blind panic was closer to what Gerry felt than mere fear. Her heart was thumping uncomfortably.

'I'm afraid that you're right,' Gerry said reluctantly, 'and I may have come to bring more trouble to you.' She saw Meraud's eyes were beginning to blaze and added hurriedly, 'It's not my doing. I don't know yet if you need my help or I need yours. Maybe both.'

'You're talking in riddles,' the healer retorted scornfully. 'As usual. Can you never give a straight answer to anything?' With that she bent to retrieve her basket with its haul of gathered plants. The stems in her hand were bruised where she had gripped them too tightly in her spurt of rage. She looked at them doubtfully but put them in with the rest anyway. Gerry moved towards Meraud as she began to turn away.

'Please, Meraud,' she begged. 'I do need to talk to you. Are we near your home?'

Meraud looked back over her shoulder, her face so fierce that Gerry was appalled.

'I don't have a home any longer,' the healer snapped. 'Only a place where I live.' She swung back to face Gerry. 'Thanks to you.'

This was terribly unfair, but she wasn't giving Gerry any chance to explain. 'Please,' Gerry repeated, 'just give me a few minutes. Then I'll go.' Perhaps it would be better not to go with Meraud to the village. Gerry didn't know who still lived there but it was plain enough she wasn't going to be welcomed. She thought with regret of how warmly they'd greeted her once, after Gerry had saved them from being poisoned. She didn't think she could bear to see them all turn on her with the same hostility that Meraud was radiating. Gerry waited anxiously for her answer.

'All right then,' Meraud replied at last, clearly reluctant. 'What do you want to know?'

'You stayed,' Gerry said. Looking away to her left she saw the long slope of Chapel Carn Brea rising from the fields around it. She could just make out the shape of the huge granite rocks at the summit. The Bees' settlement was at the foot of this hill where she'd first met them, three months, or 1400-odd years, ago. 'Did the others stay too?'

'Most of us,' Meraud said shortly. 'We weren't going to be dictated to by that woman.' Her eyes flashed again. 'May the Goddess curse her.'

This was unjust too but Gerry didn't dare argue the point. 'And the Guardians?' she asked instead, wishing she had something to lean against. Her knees had begun to tremble. 'What about them?'

'Baranwen vanished, as I just told you. Ysella left.' A wry smile suddenly overlaid the healer's anger. 'She went home to her family to get married.'

Because she had to? Gerry wondered. Their shared dislike of the vain, malicious Guardian might have formed a bridge between them, but that fleeting hope was gone at once as Meraud bit out, 'Morvoren is dead.'

'Morvoren? Dead?' That didn't seem possible. 'What happened to her?' Gerry could all but see the Guardian in front of her in her green robe, the mark of the Bees at her throat and the knife in its holder in the girdle at her waist. Dedicated to the Tegennow, the Guardian had wrongly believed Gerry to be their enemy. The last she had seen of Morvoren was her furious attack on Baranwen. She had trusted her leader blindly and had been appalled to find that her trust had been misplaced. The Chalice of the Rainbow had been kept by the Guardians to use for the common good, for everyone. Baranwen had schemed to take the Chalice for herself alone, thus betraying her calling, the other Guardians, the Gwenen, and all their people.

'Morvoren drowned.' It was clear that Meraud thought this was Gerry's fault too. 'She took one of the fishing boats out from the cove in a storm. The wreckage was washed ashore; her body came later. Her robes were waterlogged, she could not swim to safety.' Meraud's voice quivered. 'We all prayed it had been an accident. To take, or deliberately risk, her own life, except to save another, would be a sin against the Goddess who gives us life.'

Perhaps Morvoren left it to fate to decide, Gerry thought, but didn't dare say so. Was this another death she must have on her conscience? She still grieved for the one woman who she hadn't managed to save from the poison, and that grief blazed back afresh here, so near to where it had happened.

'I'm so sorry,' Gerry said, feeling her own voice shaky. 'There's only one more question. Do you know if some of the men from your neighbouring village have gone away – Talan, Kenver, Cathno or Elwyn?'

Gerry had surprised Meraud again. She creased her brow as she went over her recent visits to the nearest village. 'I was there last week when I treated the smith's daughter for a burn to her arm which was not healing as it should. The child would not leave it alone. I do not think I have seen any of those four for a while. Strange that you should ask.' She paused, then added, 'They did not say they were going anywhere. Their families are deeply distressed.'

Gerry's stomach had begun to churn. She couldn't bear to hear any more ill news. 'Thank you,' she said miserably. 'I'll go now.'

Meraud didn't even answer. She set off with determined strides towards the path, taking her day's harvest back to prepare and add to her collection of remedies. Gerry stood still, turning over what the healer had told her. Baranwen hadn't been seen since that terrible evening on the hilltop. The Gohi had vanished, and had been in her own Penzance recently. Then the image of Morvoren came before Gerry. Had she drowned herself in despair, overcome by the loss of the Jewels she too was bonded to, and the treachery of the leader she had trusted? Or had it truly been an accident? Gerry found she was mourning Morvoren. Although she had opposed and attacked her, Morvoren hadn't been Gerry's enemy in the way Baranwen had been. As Baranwen still was. At that thought Gerry came back to herself with a jolt. It was time she left. Meraud was some distance away now, marching off with angry footsteps. Her back was towards Gerry and she didn't see her disappear.

Chapter Three

Tuesday September 9th

Gerry must have slept again, because she woke late and found she had a thundering headache. Climbing reluctantly out of bed, she felt weak and shaky all over, as if she had 'flu. There was no way she'd be able to concentrate on work, not with pictures of Baranwen, the Wasps, and Meraud too, tormenting her. Gerry phoned the Cornish Studies library to say she wasn't well enough to come in. It was, after all, the first time she'd been off sick in the weeks she'd been working there. But she forgot about work again almost at once.

Claudia was at the gallery, so the house was empty, and sitting there on her own didn't do Gerry any good; she was worrying herself into what could soon become a panic attack. Towards lunchtime she decided to go into Penzance. She ought to get some shopping, and a couple of days ago she'd been thinking about looking at the new season's boots. Her headache hadn't improved, but perhaps going out would help.

When she got into town, however, it proved as hard to think about shopping as it would have been to try to concentrate at work. Gerry made herself go round a supermarket for some food, then parked down at the front and walked up to Morrab Gardens. These were semi-tropical gardens, on the same road as the public library but closer to the sea. Gerry had walked past the entrance many times, but had never gone inside.

This time she went in, passing two stone pillars supporting iron gates, then following a curving path. Palm trees, hydrangeas and other shrubs grew on both sides of it. The path passed a small pond with low railings, then came to an old-fashioned bandstand. There were stretches of grass, with flower beds and trees, and wooden garden seats placed at intervals round the bandstand. Gerry found an empty bench and sat down, looking around without taking anything in properly. There were a couple of girls sitting nearby, presumably on their lunch break. They were eating pasties out of paper bags, talking and laughing. A man walked across the path on the far side of the park, his phone clamped to his ear. Two young mothers with pushchairs crossed the grass, one calling loudly to a toddler who kept wandering off. Not for the first time, Gerry felt as if she was living in a different world from everyone round her.

She leaned back on her seat and shut her eyes; she was still desperately tired. Then she felt the slight vibration from her bag indicating a text message. Gerry would have left it till later, but she was not allowed to. The ring on her right hand started to send needles of pain into her middle finger. She pulled out her phone and read the words from Debbie: "Just seen newsflash. Truro Museum, people attacked, chalice stolen."

As the words began to register, Gerry felt everything fade around her: the girls' chatter, the footsteps of people walking along the paths, the sound of a car horn on Morrab Road. Gerry found herself in darkness as she had been before, on the times when she had travelled into the past, but now for the first time she had guidance. The Rainbow Ring had come alive. Its tiny beams of light were twining themselves round her fingers in a frenzy of agitation. The next moment Gerry found herself at the Royal Cornwall Museum. She was standing on the first floor balcony, furnished with glass-fronted cases of porcelain, pottery, plates and tiles, which circled the floor below.

She leaned over the top of the stone balustrade with its little round-bellied pillars, and found herself looking down at the gallery where she'd stood the day before, in front of the display cabinets of the early Christian era. All was quiet. People moved around on the floor below, talking and looking into the wood-framed glass cases. They raised phones and took pictures. One stepped back incautiously and banged against the old painted carriage standing near the foot of the staircase which led up to the balcony.

The Kelegel a'n gammneves was there in the centre of its shelf. Although its light was subdued, for Gerry it still outshone every exhibit in the museum. A couple had gone towards it, lifted the explanatory leaflet from its holder on the wall, and were checking the number on the little printed card beside the chalice when the peaceful atmosphere burst apart.

Four figures appeared out of nowhere and the air around them crackled with menace. The three men stood poised, weapons at the ready in their hands. Gerry recognised the faces: Elwyn with his cruel smile, Cathno, sensual and restless, and Kenver, foil to the other two; but not Talan. And the woman who stood in front of them; the one Gerry had known it must be. Baranwen, Guardian of the Chalice.

Gerry had to stand and watch as the three men leapt into action. With frightening speed, and before anyone could realise what was about to happen, they started to attack everyone within reach, their flashing blades moving almost too fast to follow. As the first victims fell bleeding to the ground, those who could run fled from the gallery in terror. It looked like Baranwen had encouraged the Wasps to create as much mayhem as they chose. Gerry saw two men hesitate near the door, obviously moved to "have a go" at the attackers, but there were three of the Gohi and all their knives were already dripping with blood. Anyone who had fallen was kicked or slashed at again.

Yet Gerry absorbed all this peripherally, for she was staring, mesmerised, at the person responsible. Baranwen, robed in green, stood before the display case containing the Chalice of the Rainbow. To anyone else she would look as Gerry had first seen her on Causewayhead in Penzance: long green dress, copper spiral earrings, hair hanging in a thick braid down her back. Now Gerry could also see the mark of the Bees at her throat, the crossed circle on the inner left wrist, the copper torc about her neck. To the Guardian there was nothing else in the room; the violence, the screaming, the wounded, and all the many objects of Cornwall's history around her simply did not exist. She had come for the Tegennow a'n gammneves.

Gerry understood in that moment that she'd been terribly wrong to assume everything was over, and to have done nothing for all these weeks. Baranwen hadn't wasted her time as Gerry had; she had been plotting, strengthening herself, gaining allies. Forcibly parted from the Jewels that been everything to her for more years than anyone had known, she had lived and breathed only to get them back. There was a deep bond between the Guardian and the Jewels, a bond forged over the decades she had worked with them. While Gerry had remained idle, Baranwen had searched tirelessly until she discovered a way to break the barrier that prevented the Tegennow from functioning in their own future.

The Kelegel had been created to enhance its users' talents for healing and knowledge. But over the centuries it had acquired other abilities; or perhaps those had always been latent within it, unknown to and never intended by its Makers. The Makers, as Gerry thought of the women who had created the Kelegel, had not intended to endow the chalice with the means to extend the lives of its Guardians, or give them the capacity to move between times. And in the course of Baranwen's long guardianship, the potential for pure good that had been bred into the Jewels had been slowly and irrevocably twisted. She had grown to crave them for herself alone, and had brought about the death of the one woman who had realised this. And whether Gerry liked it or not, she could understand Baranwen. She herself had held the Chalice in her hand and called up the rainbow light, and was bound to it for ever.

Gerry's ring blazed for a moment, then became still. Below her Baranwen placed both her hands against the glass front of the cabinet holding the Kelegel. Even from where Gerry stood she could feel something of the power the Guardian had summoned within herself, power she had absorbed from the Tegennow over the course of - *Two hundred years. For two hundred years they have been mine.* The voice rang inside Gerry's head. Baranwen had not turned, but she knew Gerry was there. *You cannot stop me now!*

With the last word, the glass before her shattered, shards flying in every direction. It would be toughened security glass, but nothing now was going to come between the Guardian and her prize. She had commanded the glass and it had obeyed her. And with a cry that must have been heard throughout the building, above all else that surrounded her, Baranwen lifted the Chalice of the Rainbow from the shelf and raised it before her in triumph.

As Baranwen's hands touched the gold, the flares of coloured light leaped out and surrounded her, like the miniature beams that had enclosed Gerry's finger magnified a thousand times. The Guardian swung round, holding the Kelegel aloft. The Gohi, weapons clutched forgotten in their hands, had turned as one at that cry. The desperate longing Gerry remembered was naked on their faces.

Baranwen looked straight up to where Gerry watched from above and this time cried aloud, 'You cannot stop me now!' And as officials raced into the room, and the first approaching sirens sounded outside in River Street, the Guardian and her henchmen disappeared.

Gerry realised that it all must have taken place earlier in real time if it had reached the local news. By now ambulances would have ferried the injured to A & E at the Royal Cornwall Hospital outside the city of Truro. The police would be taking accounts from anyone in the museum who could give them. The statements would be of little help: nobody would have seen the attackers enter or leave the building, and the descriptions would sound bizarre. No-one had stopped to film the scene on their phones; they were too busy running for their lives. And Baranwen would as a matter of course have wiped the CCTV recordings as she had done in the jewellers' shops in the summer. Those times it had been to clear any evidence of the sapphire from the 21st century. Knowing nothing of technology, Baranwen had nonetheless easily removed all traces of the jewel from modern records. With the Chalice itself involved, the Guardian would have been even more certain to obliterate any traces of her actions.

It came to Gerry with a shock that she hadn't in reality been at the museum at all, hadn't stood at the balcony railing watching the bloodshed. Her body had remained seated on the bench in Morrab Gardens, and there no time had passed at all. Yet Gerry had not only watched the attack, but Baranwen had sensed her presence and addressed her directly. This was a talent she'd never possessed before. Gerry stared at the ring as it sat circling her finger, looking so innocent. Whatever had Seona put into this gift?

Then Gerry heard a silent laugh within her head. It was more purely unpleasant than any laughter she'd ever heard.

Don't delude yourself. The tone became scornful and Gerry knew it was Baranwen. *Playing games with your Bysow a'n gammneves;*

27

you're no threat to me. She understood that the Cornish phrase meant "Ring of the Rainbow" as the Tegennow a'n gammneves were the Jewels of the Rainbow. She'd understood Baranwen, who would be speaking Cornish from her own time, as she had understood her at the museum. So the gold chain had regained its ability to translate; or was the ring now doing that? Perhaps they worked together, both being given their powers by Seona. The voice went on: *The Bysow a'n gammneves is no more than a toy. Don't think you can oppose me, or my assistants.*

Gerry clamped the fingers of her left hand hard over her ring. BLOCK HER OUT, she instructed, and felt a small shudder beneath her finger. The voice in her head was gone.

Astounded, Gerry stared at the ring, touching it gently with a fingertip. The command had been a reflex, and she hadn't in the least expected it to work. That had been an amazing achievement. To oppose Baranwen at the very moment of her triumph – and succeed? The Guardian was wrong. This ring, the Bysow a'n gammneves as she had named it, was no toy. The ring looked dulled now after its efforts. Gerry would let it rest for a bit. It was time to stop sitting around feeling sorry for herself. Suddenly restless, Gerry stood up and walked to the top of the park, past more seats placed around a fountain set in the centre of a lawn, and out through the upper gates. She headed for the public library. She needed to find out anything she could about what had happened at the museum. Hopefully there would be a computer free; if not she would beg for the use of one of the staff ones.

Gerry came back out onto the upper part of Morrab Road. As she crossed the road she spotted Ryan, who gave computer lessons at the library, and had once asked her out. He was hurrying along towards the library entrance, but saw her and stopped, looking so delighted that Gerry couldn't help smiling back at him.

'Just the person I wanted!' she exclaimed, so taken up with her goal that all she thought of at first was that Ryan would definitely give her use of a screen. 'I'm going to the library to find a computer. I need to look up something on the news and my phone's so old, the screen's just too small.'

Gerry realised as she stopped speaking that this was perhaps not the most tactful greeting for someone she'd effectively avoided for weeks along with the rest of the library staff, but Ryan took it cheerfully.

'Nice to be needed.' He gave Gerry his warmest grin. 'I've got a lesson booked in a few minutes, but I'm sure I can sort something for you first. If not, I'll put my own laptop on in the archive room, as it's for you. But if you just want to find something out – we have the technology.' He pulled what looked like the latest in smartphones out of his pocket. 'Local news, national or international?'

'Cornwall, please.'

Ryan tapped the screen for a minute, then showed her the headlines.

'Which did you want – the dog that fell off a cliff and was rescued unhurt?'

'No.' She scanned the list. 'That one, the attack at the Royal Cornwall Museum.'

'Oh, I hadn't heard about that.' Ryan located the item, brought up the details and handed Gerry the phone. 'There you are.'

She read the feature, but it was quite short and told her little that she didn't already know. There was outrage at the unprovoked attack on innocent bystanders. Witnesses agreed that there were three armed men, but they'd all been too busy trying to get away alive and in one piece to even notice Baranwen. The pictures of the scene made Gerry feel sick. It was known by now that one man had died in hospital, while a number of others were seriously hurt. As well as the knife wounds, some had been injured further by the flying glass shards.

'Gerry, what's wrong?' Ryan put his hand across the screen, covering hers in the process. 'You look quite ill.'

Gerry moved Ryan's hand away and pointed to the pictures set among the text.

'I was there myself, yesterday afternoon,' she said. 'I was actually in that part of the museum.'

And I was there today, watching, helpless.

Ryan swore violently, which startled Gerry; she'd never heard him swear before.

'Do you mean, if this had happened yesterday, you might have been -' he gestured to the image of the people lying bleeding on the floor of the gallery. Gerry nodded, finding her voice too choked to answer. Ryan thrust his phone back into his pocket, pulled Gerry close against him, and kissed her. It was a very long kiss, and wholly unexpected. When it ended, he kept his arms tightly round her, resting his face against her hair.

'You could have been killed.' He sounded devastated, and Gerry pulled back far enough to look at him. This wasn't the cheerful young man she'd joked with so often in the staff room at the library, and refused gently as a date. He seemed suddenly older, and looked serious as she had never seen him. Then he swore again.

'Gerry, I've got to get back, I'm late for my client already. Where will you be at five?'

Gerry hadn't thought that far ahead. 'I haven't got anything planned,' she told him.

'Okay,' he said, 'can I have your phone?'

Gerry handed it over and Ryan's fingers flashed across the keypad.

'Right, I've saved my number in there for you, it's under R,' he said. 'Will you call me at five? I really need to see you.'

'Yeah.' Gerry amended that to 'Yes, of course.' He still looked uncertain, so she added, 'I promise.'

'Good girl.' Ryan released her, then caught her back against him and kissed her again, this time swift and hard. Then he let her go and raced off for his overdue appointment, leaving Gerry staring after him. She realised they were virtually outside the library. Anyone could have seen Ryan kissing her. Well, she couldn't help that now.

Gerry stood on the pavement, for once hardly noticing the blue, sharp-edged horizon across the width of the bay visible at the lower end of the sloping road. Debbie had told Gerry that Ryan's last girlfriend had dumped him for someone with a lot of money. She must've have been a total prat, Gerry thought. Ryan was unremarkable to look at, except for that sudden smile which lit his face from within. He was average size and wore everyday clothes. But Gerry had just learned that he wasn't as ordinary as he looked. The passion in that long kiss had for the moment eclipsed even Gerry's fear of Baranwen and her wonder at the achievements of her ring.

Gerry walked into the Penzance library for the first time since the morning she'd limped in with her rib broken, to learn that Debbie wasn't at work. Luckily Monica wasn't anywhere in sight. The one public computer on the ground floor happened to be free, and Gerry made a beeline for it. She logged herself in using the staff password and began to search the news sites, but couldn't find out anything further. Half an hour later she was ready to give up when she heard someone say her name and felt a tap on her shoulder. Gerry looked up and saw it was Tasha, who worked in the children's department. She had blue streaks in her hair and wore a very short skirt with a bright red top.

'Hi, come and have a cup of tea,' Tasha said, beaming at Gerry. 'I've not seen you for ages, I thought you must've gone back to London.'

'No way,' Gerry said, 'I hate London,' and she followed Tasha into the staffroom.

It was strange to be back in the familiar room. Tasha made tea for them both and chatted about her summer holiday, so Gerry didn't need to talk. After a few minutes Debbie came in; her eyes widened when she saw Gerry, but she didn't interrupt Tasha. Gerry hoped Ryan wouldn't come down while Debbie was there. She could guess how he would look at her, and Debbie wouldn't miss it. Gerry knew how much Debbie liked Ryan, and that made her feel guilty. Luckily he didn't appear, but Hilary, the library manager, walked in instead and asked Gerry how she was getting on at Cornish Studies.

Trying to think about work would have been beyond Gerry but luckily she'd sent Bill an email the night before, to thank him for forwarding Seona's letter. She'd put in a few sentences about her job, so all she had to do was repeat what she'd written. The work was generally interesting, and she'd learned quite a bit about Cornwall, from the old maps to the early census returns.

'We get people in,' Gerry told her audience, 'from Australia, South Africa, America, you name it. Their great-great-great-grandparents were miners who emigrated from Cornwall. They come in and they think they can do their entire family history in a couple of hours. As if. Did you know there's a saying: "A mine is a hole anywhere in the world with a Cornishman at the bottom of it"?'

They all laughed, and Hilary, picking up her mug of tea to take back to her office, commented, 'Well, I can see you're enjoying yourself there. I expect it would feel quite dull here after all that.' She closed the door sharply behind her, and Gerry looked at the other two in dismay.

'Did I say something wrong?'

Tasha laughed.

'I think Hilary forgets there's a world outside this place,' she said. 'But don't you forget about us. We should all go out one evening.'

Gerry agreed, though she didn't suggest fixing a time. She couldn't, not just now. Tasha got up to wash her mug, and took Gerry's mug too. Gerry moved nearer to Debbie, and said in a low voice, 'Thanks for your text.'

Debbie nodded, and replied, just as softly, 'So, are you all right?'

'Not really.' Gerry couldn't say anything else there. Bang on cue, Monica came in. Unlike the others, she didn't look pleased to see Gerry, but it was Debbie she spoke to.

'Shouldn't you be on the desk now?' she asked. 'I thought I was due for my break.'

Debbie, Tasha and Gerry looked at each other. Tasha rolled her eyes, but decided it wasn't worth retorting, though Gerry could see she was tempted. The three of them went out of the staffroom together, leaving Monica alone. Gerry said goodbye to Debbie, who was looking at her with concern, then walked slowly back to Seona's Volvo. She would have loved to just sit in the car and go to sleep till it was time to call Ryan, but there was something else she ought to try to do. Gerry rested the fingertips of her left hand against the Rainbow Ring. It felt like she was connecting with Seona.

Was the ring an embodiment of Seona? No, Gerry was beginning to know its character and they were quite different. But she trusted Seona and trusted the Bysow a'n gammneves. Gerry breathed, scarcely above a whisper, *I need to talk with Hedra.* Then she closed her eyes.

Chapter Four

When Gerry had first tried to move in time by herself, rather than being brought into the past or returned to the 21st century by Justin or Baranwen, she had arrived crashing to her knees or onto the ground. And each time, the silent darkness between times had seemed to last so long she was afraid she would be there for ever and never reach any destination. Now, with the lights from the Rainbow Ring to help her and keep her company, the time gap felt shorter, and Gerry landed effortlessly on her feet.

She was not on the hillside but inside a building, close to the wall in a large room. The roof sloped up to an opening for the smoke from the fire burning on the stone hearth in the centre of the room. Gerry hoped this was the place she'd visited once before when she'd gone to the Bees' village and talked to Meraud and Hedra. The houses in this settlement were not the round houses she'd seen pictures of when she'd looked up websites about life in this century. The dwellings seemed to consist of a number of buildings surrounded by an extremely thick wall, grouped round an open courtyard. The units on one side had looked like stables for animals, others like workrooms, close to the main building.

The room where Gerry was now standing appeared to be the equivalent of a living room. Round the edge were sections divided off from the main area, presumably for preparing food, for sleeping and so on. Gerry's eye was caught by a spinning wheel, with the spindle lying in a large basket of wool, which reminded her painfully of Seona. Then she spotted a bench which she thought was the one she'd sat on during her previous visit, so this should be the right place.

Gerry saw Hedra before the teacher was aware of her. Hedra, her knees covered by a wool blanket woven in a bright pattern, was sitting in a wooden chair near the fire, gazing listlessly at the flames. Some logs were stacked within easy reach of her hand, but although the fire was burning low, Hedra made no move to replenish it. She looked older, and the lines of pain on her face were more pronounced. Hedra had been the respected instructor of the Gwenen, teaching them their various tasks and the history and rituals attached to their calling of serving the Chalice of the Rainbow. Now, with the chalice lost to them for ever, there would be no more novices among the Bees, no more ceremonies performed. Meraud still had her healing skills to occupy her, but what was there left for the teacher to do? Keep alive the memories of their glorious past? That would be bitter work indeed. It hurt Gerry to see the older woman looking so defeated.

Gerry's thoughts flew back to the day when the Makers of the Chalice had come forward from their own time to this one, and told the Bees that their revered Chalice, created centuries before to bring help and healing to their people, had been corrupted. It now posed a danger even to its Guardians; and in front of the assembled Gwenen, the Makers wiped from the Kelegel a'n gammneves all the magic they had once put into it. Then it had vanished, and simultaneously Gerry found herself in her bedroom in Claudia's house, holding the lifeless chalice. Just a gold cup, as Debbie had said, more accurately than she knew.

And it looked, from Gerry's encounter with Meraud, as if the Bees were blaming Gerry for their loss. At least Hedra was alone here, as Gerry had hoped. She hadn't expected a welcome, and didn't get one. She spoke the teacher's name gently, stepping forward into her field of vision. The light in here was poor, and the lamps probably needed filling, or trimming, but Hedra didn't seem interested in performing that task either. There was a beaker on the floor at her feet, which might have been there for hours, unnoticed.

Hedra didn't move, only turning her head to ask, 'What are you doing here, Gerralda?' The look she gave her visitor was as bitter as Meraud's had been.

Straight to the point, then. Gerry answered simply, 'I've seen Baranwen.'

At that, Hedra's head jerked up and she half rose, but stopped herself.

'And if you have, should that concern me?'

Gerry resisted the urge to shout "Yes!" She needed information, and antagonising the person best placed to give it wouldn't help. She suppressed a sigh, and tried again.

'Please, Hedra,' she said. 'You taught here for so long, you worked with the Guardians. You must have known Baranwen better than anyone else did.' *Except for one, and that knowledge cost her her life.*

That did have an effect.

'I thought I knew her,' Hedra snapped. 'It seems I was wrong.'

That at least was a start. If Hedra believed that, then she must know that Colenso, leader of the Makers, was right about the Guardians. Gerry moved forward a little, and in doing so stepped into the shaft of light that came through the gap in the roof where smoke escaped. As she stood there in the sunshine, she saw Hedra's hand go to her throat.

'What,' Hedra demanded, both anger and dismay in her voice, 'do you think you are wearing?'

Gerry gave her clothes a bemused glance; she hadn't thought about them. The smock dress, sleeveless gilet and tights, were close enough to what she'd worn to the Bees' village before. The sandals of the summer had been replaced with short soft boots, but those didn't feel out of place. She'd been taken for a beardless boy on her early visits here.

'No,' Hedra said harshly, 'there, on your hand.'

Gerry looked down, and saw that the gemstones on her right hand were glowing in the beam of sunlight. Forgetting the pain of her twisted leg, Hedra came swiftly to stand beside Gerry, catching hold of the finger bearing the Bysow a'n gammneves.

'Is this to taunt us with our loss?' she cried, trying to pull it from Gerry's finger, twisting the skin. Her hands were surprisingly strong, but the ring resisted, refusing to move. 'How could you dare to make such a likeness?'

'No, of course it isn't, please stop, you're really hurting me,' Gerry pleaded. 'It won't come off. This isn't an imitation, it's real, look.' She lifted the stones full into the rays of the sun. The shafts flared out as those of the Kelegel had done, overlapping into the seven rainbow colours but forming a curve only big enough to cover Hedra's fingers. The arc of the Chalice, on that last evening before the light was taken from it, had soared across the whole hilltop and all the crowd of watchers.

The rainbow rested briefly on Hedra's knuckles, then vanished. She stared at the ring with mingled hunger and fear, then stumbled backwards to sit down again, never taking her eyes from Gerry's hand. Gerry stepped away from the sunlight, and felt her fingers trembling.

'Can I get you anything?' she asked. 'Water, wine?' She was concerned about the effect of such a shock on a woman already in poor health and low spirits. Conceding, Hedra gestured towards a table by the outer wall, close to where Gerry had arrived.

'Both, I think,' she said. 'There's water there from the well.'

Gerry went over to the table and found a jug of water, a flask whose contents smelled like Meraud's honey wine when she loosened the stopper, and some pottery beakers. These bore the marks of the Gwenen: a circle with two crossed lines within it, and a symbol like two capital Bs joined at the spine, with small lines above and below, like a rough image of a bee. She brought some of each drink to Hedra, holding them carefully, wondering if the old teacher would try to take the ring again. But Gerry found that Hedra's anger had gone, and instead she was gently touching the place on her hand where the small arc had rested. She drank thirstily, first the wine and then the water, and finally said simply, 'I don't understand.' She reached for Gerry's hand again, this time to examine the jewels more closely.

I don't understand either,' Gerry told her. 'The ring was left to me by my great-aunt, who was a wise woman.' This was how Baranwen had spoken of Seona when she described the gold chain Gerry wore as "an object of power". Gerry didn't know the phrase in the way Baranwen used it and although she'd meant to look it up, she'd then shut it away in her mind like all else associated with that week of Midsummer. She took it that it meant more than just a woman who was wise. Yet how had even Seona known she must create this little rainbow? Gerry was more certain than ever that the Guardian in her arrogance had underestimated the Bysow.

'Hedra,' Gerry said abruptly, 'Baranwen has seized the Kelegel. She took it with violence and the blood of innocent people, and I am more afraid than I can say of what she might be planning.' Gerry hesitated, touched her ring briefly for reassurance, then went on remorselessly.

'Colenso told me that the Jewels of the Rainbow were created to enhance any woman's potential, especially for healing and knowledge. Whatever Baranwen intends, it will not include those.' Running counterpoint to her unexpected encounter with Ryan, and to taking tea in the staff room at the library, Gerry's mind had been struggling against this conviction. She found herself echoing Colenso's words on the hilltop, that fateful evening. 'Baranwen told me that she has been Guardian for two hundred years. Colenso believed that Baranwen and the magic contained within the Jewels of the Rainbow had somehow bonded, and they have changed each other. She was afraid that the Jewels are no longer a force for good but for ill, and that was why she took the action she did.' Gerry stared straight at Hedra, desperate for the older woman to understand. 'The potential of the Tegennow is frightening if, as I believe, Baranwen has somehow managed to restore the powers that they had lost.'

Hedra did not protest or argue, only nodded slightly as if this confirmed her own ideas.

'I fear you are right,' she agreed. 'Are the Tegennow in your time or in ours?' So she at least of the Gwenen accepted that Gerry came from another age.

'They have been in my time,' Gerry replied, 'since, well, since you last saw them. Beautiful still, of course, but powerless, in a place where they were, or seemed to be, safe. That's where Baranwen took them from.' She continued, relieved to be sharing this, 'I blame myself for thinking nothing further would happen. She's spent all this time working out how to restore them to what they were. I've no idea how she's done it. And she's allied herself with the men who were helping Iestyn, the ones who poisoned the wine. Three of them, that is, she's left Talan out of this. He's more decent than the others. I know you didn't believe what I said about them at the time, but -'

'Stop,' Hedra interrupted, and her voice was more like a groan. 'Slowly, please, Gerralda. I too could blame myself, but that achieves nothing. What do you intend to do?'

'I don't know yet,' Gerry admitted. 'It only happened this afternoon. I came here because I hoped you could tell me more about Baranwen.'

Hedra was gazing into the fire again. No longer listless, she seemed to be using it to concentrate her ideas.

'As you said, I have worked with the Guardians for many years,' she said. 'I have learned something of their knowledge. Tell me, the violence that you spoke of, was it these men who carried it out, not Baranwen herself?'

'Yes,' Gerry said, 'but how did you know?'

Hedra smiled, grimly pleased. 'Obsessed she might be, but even Baranwen would realise that she could not take the Kammneves with blood on her hands, however much she has changed its essence,' she said. 'She will have bound the men to her with the promise of bloodshed and, I assume, of women. The way women dress in your day..' Hedra looked meaningfully at Gerry's short smock and the brightly-coloured tights which showed off most of her legs. They appeared to be communicating with more than words, and it was unnerving; this had not happened before. Gerry seemed to receive from Hedra an image of the likely response of active men to finding themselves in a place where instead of women in gowns reaching to their calves, they were surrounded by girls in thigh length dresses. Gerry saw a picture, so vivid that she seemed to be there, of the lower part of the one-way system near the station in Penzance. It was like when she'd watched the violence in the museum; she could see everything that was happening but not intervene.

It was late, probably near midnight on a Friday or Saturday night. Three girls, dressed for clubbing, were coming down the road to the traffic lights by the railway station, near the bus stands. Their walk was a bit unsteady, they'd been drinking and they were laughing and leaning on each other. Gerry saw the low-cut tops, bare arms and minimal skirts with new and disturbing vision.

The three men came forward from the wall where they'd been standing, and blocked the way. Behind them stretched the Harbour car park. The girls stopped and eyed the men, two of them giggling, the third, perhaps more sober, hesitating. One of the men, Cathno, Gerry thought, stepped forward and put his hand on the girl's arm. They wouldn't be speaking the same language but that needn't matter. It was plain enough what was going to happen, and Gerry didn't want to have to watch it. A large clump of trees and bushes grew at the side of the pavement, completely screening that corner of the car park from the road and passers-by. And no-one returning to their car at this time of night would interfere with what some couples might be doing in a dark corner. Gerry forced her thoughts free of them and brought herself back to Hedra. The vision had only taken a minute or two.

'Well?' Hedra asked, and Gerry wondered if the teacher had seen the same as she had. Justin, and Baranwen, had been able to follow her thoughts when there was strong emotion behind them. 'Am I right?'

'I'm afraid you must be,' Gerry admitted unhappily. She didn't doubt the likelihood of what she'd just witnessed. 'Baranwen used them to help her take the Chalice. But what is she planning now?'

The old teacher's face was grim, but she seemed to have regained at a stroke the purpose she had been lacking. She gave Gerry a curious look.

'Was it true that you held the Kelegel yourself?' she asked.

That was another memory Gerry had blocked off.

41

The sense of peace that had filled her, the feeling that she could do anything.

'Yes, but not for long,' she answered. Only from the moment in the fogou when Baranwen had let her take the cup, till Gerry handed it over to Colenso soon afterwards in a futile attempt to keep it from Justin. And the time when she herself had summoned the beams of light to prove to Justin that what she held really was the Chalice of the Rainbow.

'All the same, you are bound to the Tegennow now,' Hedra said gravely. 'Even by touching them you were sealed to the stones. Gerralda,' she continued, reluctantly, as if every word was dragged from her, 'you must realise, as I do now, that there is only one thing to do. The Kelegel must be physically destroyed so that Baranwen can never restore it again. The Jewels,' her voice shook as she uttered the terrible words, 'smashed to powder if that is the only way.'

I would rather die! Gerry's reaction was instantaneous, and she looked at Hedra in silence. The words had been like a blow, although she'd been expecting them. Indeed, that was mostly what she'd come here for. She knew what must be done, but wanted to hear someone else say it, someone who knew both the Tegennow and the Guardian.

Conflicting ideas revolved in her mind. Baranwen always knew if the Jewels of the Rainbow were threatened, anywhere and in any time; she'd taken drastic action in the past to protect them. How could Gerry plan anything against her when the Guardian seemed to be aware of what she was doing and even thinking? And how could Gerry contemplate harming the Kelegel? Even if she were not bound to the gemstones, their awesome beauty and the power that radiated from them would stop anyone bent on their destruction in her, or his, tracks.

Gerry couldn't come up with any answers. She leaned back against the wall behind her. At that moment the doorway

42

darkened and a woman came in. Her braided hair, paler than that of the other Gwenen, a legacy perhaps from some Viking raider, was lit from behind by the sun. So Nessa, who looked after the sacred bees, had remained to care for her charges. Once, she'd embraced Gerry and thanked her for saving her life. Gerry waited with resignation for Nessa to go through the same change as Meraud had.

Nessa came in, pausing in the doorway to let her eyes adjust to the dimness indoors, and calling out cheerfully. Then she saw that Hedra's attention was elsewhere, and looked round to see the cause. Her reaction on recognising Gerry was simpler even than Meraud's. She came straight at her, her hand raised. Gerry sidestepped to avoid the blow that Nessa swung at her. She heard Hedra calling out, and decided she would let the teacher explain why Gerry was there, if she wanted to. That would be an appropriate task for her. Gerry wasn't going to stay and get hurt again. She touched the ring.

Let's get back to the car.

She vanished. Hedra could have the job of explaining that to Nessa as well. Gerry had too many other things to worry about.

Chapter Five

Gerry leaned back against the car seat and tried not to think. She did not succeed very well. Time passed slowly. At last it was five o'clock. She reached for her phone to call Ryan, but as she picked it up, it rang. It was Debbie.

'Hi,' she said, 'I couldn't talk earlier with the others there, but there's something I thought you wouldn't know about and perhaps you should.'

'Okay, what is it?'

It wasn't really okay. Debs sounded worried, which made Gerry afraid. What was it Debbie thought she should know?

'Well, it's about Monica.'

That wasn't at all what Gerry was expecting.

'Yeah?'

'It's that,' Debbie paused, then came out with it. 'A couple of times in the last few days I've left work at the same time as her, and I've seen a man meeting her.'

Poor bloke, was Gerry's first thought. Then, how could Monica do that, after Justin? The reaction was immediate and involuntary. And unreasonable. Did she expect every woman who'd been involved with Justin to remain single for the rest of her life? Yet she herself was still hopelessly hooked on him, despite what he'd done to her.

'He doesn't look a bit like Justin.' Debbie echoed her thoughts. 'He's big, dark and untidy and his clothes are weird.

I wouldn't have mentioned it, only -' she stopped again. By now Gerry's heart had started thumping. Whatever it was, she didn't think she wanted to know; but the suspense was scary. 'It's only that after seeing you today I realised what's odd about his clothes,' Debbie went on. 'They're like what your Wasps were wearing. I hadn't twigged before. He's not one of the two that I saw, but you said there was four of them.'

Gerry felt like a trap was closing round her. She didn't doubt for a moment that Debbie was right, and didn't like this one bit. What connection could there possibly be between Monica Fraser and the Gohi, and how, how could such a connection have been made? Gerry could only think of one possible way and that scared her so much she wasn't sure she could cope with it.

Debbie, sounding rather guilty, apologised, said goodbye and rang off. Then Gerry felt guilty herself. She had almost forgotten that she was going to call Ryan, and wondered how Debbie would react if she knew. If there was ever an example of famine or feast, this was it. More had happened in the last two days than in all the weeks since she gave away the Kelegel. Gerry took out her phone and pressed the number which Ryan had saved onto it.

Ryan answered at once, and when Gerry confirmed she was free, suggested they met at the Long Rock car park. He told her how to get there and said he'd be there in half an hour. That gave Gerry time to get a cup of coffee somewhere. She hadn't had lunch, but felt too stressed to eat.

After a very welcome mug of coffee Gerry drove along the front, past the railway station and the out of town supermarkets to the Long Rock industrial estate just east of Penzance. The entrance to the car park was on the seaward side of a level crossing where the main line ran to and from Penzance station. Although Gerry had passed the turning to this car park a few times,

45

she had never gone in. As soon as she got out of the car she felt that she should have come here before. The car park was directly above the beach; large misshapen boulders of grey granite formed a barrier between the cars and the beach, and lined both sides of a path sloping down to the sand.

Standing here Gerry was unexpectedly close to St. Michael's Mount. Although dusk was starting to draw in she could easily see the familiar shape of the little island, with the gradual slope on the right and the steep slope on the left. Lights were showing in some of the windows of the castle on top. The lights of Penzance were strung out on her right, curving round to the Battery Rocks and the Jubilee Pool, with the walls of Newlyn harbour and the road to the village of Mousehole beyond them forming one arm of the bay. A cluster of lights on her left indicated the village of Marazion. The tide was nearly full, with the causeway to the Mount, which was accessible at low tide, lying invisible under the water. Gerry had never walked across it, though she had intended to. A public footpath parallel with the railway line led from here back to Penzance in one direction and to Marazion in the other. It ran just above the beach, and Gerry promised herself that if her life ever returned to some semblance of normality she would take that walk from end to end.

Gerry turned at the sound of a horn, and was surprised to see Ryan at the wheel of a very grimy transit van. It had the name and contact details of a local plumbing firm on the side, just visible through the dirt. He parked the van next to the Volvo and came over to where Gerry stood.

'Hello,' he began, and waved a hand at the van. 'No, it's not mine, I share a house with my brother Connor, you see, and Jez who's a mate of his. This is Jez's, I begged it off him, he didn't need it tonight.'

'Right.' Gerry wasn't sure what to say. After his flood of words Ryan didn't seem to know what to say next either. Gerry had never seen him at a loss for words before.

'Ryan, are you all right?' she asked him, surprised.

He gave a sheepish grin and looked a little more like the Ryan she was used to. 'Well,' he admitted, not really looking at her, 'I know I got a bit carried away this afternoon. I didn't mean to do that. Afterwards – well, I didn't think you'd even call me tonight, let alone turn up.'

'I told you I'd ring,' Gerry said. 'If you remember, I promised.'

'I know,' he said, 'but still..' And Ryan looked at her, a question in his eyes.

'It's all right,' Gerry told him, and was pleased to see him relax a bit. There was no wind, and although the tide was in, the sea was almost flat and the waves, lapping the small strip of sand that was still visible below the wall, curled over in tiny rolls of creamy white. Ryan moved closer and took her hand.

'Come on,' he said, and drew Gerry towards the concrete slope that led down to what beach there was at high tide. She noticed him giving her boots a quick glance, as if to check they were okay for walking on sand. Luckily some of the boots in fashion this year were flat, and that was what she was wearing. She wondered if his ex was the sort of woman who went around in heels all the time, whatever the current trend. Was everyone haunted by their exes? But then, who was she to talk, with Justin's image still coming between her and any peace of mind?

There were a few people on the beach as well as a couple of dogs, but not so many as to make it feel crowded. Ryan stopped walking, and began speaking again, not looking at Gerry, although he kept hold of her hand. She had never held hands with Justin.

'I thought I'd better explain,' Ryan began. 'I haven't been able to think about anything but you since this afternoon when you told me about – well, what happened. When I thought you could have been killed, I -' he stopped, then started again. 'I knew I couldn't bear to think of the world without you in it.' He wasn't looking at Gerry as he spoke, but out across the bay. 'You see, I'd always wanted to kiss you.' He stopped again, then gathered his confidence and went on with more assurance. Gerry listened, completely taken aback at what she was hearing.

'I'd wanted it from the day you first walked into the staff room at the library and Hilary introduced you,' he said. 'I'd never seen a woman like you – your smile, your beautiful hair, that lovely Scottish lilt to your voice. But I saw almost at once that you were only comfortable with the other girls, and seemed to shy away from men. I guessed you'd had some sort of bad experience?' He looked at Gerry then, and she nodded wordlessly. 'So I thought I'd better not try to rush anything, but just be friends and perhaps you'd learn to trust me.'

No man Gerry had known would be as honest as this, and she liked him all the better for it. She remembered that Debbie had said back in the summer that Ryan fancied her. Only then she'd bought the sapphire - and met Justin.

'The day you came in and you couldn't walk properly,' Ryan went on, 'you know, when you said you'd fallen downstairs, it was all I could do not to just pick you up and take you straight to hospital and hang the job.' Ironically Gerry too had been very tempted to let him take care of her then, but knew it wouldn't be a good idea. She stayed silent and let him talk on. 'Then overnight you went off to work in that place in Redruth and never came into the library. And I'd never forgotten what Ernie, you know, the agency guy, had said in the staffroom, about seeing you with a man at the fireworks. He was telling everyone about it that day, said you were "all wrapped round each other".'

What a bastard, Gerry thought. But of course everyone likes gossip.

'I think I lost hope then,' Ryan continued. 'Connor and Jez told me I should forget it, go out with someone else. But I couldn't; there was only one woman I wanted.'

Now he could look her straight in the eyes. 'I did see you in Penzance a couple of times in the summer. You looked all lost, and – I dunno, like, haunted. It scared me. I wanted to go up to you and say hello, but you were, like, wrapped up in a world of your own. I was afraid if I spoke to you, you might look right through me and not know who I was, and I didn't think I could bear that.'

'I'm sorry,' Gerry said helplessly. No wonder he had looked so delighted when she had smiled at him on Morrab Road – was it only this afternoon?

'Sorry?' Ryan gripped her hand harder. 'What on earth have you got to be sorry for? I suppose he ditched you.'

Gerry gave a rather shaky smile. It wasn't quite that simple.

'Not exactly.' She had better tell him. Ryan deserved the truth; at least what she could reasonably tell him. 'He died - he was killed.' Gerry got stuck at that.

'Oh God. Was it an accident, was he driving? Were you there?'

'No, it wasn't that.'

Gerry didn't know how to reply to Ryan's questions. Anything she said would be wrong: that she and Justin hadn't been an item, or that she was over him. Ryan was still gripping her hand. She was tempted to kiss him, just for reassurance, but felt too visible. At the sidings by the level crossing there were rows of bright overhead lights which shone over the car park, and there were people on the beach not far away. Martin, her so-called boyfriend in London, had once called Gerry a prude; perhaps he was right. But she was thinking of her vision of the Gohi at the Harbour car park with the girls from the night club. And then of Justin holding her close at the fireworks amid the teeming crowds there. Gerry wondered bitterly if she would have protested at anything Justin might have done there, despite the hundreds of people around them. She knew the answer was no, and despised herself for it.

'Look,' she said, 'it's getting colder. Why don't we go for a drink somewhere, at least we can talk.'

They settled on the Godolphin Arms at Marazion, just up the road, and took the Volvo. Ryan got a ticket for the van, leaving it in the car park to collect later. During the short journey to Marazion Gerry reflected that it was totally unlike her to take the initiative with a man, and also that Ryan was the only person other than Debbie who she had taken in Seona's car. Further, he had not suggested, as most men might, that he should drive. Gerry had a feeling Seona would have approved of him.

As the main holiday season was pretty much over, the bar wasn't too busy and they were able to get a table by the window. There were enough customers to create a pleasant buzz of background noise, so they could talk easily enough. Gerry didn't recognise anyone, and guessed that most of the people here were locals. Ryan ordered a beer for himself and Gerry stuck to her usual Diet Coke. Neither wanted to eat.

When they sat down, Gerry looked out of the window and saw that the hotel was almost opposite the Mount, about as close as you could get and still be on the mainland. It was nearly dark now and the lights in the bar made it seem darker still outside. There were more lights in the windows of the castle on top of the Mount. Looking across the water Gerry could just make out the island's little harbour and the row of houses behind it. She thought she could see a couple of small boats there, perhaps the ones that ferried passengers across in the daytime when the tide came in and the causeway was under water.

Gerry felt awkward again with the change of setting, and wondered if it had been a mistake to suggest coming here. If

Ryan felt the same, it didn't show. He leaned forward a little, took her hand in his again, then said, 'Tell me about the place where you live.'

That was easy to begin with, and Gerry waxed enthusiastic about the view along the north coast, the gardens on all sides of the house, and the absolute silence apart from the birds. It was harder to explain what Claudia was like: smart, self-contained, polite but not exactly friendly. Ryan was a sympathetic listener and after a while Gerry found herself telling him about the man who was haunting Claudia's gallery, the 'stalker' as Debbie had named him. Ryan drank his beer in thoughtful silence for a few minutes, while Gerry sipped her own drink and watched the familiar face in these unfamiliar surroundings.

Finally Ryan said, 'I've got an idea. I might be able to help your Claudia with this Stork character.'

'I said "stalker", not "stork",' Gerry protested.

'"Stork" will do,' Ryan replied. 'Do you think I could come to your house and talk to Claudia tomorrow after work?'

'I'll suggest it,' Gerry said doubtfully. No-one invited themselves to visit Claudia. Yet Gerry didn't see how her landlady could take exception to Ryan; no-one could. 'I'll speak to her when I get home,' she promised, 'and I'll text you. But I warn you, Claudia's the most private person I've ever known.'

'Yes, you have kind of indicated that,' Ryan agreed with a smile. 'And you say she's beautiful, but you haven't mentioned a boyfriend. Or, maybe, a girlfriend?'

Gerry didn't know what she could say. She didn't think Claudia was gay; after all, she'd been involved with Justin. She had implied early on in their acquaintance that she avoided men, believing they were only interested in her for her looks or her money. If that was true, that was Claudia's own affair, and Gerry wouldn't repeat it, even to Ryan. But then Justin had come into her life. Claudia had never said how they had met, but had told

Gerry that she'd made it clear to him that she wasn't interested. Gerry knew Justin well enough to be aware that a woman so lovely and so aloof would present an irresistible challenge for him. He wouldn't have given up until he'd got what he wanted.

Ryan had been so open about himself earlier that Gerry felt she owed it to him to explain. Unconsciously she pulled her hand away from his.

'She did have someone,' Gerry said, and stopped, trying to work out how to say this. Ryan looked surprised, as she had been talking readily enough up to this point. 'It was – oh, sod, it was the same man, the one I just told you about, the one who was killed. The one Ernie saw me with at the fireworks. He was called Justin.'

Gerry realised at once that she had just made a serious mistake, misled by how easily they were talking. She saw Ryan's expression change, and as the implications of her words sank in Gerry saw his image of her start to shift. She nearly said, 'No, it's not what you think', though that was only partly true, as well as sounding like an excuse. But Gerry couldn't bear the disillusion she saw beginning on Ryan's face. For a dreadful moment she thought he was going to get up and walk out of the bar.

Gerry had stayed silent for too long. She wanted to assure Ryan she really was the person he had thought she was, but that wasn't true either. She didn't go around stealing other women's boyfriends, but she was so different from what he believed that she could have come from another planet. She would just have to fight fire with fire.

'Ryan, please don't look like that,' Gerry said desperately. She could feel him retreating and his face had grown cold. 'No, listen, this is important. Did you look at that feature about the theft at the museum?'

Whatever Ryan had expected her to say, it certainly

wasn't that.

'Yes,' he said, but all the warmth had gone from his voice. 'It was a dreadful business.'

'Please, Ryan, you need to understand this,' Gerry said. 'I know the people who did it. Justin knew them too. They're really dangerous, like he was. And they know that I know about them. I'm not a safe person to be around.'

Gerry stopped, wondering if she'd made things worse. Did it sound as if she was asking for protection?

'I can look after myself,' she added hastily. 'Only, the chalice that they stole in that break-in today, it was mine for a little while. I gave it to the museum to try and keep it safe. It was very old, very special, and worth a bomb. Justin tried to get it from me. He nearly throttled me once.'

Gerry stopped, horrified. She hadn't meant to say that.

Ryan said nothing. After a while he drank some more beer, though the action seemed mechanical. Finally he raised his head and looked at Gerry as if seeing her for the first time. She was afraid she'd damaged something in him for ever.

But when Ryan did speak, it was his turn to surprise her.

'Did Debs know about this?' he asked.

'Some of it – why? What did she say?' Gerry had thought she could trust Debbie.

'Nothing very much,' Ryan said, seeing her concern. 'And I was the only one she spoke to. After you stopped working at Penzance, Debs gave me a couple of hints that you had problems and wanted to be left alone to sort them out. I naturally assumed it was a man.'

'It was,' Gerry said, 'but it was the other stuff too. Debs knew a bit about it, 'cos they're all mixed up with each other. It's part of why I might have looked as if I was walking around in another world, like you said.'

There was another silence, then Ryan asked, 'How the hell did you come to have something like that? Was it a family heirloom? No, it couldn't be, you're from Scotland and the news thing said it was Cornish.'

'The woman who had it gave it to me to try to stop Justin getting hold of it.' Gerry knew that sounded unlikely, but she hoped Ryan wouldn't ask for explanations just now. 'I didn't make a very good job of that.' She might as well tell him the rest. 'That was why Justin made up to me in the first place.'

'And did your Claudia know about this?' Ryan was frowning.

'No, at least she wasn't involved in any way,' Gerry said. 'I showed her the chalice, before I gave it to the museum. I told her Justin had been after it, and she wasn't surprised, said it was just the sort of thing he would go for. She knew he was ruthless and would stick at nothing. But don't get me wrong,' she added hastily. 'Claudia's as straight as they come, she'd never do anything illegal or underhand. Only I'm worried about her. Justin made enemies. I'm afraid she may get targeted because of him, even though they were finished.' Gerry fought back a gasp of shock at her own words; she hadn't consciously thought this through. 'Perhaps that's why I'm so worried about the man in her gallery.'

Ryan's brows were drawn together, but now he seemed confused rather than angry. Gerry was glad that he didn't ask why her upright landlady had ever had anything to do with someone like Justin. She took it that he had worked out that much.

'It sounds,' Ryan said, 'as if you're more concerned about Claudia than about yourself.'

'Of course I am,' Gerry said. 'She's an innocent. After what happened to me in the summer, I at least have some idea of what I might be up against.'

'What are you saying?' Ryan's voice was very low. 'That you're setting yourself against these murdering thieves?'

'Yes,' Gerry said simply. 'But that's my choice. I don't want to involve anyone else. I've got to do it, you see. I feel it's partly my fault that man died today in Truro.' It was the first time she'd acknowledged that. 'I'm afraid I'll have bad dreams tonight.' She doubted if even the Bysow a'n gammneves could keep Baranwen out of her head once she was asleep. Remembering the pictures of people lying bleeding on the floor in the Museum wouldn't help either.

'Would you like me to come back and sleep with you?' Ryan asked. 'It might help. At least I'd be there if you woke up out of a nightmare.'

Gerry giggled; she couldn't help it. The offer had been made with a straight face, but there was a private smile in his eyes. She knew then that the worst was over. Ryan no longer thought she went around wrecking other people's relationships.

'No, you can't,' Gerry told him, in the same tone of voice as she'd have used to her little niece if she asked for a third helping of ice cream. 'But it's good of you to ask,' she added, keeping her face straight too.

They were both quiet for a while, but the tension had gone. They reached for each other's hands again, and Gerry began to notice what was going on around them. A tall young man brought a tray of drinks from the bar to three men sitting nearby. A woman from the kitchen in a white overall was serving large plates of food to two middle-aged couples. These were sitting at tables further along the window, talking and laughing. Ordinary people on an ordinary, pleasant evening out. Two women sat chatting near the bar, one holding the leash of a golden retriever. The dog was lapping water eagerly from a bowl on the carpet beside them.

Ryan followed her gaze.

'I suppose you're not making all this up?' he asked. 'It just seems so fantastic. I mean, here we are, sitting in a pub having a drink, and you're telling me a man tried to kill you because you had a precious chalice. And now someone else really has killed one man and injured a load of others to get hold of it, and you're planning to go against them? And you say you're a dangerous person to know? No,' he said, half to himself. 'If you just didn't want to see me you needn't have rung me tonight. You wouldn't have to invent all this.'

Gerry sighed. 'It's all true enough. I wish it wasn't. But I meant it, you'd be better not getting involved. Remember those pictures.'

Ryan made a strange, choking sort of sound, pulled out his phone and called up the feature he'd shown her earlier.

'What do you think you can do against people who do something like this?' he pleaded. 'Leave it to the professionals, Gerry. You said you knew the men. If there's anything, any info, names and stuff you can give, then do it. But surely that's enough.'

Gerry imagined herself going into Redruth police station in her lunch hour the next day. She had four first names which were strange in themselves, but no surnames, no addresses and above all no proof. She knew how they'd got in and out undetected, and how the security glass had been smashed, but Gerry couldn't explain that and be believed. The police would think she was on drugs or something.

Gerry couldn't talk about it any more.

'I'll tell you something else about me,' she said, hoping to lighten the tone a bit. 'My real name's Gerralda, it's only Gerry for short. No-one down here knows except Debs. I never used it in London either, it didn't feel right there.'

'Don't try and change the subject,' Ryan retorted. 'It won't work. But Gerralda's a beautiful name. Beautiful and special – like you.'

Gerry couldn't help feeling warmed, even if she was sure he was exaggerating; she wasn't used to compliments, and no-one had ever called her beautiful. She finished her Coke and stood up.

'Let's go back to the car park,' she said. 'I ought to go home and talk to Claudia.'

Ryan gave that smile again, and drank the rest of his beer in one go.

'Yep,' he said. 'Let's do that.'

They said very little during the short drive back. When they reached the car park, Gerry saw that some of the cars had gone while they'd been at the pub, the beach was empty, and the moon had not yet risen. The lights above the sidings blazed out, illuminating the whole area now it was fully dark, but she wasn't bothered any longer. Gerry parked by the plumber's van and they both got out. This time when they kissed it was gentle, but warm. Gerry never been kissed by a man she could relax or laugh with. She wanted it to last longer, but Ryan stopped.

'I don't want to get carried away again,' he said. He gave a quick glance at the van, half raising an eyebrow with a hopeful query, but Gerry shook her head.

'Definitely not.'

Ryan gave a rueful smile. 'No, I agree, the inside's far worse than the outside.' He grinned, and added, 'I ought to tell you I drove round the industrial estate across the road before I came over here. I know it, it's where Connor works, but that's no good either. Street lights all over the place, lorries parked up everywhere, with their drivers inside for all I know. Plus a gang of kids up to goodness knows what, and a cab firm with drivers coming and going that looks as if it's open all night.'

They looked at each other and laughed. Both knew they wanted the same thing, and sharing that felt good. 'I can't ask you back,' Ryan added gloomily. 'Connor and Jez are both in, I mean, of course I've got my own room, but - well.' He didn't need to explain; Gerry could picture the set-up perfectly. His ex must have had her own place. 'And I suppose you'd think the house was a mess,' he finished. 'I don't think so, but my mum's always moaning at me and Conn.'

'And I can't ask you back either,' Gerry said. It felt like being a teenager again, but she couldn't see herself casually bringing a man back to Windhaven and vanishing up to her room with him.

Ryan sighed. 'I'd better take myself off then,' he said, then asked, 'What are you doing tomorrow?'

It took Gerry a minute to remember.

'I'm working at Redruth, at the Cornwall Centre.'

'Well, I don't suppose you can get into much trouble at work.' Ryan pulled the key to the van out of his jacket pocket and grinned, his face a strange colour in the orange-pink glow of the floodlights. 'Conn was talking about getting a car. I mean, he works in a body shop, he ought to know where there's one going. I could always offer to help with the payments so we could share it. I've got a real reason now. They'll tease the bol-,' he corrected himself, 'tease the hell out of me, but it's worth it. I don't know if I'll believe all this myself when I wake up tomorrow.'

Ryan gave Gerry a last hug, then got into the van and started the engine. He lowered the window and leaned out, calling above the noise, 'Let me know what Claudia says. I'll see you tomorrow evening, there or somewhere else, we'll sort it later. And remember, don't do anything stupid.'

He drove off with a wave, the van's exhaust roaring. Gerry winced at the sound, then turned and stared out at the dark water of the bay and the few stars coming out in the blackness above it. After that last kiss in the car park Ryan had said he loved her. That he thought he'd fallen in love with her on her first day at the library in the summer, though he'd never believed in love at first sight before. Gerry couldn't in all honesty say she loved him too, but perhaps soon she might be able to. It looked like maybe there could be life after Justin. That reminded her of Monica, and suddenly the warmth Gerry was basking in vanished. Who was the man Debbie had seen Monica with? Was he really one of the Wasps?

She drove home very soberly. Ryan had said not to do anything stupid. Unfortunately, Gerry was thinking about doing something that might be really stupid, but she had no choice that she could see.

Chapter Six

'Claudia, I've invited someone to come over tomorrow evening after work, to meet you.'

Gerry had known Claudia wouldn't like this. When she first moved in, it had been on condition that she didn't bring her friends to Windhaven. It had never been an issue so far, as Gerry had been avoiding her few friends. And beautiful as the location was, Windhaven didn't lend itself to casual chat and laughter.

The kitchen was filled with the smell of ham and vegetables, and some freshly cut chunks of bread sat in an individual bread basket on the glossy granite work surface. Claudia's hand was arrested in the act of stirring some soup she was warming through, which was where the appetising aroma came from. Her face went still as she turned to look at Gerry.

'I know I said I wouldn't,' Gerry hurried on, 'but this is a one-off. His name's Ryan and he works at the library. I know him, and he's totally trustworthy.' She stopped, but still Claudia didn't speak. 'It's, I was telling him about what's happening at your gallery, and he thought he could help.'

Claudia switched off the soup and turned away from the stove, her eyes half closed for a moment as if in pain. Gerry felt that the fragile confidence which had been restored so slowly between them since Justin's death had been shattered again, but all Claudia said was, 'Well, if you've invited him, he'd better come. But I wish you'd asked me first.' Then, abandoning her supper, she went off to the lounge, picking up her glass of wine from the work surface and taking it with her.

Gerry was mortified. She was sure that once Claudia had met Ryan it would be all right; no-one could help liking him. And Claudia would understand why Gerry felt she would be able to trust him. She hated the idea of Claudia sitting on her soft leather sofa in the lounge, sipping her wine, looking at the large, high-definition tv screen but oblivious to her surroundings, lost in bitter memories.

Gerry went off to her room early, then lay on the bed fully dressed, but with her eyes open to help her stay in place. In the silence she was bombarded with images: Ryan's face earlier when he thought she'd seduced Justin away from Claudia; Monica and the unknown man she was seeing; Baranwen's shout of triumph as she lifted the Kelegel in the Museum.

Baranwen. Gerry should be thinking about her, not the rest; everything revolved round the Guardian. If her guess was right, Baranwen had not only brought the Wasps forward in time, but had somehow got Monica together with one of them. Debbie didn't know him, so if it was one of the Gohi it must be Kenver. Talan didn't seem to be with the rest. Anyway, he had fair hair, and was neater in build than the others, so didn't match Debbie's description.

And how could she involve Ryan in all this? Gerry doubted if Ryan had met any more violence than maybe a Saturday night pub brawl. Gerry remembered the Guardian brandishing her great double-headed axe, the one Rosenwyn the Maker had called a Labrys, whatever that was. That was yet another thing she'd meant to look up, but had shut away after Justin's death like everything else.

And at the memory of the confrontation between the Guardians and the Makers, Gerry sat up sharply, her simple supper suddenly churning inside her. She must go back to the Makers. That was the name she used when she thought of the three women who had made the chalice, six or seven centuries before the time of Baranwen, Hedra and Meraud. Gerry no longer expected them to help her, or to have any ideas how she could contend with Baranwen and the Gohi, but they ought to know what the Guardian had done. They believed the Kelegel could never be used again; they needed to be told that it had come back to life. The Chalice had been restored, and it was now tainted with blood.

Gerry switched off the lights, lay down again and this time, with two fingers closed round her Rainbow Ring, she closed her eyes. She rested her other hand on the gold chain Seona had given her. She only needed to picture the entrance to the fogou and she was there; and she knew at once that she'd come too late.

Gerry found the Makers near the top of Chapel Carn Brea, close to the entrance to the short tunnel leading into the round, stone-walled chamber. In this earlier century the village was further up the hill, before the people had moved down to better lands for farming, but the cave known as the fogou was hardly altered. The air was cold and it was almost too dark to see, although streaks of apricot light on the eastern horizon over the distant Mounts Bay showed that dawn was not far off. One of the enormous slabs of granite which stood close to the hill's top reared up behind the three women. Gerry could just make out that they were wearing ordinary gowns rather than their formal green robes. Rosenwyn the Mother stood leaning back against the near-vertical surface of the stone. Colenso the Wise Woman was standing nearby, but Keyna the Maiden knelt on the damp grass, her face buried in her hands. Gerry's first impression was that they were unharmed; yet the sagging of their bodies and what little she could see of their expressions indicated only hopelessness.

Gerry had arrived almost directly in front of them, yet she could not be sure that they were even aware of her. Then Colenso raised her head and looked hard at Gerry, but said nothing. Keyna remained kneeling, seemingly oblivious. Only Rosenwyn spoke, and her habitually compassionate voice was harsh.

'Gerralda Melinda Hamilton,' she said. 'You have picked the time of your return with care, I see. We were not kind to you. Have you come back now to deride us?'

Colenso still did not speak, but at Rosenwyn's words, Keyna made a sound like a choking sob, or a painful laugh. Her strong young form seemed to have collapsed in on itself, and she was rocking backwards and forwards. She looked even more helpless than her two companions. She took her hands from her face, but her eyes were closed.

'No, of course not,' Gerry faltered. 'I came to warn you. About – Baranwen?'

'Then you should have come sooner.' Keyna's tone was beyond bitterness. There was a bleak acceptance in it which hurt more than if she had screamed aloud. 'Ah, no, we thought we had prevented you from moving in time again.'

Keyna did not ask how Gerry had overcome their barrier. Instead she raised her head, opened her eyes and turned her face directly towards their visitor, or to the sound of her voice. In the dim light Gerry must have sensed rather than seen what was wrong. The Maiden's eyes were sightless.

Gerry found she had covered her mouth with her hand, pressing hard. She didn't know if she was trying to stop herself from crying out, or from throwing up.

'She did that.' It was not a question. Gerry looked at Rosenwyn.

'I see that you have understood,' she said. Her phrasing was odd, deliberate. The harsh voice went on, devoid of tone. 'She came to us like a storm in the night. Summoned us as she did before, drew us out here using the Kelegel a'n gammneves, the precious creation that we had believed would bring light and help to our people. She taunted us, held us bound and helpless solely by her will. She came alone but outmatched all of us together. Then she showed us what she could do.' Rosenwyn rubbed her ear absently. Gerry looked at Colenso who was watching intently. By now her silence was terrifying.

'Baranwen told us,' Rosenwyn continued, 'that when we destroyed the powers of the chalice, it was as if we had left her blind, deaf and dumb; so she would return what we had given her.'

Keyna rose, turning towards Rosenwyn, took a few steps and stubbed her toe against a large stone in the path. Gerry had never heard the words she used, but she was obviously cursing. Perhaps it was not only the stone she was swearing at. Rosenwyn came to her and wrapped her in her arms, holding her like a mother whose child has suffered the worst pain imaginable. Over Keyna's shoulder she looked at Gerry.

'Baranwen took Keyna's sight,' the Mother said. 'She said that as she was the youngest of us, she would be the one who would miss it the most. Then she told Colenso that because she was the one who had pronounced the words that had caused the harm, she would deprive her of speech. I am the most fortunate; I have merely lost my hearing. This will not be all that your Guardian will do to us. She has left us like this to wait. We have been here for most of the night, but we cannot guess when she will return. In the meantime we can only endeavour not to imagine what she might do next. Nor,' Rosenwyn added after a pause, 'can we begin to comprehend how she has brought the Stones back to life. There was nothing of power left in them. Nothing.'

Keyna pulled herself out of Rosenwyn's grip, but seemed reluctant to try walking again. Gerry went to her and took her hand, which was ice cold. Keyna snatched it away.

'You're freezing!' Gerry exclaimed. 'Shouldn't you at least go home and get warm?'

'And face everyone?' Keyna turned her ravaged face towards Gerry. 'The people who have trusted us, respected, even revered us? Let them see us like this?'

Colenso the Wise Woman came over and put her arm round the young woman's shoulders. Gerry could hardly bear what she was seeing, and could think of nothing that would help. Then she felt the Bysow a'n gammneves begin to pulse steadily. Colenso swung sharply towards her. Rosenwyn moved too, as if, impossibly, she had heard a call. Keyna lifted her head, staring towards Gerry with those dreadful unseeing eyes. Colenso's lips moved, but no sound came out.

Little rainbow lines were moving around Gerry's finger. She covered them with her other hand to keep them out of sight, feeling the beginning of an idea.

'Baranwen did this just with the Kelegel?' she asked Keyna. 'I mean, it's not physical?'

'You are correct,' came the reply. 'She had no need of hot irons for my eyes, nor to cut out Colenso's tongue.' Colenso nodded in confirmation.

Keyna burst out passionately, 'That was what made it far worse than anything else she could dream up, and she knew it. We created the Chalice for the benefit of all; and she enjoyed using it to torture us. That she could do that – you could never imagine, it was like she was burning our hearts out. Deliberately showing us the wreck of everything we had hoped for.'

Any bitterness Gerry might have felt towards the Makers for their former treatment of her had evaporated at the sight of their anguish. To see this proud, confident, powerful young woman reduced to such helplessness was appalling. Gerry touched her ring. The pre-dawn light was too dim for the beams to form properly, but she could feel it was trying to tell her something. She said nothing of it to the Makers; she didn't want to make promises she might not be able to keep.

'I'd better go,' Gerry said instead, 'and I'm so very sorry.' She prayed that they could see or hear how earnestly she meant that. Gerry didn't say she would come back; but she had every intention of doing so.

There was one more thing she could attempt. She had tried Hedra, Meraud and the Makers. The only person remaining who could give her guidance was Seona. Gerry had been warned emphatically against changing anything that had already happened within her own life, and had finally been convinced of the truth of this. It was, after all, why she had tried to keep the Chalice from Justin. Justin wanted revenge on the brother who had cheated him out of his inheritance. He had planned to alter his own past, and the consequences could have been unthinkable. But if she went back to around thirty years before her own birth – surely that couldn't do any harm?

Gerry had never gone in person to anywhere in the past except Chapel Carn Brea, and the nearby village where the Wasps lived. Baranwen and Justin had initially brought her to and from the time of the Bees, and the Chalice itself had taken her back to its Makers the first time. But almost as soon as she had received the Rainbow Ring from Seona, Gerry had found herself watching, mentally but not physically, what had happened in the Museum forty miles away and perhaps forty minutes earlier. Moreover, Baranwen had been aware of Gerry observing her. Then when Gerry had gone to visit Hedra, she had visualised the Wasps with the girls in Penzance. She had no doubt she'd seen something that had actually happened, seeing with her mind's eye alone. The ring plainly had powers different from those of the sapphire, the Chalice or Seona's gold chain. And maybe, as she'd conjectured earlier, Seona's two gifts, the ring and the chain, were working together, augmenting each other. So perhaps between them they could help her go to a totally different time and place. The Chalice had taken her to the women who made it. The ring and chain could return to the woman who had not physically made them, but had at least chosen or ordered them. And endowed them with all the powers they had. Gerry had seen that, after working with the Kelegel, the chain could take her back and forward in time and translate between modern English and old Cornish. The ring, she suspected, she was only just beginning to learn about.

Once Gerry was back in her room, she opened her laptop and called up pictures of the clothes that women were wearing in the nineteen sixties. She couldn't imagine Seona in any of them: short straight mini skirts above long thin thighs; white boots, big chunky jewellery, thick bobbed haircuts. These must be London fashions for girls in their teens and twenties. No one in Oban, perhaps not even in Edinburgh, let alone the remote village of Lochallaig, would have dressed like that. Gerry had hardly seen any pictures of Seona as a younger woman; there were no photos in her cottage, and even in the family album there were only a couple. Her clothes in the latter were just like anyone else's. If Gerry's adding up was right, Seona would be somewhere in her thirties at the time she was looking to go to, while Gerry's mother would still be at school.

And with that thought, Gerry was engulfed in an unexpected wave of homesickness. She remembered the sound of the children in the playground at the village school: laughing, shouting and racing around. The soft accents of the Western Highlands were higher, shriller in their young voices, but the memory hit her with a nostalgia she had never experienced during her self-imposed exile in London.

Then, even more startling, Gerry had an image of going back home with Ryan. Gerry knew everyone would like him: her parents, her brothers and their wives, people she'd been at school with. The long journey, a good 650 miles, would pass easily, talking and laughing, whether they drove or went by train. She would never have gone to Lochallaig with Justin.

This was stupid. Justin was dead; and she needed to get some sleep. Tomorrow night she would do her best to go to see Seona. And before that she was going to introduce Ryan to Claudia.

Chapter Seven

Wednesday September 10th

At work the next day, Gerry made sure she got put down for all the most routine jobs which involved the minimum of concentration. All she could think of was the Makers and their torment, as well as Baranwen and Seona. It would be a miracle if she even managed to get things in alphabetical or numerical order.

Ryan called her at lunchtime while she was out buying a sandwich. Gerry was never organised enough to bring her own lunch.

'I've been thinking about you all morning,' Ryan said. 'Tell me I didn't imagine it, that yesterday really happened.'

'It happened.' Gerry felt guilty as she realised she'd hardly thought of Ryan, being too overwhelmed with harsher issues. Now it all rushed back: the kiss in the street outside the library, the talk at the pub in the evening, and the car park afterwards. Gerry remembered the look on Ryan's face as they said goodnight. She'd never seen a man look so loving, or so happy.

They arranged that Gerry would pick Ryan up at the station car park in Penzance on her way back from work.

'I'll be waiting for you by the entrance,' he said. 'I can't have the van tonight, Connor wants it. Anyway, I'm not sure it would make a good impression on your dragon landlady.'

69

Gerry laughed, but he was probably right.

When she came back into the staff room at the library ten minutes later, clutching her sandwich and a banana, Lowenna, the senior assistant, was at the microwave and Mark was sitting opposite the door, holding a mug of tea. He was a lanky young man on work experience, who dressed like a student and talked with a pronounced Northern accent.

'You're looking very cheerful all of a sudden,' Mark said. To her annoyance, Gerry felt herself blushing. Surely she was too old for that?

Lowenna turned round to look.

'You're right,' she agreed, 'I hardly recognised her. Thought it must be some member of the public coming in here by mistake.'

Gerry knew Lowenna was only teasing, but even so – had she been as miserable as that for all the weeks she'd been here? She liked the others and got on with them well enough in the course of her work, but that was all. She'd just kept her head down and got on with the job.

'I'd say she looks like she's in love,' said Mark.

It wasn't worth protesting. Whether Gerry said she was or wasn't, Mark could keep up the banter all afternoon.

'No,' Gerry told him instead, 'actually I've just won the lottery. I'll buy you that bike you're always going on about.' Then she unwrapped the sandwich and bit off a large chunk. She couldn't be expected to talk with her mouth full.

'So, how was your day?'

Ryan smiled at Gerry as he fastened his seat belt, and she found herself smiling back.

'Oh, it wasn't very exciting' she said. 'Just all the usual, you know – filing, shelving, helping people with the film readers for the old newspapers. Very 1970s.'

'Sounds like fun,' Ryan said, settling back and turning his head to watch Gerry as she started the car. 'I'll have to get some time off and come and give you a hand. Anyway, now I've got you here, I was going to say, you remember when I asked you to go to that jam session with me?'

'Yes, of course' Gerry said. 'Then I fell downstairs and couldn't go.'

That was only a fraction of what had happened but she couldn't say anything about the rest.

'Well this time I'll ask if you fancy going to the pictures,' Ryan said. 'There's one rom-com, one adventure movie and one sci-fi on in Penzance this week. Which would you prefer? Are you free tomorrow evening?'

'Sci-fi,' Gerry said. Perhaps it would give her a chance to sound him out on time travel and mind reading.

'Just as well I asked, then,' Ryan said. 'I'd assumed it would be one of the other two.'

'You're right, usually it would be.' Gerry didn't like telling Ryan half-truths. 'I just felt like a change. Anyway, I'd probably better not talk any more for now. I'm not used to driving with a passenger.'

Ryan obediently kept silent as she drove through Penzance and up the road towards St. Just. Finally she took the Pendeen turning and then headed left at the milestone. Once they were on the lane to Windhaven she stopped for a moment and turned to Ryan.

'I'd better warn you,' she told him, 'Claudia will know we've arrived and will probably be waiting on the doorstep. If it was a bit warmer she'd be out at the gate of the courtyard.'

'How does she know?' he asked. 'Has she got a sixth sense or something? Spooky.'

Gerry winced at that. She wondered how he'd react if she said 'No, but I have.' Instead she explained about the hidden security camera.

'Sounds very up country,' was his response. Then they had crossed the cattle grid and Ryan got his first sight of the view of the coast. Gerry heard him gasp, and looked sideways, hoping he was as impressed as she'd been the first time she came here. Then she saw that she'd been wrong about Claudia not coming outside. She was standing in front of the gate with a loose jacket over her habitual tailored shirt and slacks, watching the car approach. Her hair in its neat copper layers ruffled slightly in the light breeze. Her fine cheekbones had become more pronounced since Justin's death. She stood watching them, elegant, slender and unsmiling. Ryan let his breath out again.

'That,' he asked, staring, 'is your landlady?'

Gerry could tell she hadn't made as good a job as she'd thought of preparing Ryan for what Claudia was like. Or maybe she'd got so used to her that she'd forgotten the effect Claudia was likely to have on strangers.

Gerry and Ryan got out of the car and walked over. Claudia's expression was completely neutral. Gerry wondered what sort of person Claudia had expected her to bring. Claudia held out her hand formally and Ryan shook it. Gerry introduced them then remembered she'd left her jacket in the car and went to get it. By the time she got back to them, Ryan was waving an arm at the view and Claudia was looking more relaxed already. Gerry felt herself unwind a little too. Ryan, as she'd seen at the library, could always disarm people.

'You haven't seen it properly till you've seen it in the sun on a clear day,' Claudia was saying. 'Then you understand why all those artists came to paint the light on the north coast. You'll have to come back when it's not so grey.'

This, from Claudia, who'd told Gerry when they first met that she didn't want her to bring friends to the house? Claudia led them indoors, and Ryan took Gerry's hand and gave it a squeeze. She looked at him, but he'd already let go and was following

Claudia into the long kitchen and through to the conservatory.

Gerry could smell hot soup, and the table was laid with cold meat, bread, cheese and butter. On the side was a dish of salad and a bowl of fruit. Claudia didn't cook; the soup would be "home-made" but bought from one of the delis in Penzance.

Ryan shook his head, disconcerted.

'I'm sorry, I wasn't expecting this or I'd have brought something for you. I thought we were just going to have a cup of tea and a chat. Like I told Gerry, I've got an idea I wanted to run past you.'

Claudia waved a hand dismissively.

'It's nothing,' she said. 'It's the least I could do after dragging you all the way up here at the end of a day's work. Would you like some soup, or do you want a look round the gardens?'

'No, I don't know anything about gardens,' Ryan said. He smiled at her. 'I can see them pretty well from here.' From his place by the window, he was looking over the gardens to the north and east sides of the house. They were full of flowers and shrubs, with trees behind them to protect them against the fierce winter winds which gave the house its name. 'Soup sounds good.'

While he and Gerry sat down, Claudia went to get warm plates out of the oven, then served them. Once they had all started to eat, Claudia asked Ryan about his job. He sketched it briefly, giving an example of an elderly couple who'd come in earlier in the week. Their grand-daughter was going backpacking in Australia and had promised to email, but they had never used a computer and were nervous of them.

'You don't often have to start at the very beginning,' he said, 'but to them a mouse was something you don't want to find in your kitchen, and a screen is what you watch at the cinema. And a keyboard belongs on a piano.'

Then he made them both laugh with an account of a particularly irritating customer who was a classic know-it-all.

'Of course, with all the talk of cuts that's going on, I don't know how long I'll have a job,' Ryan said. 'They might put up the cost of lessons, but then some people will decide they can't afford them.' He finished his soup, and Gerry handed him the plate of cold meat. She'd finished her own soup without noticing what flavour it was. 'Anyway, that's enough about me. Do tell me about your work.'

So while they all passed round the bread, butter and salad, Claudia outlined her career.

'I took a degree in Fine Arts,' she told them, 'and I always hoped I'd be an artist, but in the end I had to accept that my talents lay in the direction of promoting people who really can paint.' She stopped to take a mouthful of bread, and Gerry remembered to eat some herself. She'd never seen Claudia so expansive, or prepared to talk about personal things. It was good that Ryan was gaining Claudia's confidence so easily, but something she couldn't yet identify was beginning to nag at her.

'I worked in a couple of the galleries in London, in New Bond Street,' Claudia went on, lifting her glass in one perfectly manicured hand. 'I met a lot of useful people and learned the ropes, but I didn't see myself working there for the rest of my life. I'd done a module in my course on the artists of the St. Ives school between the wars, and the Newlyn and Lamorna ones as well. I came down to Penzance to see all the places, and decided what I really wanted was to set up on my own here. There were quite a lot of galleries already, though not as many as there are now. But I had my London contacts and I was sure I could find outlets for some of the people whose work I was seeing.'

Gerry had learned more about her landlady this evening than in all the time she'd lived here. Claudia didn't talk about herself. All she had ever said up till now was that her father, the banker, had bought the house as a tax dodge or something.

'So that's what you did?' Ryan asked.

'Pretty much, yes.' Claudia smiled at him, and it was a smile Gerry hadn't seen before. 'It's a challenge, of course, but I enjoy it. And the internet has completely changed the way you can promote works of art since the days when I was at university.'

Ryan laid down his knife and fork.

'Thanks, that was great. Now, I hate to spoil the party, but will you tell me about this man who's been coming to your gallery?'

Claudia's face went hard for a moment, then her expression became resigned instead. She summarised what she'd already told Gerry, about the man coming in every day and hanging around.

'If I'm in my office, I can see him on the CCTV screen, and if I'm in the gallery it's hard to avoid him,' she said. 'It's only a small place. He never stays more than an hour but by now even ten minutes would be enough to set me on edge for the day. He doesn't say anything, and technically he's not doing anything wrong, but it's,' Claudia paused, and Gerry wondered if she was going to say 'driving me nuts', but she settled for, 'it's begun to really get under my skin. He never comes in if Ethan, my assistant, is there. It's only when I'm on my own.'

Ryan nodded.

'That fits. Your gallery's in Chapel Street?'

'Yes,' Claudia confirmed. 'Why?'

'There's some little side passages there as well as other shops and some other galleries too,' he said. 'My guess is that he's watching your place, checking you're alone before he comes in.'

Claudia shuddered. So did Gerry, but she didn't think either of them noticed. The idea of the man watching and waiting for his moment was horrible.

'That makes me feel as if I've got insects crawling under my skin,' Claudia said. Her face had become haggard.

'I'm sorry,' Ryan said quietly. 'I didn't mean to make it any worse, or to upset you.' For a moment Gerry thought he was going to reach over and take Claudia's hand. 'It's just, you see,' he went on, 'that he's seeing you as vulnerable. If you react in any way when you see him, then that reinforces it. Even if it's just an expression of distaste or annoyance. If you looked afraid, then that would suit him even better.'

There was a sudden flash of anger in Claudia's eyes, replacing the fear of the moment before. Ryan's job entailed not just knowing a lot about computers, but setting people at their ease. She could picture him doing just that with the two grandparents he had described earlier. But he wasn't being gentle with Claudia. Perhaps that wasn't what she needed.

'So what was this idea of yours?' Claudia asked. 'I don't see that I could put in a complaint against him.'

'Well, I suppose you could say he's stalking you and that's a crime. But that wasn't what I had in mind.' Ryan looked straight at Claudia. 'If he thought you had someone else around who would be prepared to look out for you, if he didn't see you as isolated, he might back off. I'll tell you what I thought of, and if you don't like it you can just say no. I won't be offended.'

'Go on.' At least Claudia didn't look angry. Gerry wondered what Ryan was going to suggest. Then she found out.

'Well, you know I work just a few minutes away from Chapel Street,' Ryan said. 'My idea was that I could stop by and see you in my lunch hour, and call in again when I finish work. Look around, like I'm checking to see if he's there, ready to have a word, put him in his place or report him. Assuming he's watching, he might get the message.'

He could have warned me. Gerry glanced at Claudia, who appeared to be considering the idea seriously. Ryan was looking at Claudia to see her reaction. Gerry wasn't sure either of them even remembered she was there. She felt like she'd been hit in the

76

stomach. Ryan had said the night before that once he'd met her he couldn't go out with anyone else. He'd told her he loved her and called her "beautiful and special". He'd phoned to check that their evening together hadn't been just a dream. Now she was watching him concentrating on another woman. Was she jealous, after one evening together? Gerry hadn't felt this bad when she'd thought of Claudia and Justin together. Nor when Martin, her supposed boyfriend in London, had coolly confirmed that he was going back to his real girlfriend now she had returned from her holiday.

Gerry knew that Ryan wasn't asking Claudia to go out with him. He was suggesting coming to her workplace, in order to frighten off this horrible man. But knowing that didn't get rid of the churning inside her. It wasn't as if she was in love with Ryan. It must be that she hadn't got over the way Martin – and Justin - had treated her.

Claudia was silent, thinking through Ryan's suggestion. Gerry was pretty sure her landlady wouldn't like owing anyone favours. Feeling superfluous, she got up from the table and went through into the kitchen to put the kettle on. The long kitchen was divided from the conservatory by sliding glass doors with wooden frames. These took up almost the whole wall between the two rooms and had remained open all through the summer. Now it was autumn they were usually closed after dark and the curtains drawn. Tonight, however, they were still open, although the evening was drawing in. Claudia had switched on the bronzed standard lamps at the far end of the conservatory, so from where Gerry stood, Claudia and Ryan, sitting at the table, were illuminated as if they were on a stage. The floor length curtains, pushed back on either side of the sliding doors like stage curtains, completed the image.

With the noise of the kettle coming to the boil beside her, Gerry couldn't hear what they were saying. Or perhaps Ryan was sensibly keeping quiet, leaving Claudia to think, rather than trying to push her into agreeing. As Gerry watched she saw Claudia's expression finally relax from consideration into acceptance. Ryan leaned back in his chair looking relieved. Gerry went back in to join them.

'Does anyone want a cup of tea?' she asked.

'If I'd ever met her, or even seen her before, I'd never have had the nerve to come up with an idea like that,' Ryan said, turning in his seat for a last look back as Gerry drove up the lane. 'I know you said she was beautiful and very self-contained, but I didn't expect her to be quite so,' he stopped, searching for the right word, 'so overwhelming.'

Gerry tried to keep her voice normal.

'Well, she's agreed to try it.'

'Yeah, that's great, I really didn't think she would,' Ryan said. 'Let's just hope it does the trick. I'll start tomorrow lunchtime.'

Gerry glanced sideways at him. He was looking unusually serious.

'I thought I'd try and get a picture of this man if he's still there when I arrive,' Ryan said. 'If he's not, I'll just have to act as if he was and hope he's watching and sees me with her, like checking the place out. Then I'll have achieved something by being there. But if I do see him I'm sure I can get a picture, like I said, without him knowing. Then I'll text it to you, and you can tell me if you've ever seen him hanging around.'

They had reached the top of the drive from Windhaven. Gerry was about to turn onto the bridle path which led from the drive up to the road, but at Ryan's words her foot hit the brake without conscious decision. Luckily she was going very slowly, as this bit of the lane was uneven. Even so she felt her seat belt tighten as she jerked forward.

The same thing had happened to Ryan. He straightened up in his seat, adjusting his own belt.

'Hey, what's up?' he asked. 'What did I say?'

'That's a scary idea,' Gerry said slowly; she was thinking aloud. 'He's not anyone Claudia knows. But,' she stopped. Debbie had suggested the man in the gallery might be connected with the Wasps. Belatedly things began to click into place. Debbie had seen Monica with a man who might be Kenver. Monica hated Claudia, and was mean enough to have dreamed up something like this. If Baranwen didn't need him, there was nothing to stop Kenver spending his time as he wanted. And if it was him, Gerry would recognise him.

And if Baranwen didn't need the Wasps round her right now – then what was the Guardian doing?

'Gerry?' Ryan put his hand on her shoulder. 'You've gone away from me. Tell me, what is it?'

Gerry had to play this down. She restarted the engine; it had stalled when she braked so suddenly.

'I'm sorry,' she said, trying to keep her voice from shaking. 'You just reminded me of that trouble back in the summer. Do you remember, I told you I was afraid Claudia might get targeted because of Justin?'

This was getting worse. Now she was making it sound as if Claudia really did need someone to protect her. Well, to be fair, perhaps she did. Only – did it have to be Ryan?

Ryan put his hand on the steering wheel.

'Gerry, wait.'

She switched the engine off again.

'Yes?'

'Do you mean,' Ryan spoke levelly, but his eyes were appalled, 'that this Stork character could be connected with the robbery at the museum yesterday? If he was then I'm definitely calling the police. Did you go to them today?'

'No.' Gerry turned the ignition key and repeated what she'd told herself the day before. 'I only know the men's first names. No surnames, no contact details, nothing.'

'Not where they work, what they do? Gerry, how do you even know who they are?' Ryan asked.

'I met them when I was with Justin that evening, after the fireworks,' she replied. 'He knew them. If you send me the picture I'll be able to tell you if the man's one of them or not.'

Gerry had been more brusque than she'd intended, but she couldn't tell Ryan the truth about the Wasps – and she didn't want to talk about Justin. Ryan looked startled at her tone which had verged on sharp. Gerry wanted to apologise, but if she said she was sorry she'd have to say what she was sorry for, and she couldn't explain that. Miserably, she began to turn out of the bridle path onto the hill.

Ryan remained silent as she drove. Gerry hoped that was only because she'd asked him earlier not to talk while she was at the wheel. She didn't dare even look at him. When they got to the roundabout on the edge of Penzance she took the turn towards the sea rather than going round the bypass. As Gerry drove along the front, she spotted a good-sized parking space and pulled over into it.

'Where do you want to be dropped?' she asked. 'I mean, I don't even know what part of town you live in.'

'It's all right,' he said. 'I can walk from here.'

He just wants to get away from me, Gerry thought. She could see Ryan looked preoccupied. Then she thought, now he's met Claudia he's probably wondering why Justin would look twice at me.

Ryan unfastened his seat belt and began to open the car door.

'Don't forget to send me the picture if you get it,' Gerry said, hoping she didn't sound as desolate as she felt.

'Of course.' Ryan leaned over and kissed her, but it was hardly more than a brush of his lips across hers. 'Take care.'

And he was gone. Gerry watched him cross the road and walk as far as Queen Street where he turned left and disappeared. She saw that his steps were slow instead of his usual jaunty pace. He didn't look round or wave at her. Yesterday, he would have done.

If a week ago Gerry had met up with Ryan and told him about Claudia's situation when they were still just friends, how would she be feeling now, she asked herself? If he'd had the same idea and she'd taken him home, and Claudia had agreed – would she still have minded about the way he'd looked at Claudia? A beautiful "damsel in distress" – what man could resist? Gerry wished fervently that she could appeal to Ryan to help her against Baranwen and the Wasps. She could tell him what a desperate situation she was in, and he would come back to her. But that wasn't what she wanted, or rather that wasn't how she wanted it to happen. She wanted him to look at her the way he'd looked at her in the car park the night before, shining with love and happiness.

Gerry told herself she was not going to cry. She would go home and rest for a bit before making her attempt to see Seona. After all, that was more important right now than anything else.

But thinking about Ryan still hurt.

Chapter Eight

It was only when Gerry found herself actually standing in Lochallaig in the 1960s that she realised she hadn't thought through what this visit truly entailed. She'd been thinking only about how desperately she wanted to see Seona. She wanted the comfort of the familiar presence, and the reassurance of her great-aunt's advice which she'd always trusted, based as it was on decades of knowledge and experience. But the Seona who Gerry was about to confront would only be ten years or so older than she was now herself, and would be a complete stranger instead of someone she'd been close to for much of her life.

Gerry had prepared as well as she could for this trip. Knowing that Scotland would be much colder than Cornwall, she'd put on jeans, a warm sweater, boots and a jacket which she hoped would all be neutral enough to pass unnoticed in the earlier decade. She had tried to 'speak' to the ring and the chain, as she'd done with the Kelegel when she first went to the Makers. Putting all her faith in the two, she'd let them pick the precise time and place to go to.

Now she was standing on the road that ran through the centre of the village. Lochallaig was at once reassuringly familiar and disturbingly altered. The stone houses and cottages were the same in their layout; she'd known them all her life and they all dated back to well before the sixties. From where Gerry stood she could see the slopes of the mountains and the deep pine forests surrounding the village on every side. At the sight she realised, with an unexpected ache, how much she'd missed them in the months since she'd last gone home. It was just getting light but there was no-one about, so it must be very early on a summer morning. Gerry rested her left hand over the Rainbow Ring. She hadn't even considered what would happen if she arrived in a street full of people.

There were hardly any cars, and the handful she could see looked like museum pieces to her twenty-first-century eyes. The houses sprouted tv aerials on the roofs, and most of the doors, fences, curtains and gates were different from the ones she knew. The whole had an old-fashioned aspect which Gerry didn't try to analyse but which she found disconcerting. This wasn't like going back centuries at Chapel Carn Brea; this was literally too close to home. She found she was shivering, and not just from the cold air.

Gerry was certain that Seona would be in the same cottage. As far as she knew, her great-aunt had lived there all her adult life. She touched the ring again, and hurried towards the door before an early-rising farm worker could come out of any of the houses. As Gerry unlatched the gate, which wasn't the one she knew, a grey cat streaked across the road and shot ahead of her to the mat where she stopped and let out an imperious cry. That was reassuring – Seona always had a cat. Gerry raised her hand to the knocker, but that loud miaow had done the job. The door opened and a woman stood on the threshold.

She had begun to stoop down to stroke her pet, but on seeing Gerry she straightened up at once. For a few seconds, which felt like much longer, they simply stared at each other. Then Seona reached out a hand and drew Gerry inside.

'Dinna stand out there on the doorstep,' she said. 'Come in, sit down and I'll make you some tea.'

83

Gerry found she couldn't speak. She just followed, and sat down on an unfamiliar chair at the kitchen table, while Seona went to the stove. She used a push-button device to light the gas then put the kettle on the ring. While it heated she moved around the kitchen, fetching the tea canister, milk, cups and saucers. Anyone else would have thrown a barrage of questions at her visitor: who are you, where have you come from, what do you want? And - given the absence of any visible means of transport - how did you get here? And asked them on the doorstep, not inside. Seona had simply seen someone in trouble and taken her in. Now she let Gerry sit in the warmth of her room while she busied herself around the cooker.

Seona was an early riser, then, as she always had been when Gerry knew her, and was dressed not in a 1960s mini-skirt but a countrywoman's sensible skirt and blouse, with a hand-knitted cardigan against the early morning chill. Gerry touched the ring again. Seeing Seona had been a shock; they were more alike than she had dreamed. This Seona's hair wasn't the grey Gerry was used to but as red-gold as her own. Her eyes, free of glasses, were the same as Gerry's too; the green-grey which mostly looks hazel and only shows its true colour in sunlight. They were much of a height though Gerry was thinner, as she still wasn't eating properly.

The kettle began to whistle, and Seona poured hot water into the teapot to warm it. Gerry knew she would make the tea using tea leaves, not tea bags, and would put a home-made cosy over the pot as her mother and grandmother had done. Details Gerry had forgotten, so poignant that they hurt as she watched. When she decided the tea had brewed enough, Seona poured it and brought a cup to Gerry. Then, fetching her own cup, she sat down on the opposite side of the kitchen table and smiled at her visitor.

'Are you feeling better now?'

84

The rhythm of her voice was just like any woman's in Lochallaig; like Gerry's mother's. Gerry nodded then sipped some tea, trying to find the right words, taking the excuse of drinking to wait for a few minutes more. Seona drank her own tea, watching but not pushing her visitor. Finally Gerry put the cup back on its saucer.

'Thanks so much for that, and for letting me come in,' she said. 'My name's Gerralda and I'm from Cornwall. I'm one of your family, though you wouldn't have heard of me, but – well, I wanted some advice and I was sure you would be the best person to talk to.'

Seona put her own cup down and smiled at Gerry.

'Of course you're family,' she said. 'I saw that at once. You're right, I've never heard of anyone called Gerralda. I didn't know we had any lost relations; perhaps you're a black sheep and no-one mentions you. But you look more like me than my cousins do. Now, I know you're no' staying at Bill's house.'

That caught Gerry off balance till she realised Seona must mean her brother Bill, Gerry's grandfather, who her own brother was named after. Gerry had never known him. By the time she was five, her mother's mother was the only one of her grandparents still alive; but Seona had more than filled that gap. Gerry looked at the woman opposite who was, impossibly, her great-aunt.

'Well, we'll leave that for the moment.' Seona put her cup down and settled back to listen. 'So what did you want to ask me about?'

It was like jumping off a diving board; the only thing was to do it without thinking or hesitating. Gerry did it.

'Do you believe in what's called "second sight", or just "the Sight"?' she asked. She watched Seona nervously, but she seemed no more fazed than if Gerry had asked her if she knew what time the post arrived.

'Of course I do,' Seona said. 'I have some of it myself.

85

And so do you – I could tell that as soon as I saw you.'

As matter-of-fact as ever. Gerry was so relieved she could have laughed. How simple Seona made it seem. But that was the miracle about her great-aunt; she always had made it seem ordinary. Gerry realised how tense her whole body had been as she felt it start to relax.

'Now,' Seona continued, 'you say you want advice. Will you tell me what it's about? Sometimes just explaining can help to put things in place. Or would you like some breakfast first? You must have had quite a journey.'

Gerry shook her head.

'Not just now, thanks. Maybe later.'

Seona gave her a quick up-and-down glance, but didn't insist, to Gerry's relief.

'Maybe later,' she agreed. 'I'll just pour some more tea for us both.'

A warmth that came from more than the fire and the tea Gerry had already drunk had begun to spread through her. Gerry watched Seona go through the simple action of pouring, feeling safe for the first time in months. Nothing could touch her here. She took the full cup gratefully, and began to tell her story.

It was very easy to talk to Seona. She didn't interrupt or ask questions, just gave the occasional nod to indicate she was following. And Gerry was sure Seona could read between the lines, pick up much of what she wasn't saying. Gerry did her best to keep to the bare bones of the story: how she'd bought the sapphire, been drawn into the past, first heard of the Kelegel a'n gammneves, the Chalice of the Rainbow. Baranwen she described as the Guardian of the chalice, and Justin as her landlady's ex, though it didn't take second sight to tell that wasn't all. However, she hadn't come here for advice about her tangled love life.

As the story progressed Gerry realised she'd told Seona about travelling to the past as simply as she'd spoken of going to the jeweller's shop, and Seona hadn't queried it. Gerry found herself shaking when she got to the violence that she'd met: a knife at her throat; watching helplessly as a friend drank poison; and Justin's murderous attack on her following his discovery that he couldn't use the Kelegel in Gerry's time or in his own.

They were on their third cup of tea by the time Gerry was nearing the end. The final confrontation between the Guardians and the Makers, Colenso stripping the chalice of its powers, and then Justin's death. She finished with the most recent events: the theft of the Kelegel from the museum and what Baranwen had done to the Makers. She'd made no mention of the gold chain or the ring, Seona's gifts. She'd indicated that Justin and Baranwen had helped her time travel, and the sapphire had helped her in some ways while she had it; and hadn't offered any explanation of how she'd "seen" Baranwen at the Museum.

When Gerry finished, Seona spoke at last.

'That's a very clear account,' she said. 'And now do you feel able to tell me what it is that you most want advice about?'

Gerry hadn't been sure before which of her many concerns came top of the list, but at Seona's question she knew there was only one answer.

'Baranwen,' Gerry said. 'She spoke to me as she took the Chalice in the museum, so she knows that I know she's got it, and that she can use it again. She went to the Makers and took her revenge on them, but she's done nothing since then that I know of.' Gerry stopped and did some adding up. 'Mind you, she's hardly had time to do anything else yet. It feels like much longer ago than it really was.'

As she stopped speaking, Gerry noticed that her own Scots accent was becoming more pronounced the longer she talked.

It had become fainter during her time in London and then Cornwall. Here it had come back, apparently of its own accord.

Seona rose.

'Well, after all you've told me,' she said, 'I think I could make some suggestions about Baranwen which you might like to think about. First, though, I'm going to make some porridge. I want my breakfast, and you certainly need yours.'

She was right, of course. Gerry was ravenous, but she'd got used to ignoring hunger. She watched Seona measure oats from a large earthenware crock into a saucepan, add water and a little salt, and place the pan on the gas. Seona stood by the stove, stirring the mixture with a wooden spoon as it began to heat, and looked at Gerry very directly.

'Are you expecting me to guess who you are?' she asked. 'Maybe I should explain, you canna use the Sight like that. It comes to you; you don't ask a question and get an answer like asking the price of eggs.'

'No, I know that.' Hedra had told her, a long time ago, and Gerry had put that aside like everything else. She'd never intended this to be a guessing game, but hadn't known it would be so hard to say who she was. If Seona had believed her about the Chalice and the Bees, she should believe this too. But Gerry remembered the times she'd been warned against interfering with the past, and was becoming afraid that by being here she could be committing just such a breach of the unwritten rules, for all she'd persuaded herself otherwise.

'All right,' she said reluctantly. 'I'm your great-niece. My mother's Margaret, your brother Bill's daughter. She'll be a schoolgirl if I've got my timing right.'

Seona's hand had stopped in mid stir, letting the spoon clatter against the side of the pan.

'You're Margaret's daughter? Our wee Maggie? So where, or should I say when, have you come from?'

'The next century,' Gerry told her, wondering why Seona

suddenly looked so stricken. 'The year all this happened was – is – 2014. The present-time bits, that is.'

Seona began stirring the porridge again, but it was an automatic movement. She looked ill. Alarmed, Gerry got up to go to her, but Seona waved her away.

'No, sit down,' she said, 'I'll be just fine in a minute.'

Gerry sat down again at the table in silence, not knowing what she'd done. Whatever mistake she'd just made must have been catastrophic. Seona, always so reasonable, so practical, had for that moment looked wretchedly frightened. Gerry had never in her life seen her great-aunt look like that. She sat helpless, afraid too, and unable to do anything.

After a while, however, Seona's face reverted to its habitual calm. She inspected the porridge, decided it was ready, fetched bowls and ladled out two generous portions.

'You've been living away from home for quite a while,' she said. 'Did you start taking sugar with your porridge?' It was like a brave attempt at a joke, and it burned Gerry, though she didn't yet know what had brought that look of fear to Seona's eyes. 'Somehow I knew that you wouldna be taking sugar with your tea.'

Of course – she hadn't put sugar on the table, or offered it, and in this almost-familiar place Gerry had taken that for granted. There were many small things in this kitchen, and one or two pieces of furniture, which were strange, but overall everything felt right.

'I wouldna dare,' Gerry replied, trying to keep her voice light as Seona put the bowl of porridge, a spoon and a jug of milk down in front of her. She took a mouthful and was suddenly flooded by memories. It was like that French author she'd heard about who describes how a mouthful of cake takes him back to his childhood. In one spoonful this porridge brought back countless breakfasts before school. Gerry was about to say how much better it was than the instant microwaved porridge she'd had last, but stopped herself in time.

Gerry had emptied her plate before she knew it, and looked up to apologise for her bad manners. She'd had it drummed into her as a child that it wasn't polite to wolf down food, even less so as a guest. Then she saw that Seona had hardly touched her own breakfast.

'That was really good,' Gerry told her. 'They don't make it like this anywhere else.'

'Would you like any more? There's another portion still in the pan.'

'No, I'm fine, thanks.' Gerry didn't dare ask what had upset her great-aunt. 'You were going to say something about Baranwen.'

'Oh, yes.' Seona pushed her plate away and became business-like, but Gerry could tell the effort it cost her.

'Baranwen,' Seona said. 'I'm only going on what you've said, but that's given me a fair idea of the woman. First, now, she has been planning this for a very, very long time – I mean, having the chalice to herself. She has killed for it, or at the least caused the death of anyone who stood in her way. She may even be implicated in the death of the man Justin.'

That was something that had never occurred to Gerry.

'But he couldn't use it,' she pointed out.

'No, but he took it, and meant to hold onto it, which would have kept it from her. But we'll leave that for the moment.'

Seona was looking more like herself, at least like this self, as she thought through Gerry's problems.

'Now, you said that your – Colensa, was it?'

'Colenso,' Gerry corrected.

'Colenso then,' Seona went on. 'She thought that Baranwen would claim that you had stolen the chalice and let her fellow Guardians kill you in their fury, which she would deliberately fuel, before you had a chance to say where you had supposedly concealed it. Then she could keep it herself and no-one would be any the wiser. All the – Bees?'

'Yes.'

'They would believe it lost.'

Gerry shivered as Seona said it, for all that she'd heard this before from the Makers.

'And if that's right?' Gerry asked. 'What now?'

Seona leaned forward, resting her elbows on the table, chin cradled in her cupped hands. It was a gesture Gerry had seen her great-aunt make a thousand times, when she was thinking hard. She felt her heart twist at the familiarity of it.

'Well, I'm only guessing,' Seona said, 'but I'd think that she's been brooding about the Makers all the weeks she and the Kelegel – is that the word?'

Gerry nodded.

'All the weeks they have been parted.'

'You make them sound like a couple,' Gerry said, surprised.

'Oh, but they are, you see,' Seona said. 'Whoever said they had twisted each other was quite correct. Didn't you say Baranwen told you they had been bound for two hundred years? But she has been cunning, and barring that one woman, Del – what was her name?'

'Delenyk,' Gerry supplied.

'No-one else among the Bees, from the guardians to the novices, suspected,' Seona said. 'They stood in too much awe of the Chalice and its chief guardian. I would say that since she paid her visit to the Makers, Baranwen is now hiding somewhere with her prize. She has damaged and humiliated those three women, and I don't suppose she feels any need to go back to them again. They are suffering enough, expecting her to return. I can picture her gloating over the cup. She has devoted most of her long life to reaching this moment. Only, I don't think she is in control any

91

longer. She thinks she is, but in reality the chalice is manipulating her. She has poured so much into it that now it can use her as she used the Wasps. I suspect that the Kelegel itself instructed Baranwen on how to free it.'

Seona frowned a little, trying to explain the steps of her argument.

'Even the novices you met knew that the Kelegel has powers most people don't know about. The Makers themselves acknowledged it could do things they hadn't devised for it.'

'Yes, but how –' Gerry began. Seona held up her hand.

'In a minute,' she said. 'Magic is dangerous. Throughout the ages men, and women, have believed they were controlling it, only to find to their cost that they were wrong. There are endless stories on that theme. Think of King Midas, or the Sorcerer's Apprentice. The explanation as I see it is that there was some germ of magic left in the chalice, something that got in, so to speak, when the Makers created the powers for learning and the rest. So when Colenso removed the powers she had given the Kelegel, there was something beyond, that she had not put there. Something that has grown within the chalice, growing each time Baranwen used it. I wonder when the Jewels of the Rainbow were last used for healing in Baranwen's time? Not for a long time, I would imagine. And the only reasonable explanation for what happened this week must be that it, whatever it is, reached out to Baranwen and brought her to your museum to free it.'

Gerry looked at Seona, stunned. She had never dreamt of anything like this.

'And next?' It came out as little more than a whisper.

'Next?' Seona looked at Gerry, face to face. 'That depends on whether she sees you as a threat or if she has truly dismissed you as ineffectual.'

'I hope she has,' Gerry said. 'Dismissed me, I mean. If you're right, it explains what she did the times when the Jewels were in danger. The Chalice itself summoned her. Hedra, that's the teacher I told you about, she said the Jewels must be utterly destroyed. Physically destroyed, that is. But I can't do it.' Gerry could feel herself panicking. 'I can't even try. Baranwen told me that she always knew if they were threatened, and that makes more sense now. They'd call her. Even the sapphire alone did that. I couldn't get near them without her knowing. And I'm bound to them too. Not like she is, but I've used them. Anyway can you see me trying to smash them with a hammer or cut them up with a hacksaw?' Gerry's voice was rising, and she stopped. 'I'm not trying to be difficult,' she finished. 'Really I'm not.'

Seona looked at Gerry as if she were assessing her strength.

'Isn't there anyone who could help you? Anyone who knows about this?'

Gerry shook her head. 'My friend Debbie, the one the Wasps tried to kidnap at the fair, she knows I found the chalice and gave it to the museum, but that's all. And Claudia knows that too. She'd probably know a jeweller who could cut the stones up if I had them, which of course I haven't. And besides,' she added bitterly, 'I expect it would be like that jeweller in Redruth all over again, the man who tried to steal the sapphire. Anyone I took them to would want the stones himself. Or herself,' she added as an afterthought. She supposed there were women jewellers. 'And it's not as if I've even got the Jewels,' she finished. 'I don't even know where they are.'

'No, you're right,' Seona said with a sigh. 'Of course no professional would want to harm such beautiful, valuable gems. Still, a reputable jeweller might be prepared to cut them down to smaller stones. Separately they might even be worth more if it were done well. I assume once they were cut up they would truly lose their powers. Those were invested in the gemstones in their original, complete condition. Even separated from each other, I don't see how they could function. When you had the sapphire alone, you told me its powers were limited. I'm afraid I can't be certain of this. I can only tell you that you must succeed. I would like to think that you will.'

She rose and leaned on the back of her chair for support. Gerry got up too, worried afresh at how sick she appeared.

'Seona, what is it?' she begged. You look like,' she faltered, unable to find the right words.

'Like someone who's been told that their illness is terminal?' Seona said. 'But that's just what I am.' Gerry stared at her, still not understanding.

'Didn't you realise,' Seona said sadly, 'that when you told me about all the things that had happened to you over the summer, it sounded as if it was this summer? I knew that you'd gone back many centuries in Cornwall, but,' her voice quivered, 'I thought you were a distant relative, whose parents or even grandparents left here under some sort of cloud a long time ago. Something so bad that no-one even talked about them, so it was a branch of the family I didn't know existed. Nowadays it's not like when I was younger, I know girls do go to London to get jobs, share houses with other girls. Even from here I've heard that it happens. And a library is a respectable place for a young woman to work. So I had no reason to suppose you were from the future.'

'No,' Gerry protested, 'I never meant it to sound like that. I didna do it on purpose, I assumed you knew.' She was growing more worried by the minute. 'But why does it matter so much? You didn't have a problem believing I'd gone back to the Dark Ages in Cornwall.'

'Gerralda,' her great-aunt said, struggling now to keep her voice steady, 'you came to me for advice, because I was the best person to come to. That was the first thing you said. You knew I was someone who would accept the story you wanted to tell me. So it follows that you know about me. And unless Maggie moved away from here when she married, which I dinna think she would, you have come to me before with your troubles. So if I were still alive in your year of 2014 you would have come to me there. Now do you understand?'

And at last Gerry did. Now, when it was too late, she saw what she'd done. Done to the woman who'd helped her, supported and encouraged her so much. The Makers had warned her against meddling with time, but she'd thought this would be all right because it was outside of her own lifespan. This wasn't like stories of people going back in time and killing their own parents, or preventing them from meeting. It wasn't as if she'd gone back and changed something her younger self had done. That could have altered her life and might have meant she would never have gone to Cornwall and gone back in time to make that change. The classic time paradox. But Gerry had convinced herself that going back to before she was born couldn't do her own life any harm. And it hadn't harmed her. Only Seona.

And the reason Gerry had tried so hard to keep the chalice from Justin was because he wanted to change things in his own past, to get his revenge. She was no better than he.

Gerry looked at Seona again, and couldn't bear it.

'I'll go,' she said miserably. 'I'm sorry, I never meant,' but saw Seona's face and stopped. Words were useless. 'I'll go,' she said again, wishing she could hug her great-aunt and not daring to.

Gerry took herself out of the kitchen into the front room. There was no separate entrance hall; the front door led straight into this room. Telling her story had taken a long time. The men would be on their way to work already, the children walking to school. Maybe her own mother was among them. Gerry couldn't let anyone see her coming out of the house, knowing they would ask Seona later who the red-haired stranger was, so she would have to leave from this room.

Gerry was about to disappear when she heard footsteps behind her and Seona came through the door from the kitchen. There were tears in her eyes, something Gerry had never seen before, but Seona came up to her with a firm step.

'Gerralda,' she said, and put a hand on Gerry's shoulder, 'I don't want you to leave like this. Of course it was a shock. No-one alive wants to be told when they're going to die. But there's many sick people who have only weeks or months left to them.' She rubbed her eyes with the back of her hand. 'I know I'll live to see you at least begin to grow up. And as our Maggie's still a child, I've got a fair few years ahead of me yet. But don't tell me any more. Didn't you say your Makers had warned you about the dangers of time travel?'

Gerry nodded, feeling tears starting in her own eyes.

'Yes. That's why I came back this far, so it wouldn't be within my own lifetime.'

'No,' Seona agreed, 'I can see you didn't mean to do any harm.'

'I never do mean to,' Gerry said bitterly. 'I can see that being my epitaph: "She never meant to do any harm".'

'There are worse things that could be said,' Seona replied. 'Now, you must go, before anyone comes knocking to say good morning. We'll see each other again.' She gave Gerry an odd smile. 'In my future and your past.'

This time Gerry did hug her. Then she let go and took herself back to her room at Windhaven. Seona had given her a lot to think about, more than she'd expected. Gerry had guessed that Seona would confirm Hedra's instruction to destroy the Kelegel, even if she had secretly hoped there might be an alternative. But Seona's suggestion about the Kelegel having a magic outside of the magic that the Makers had put into it and then destroyed, a separate life within it, that was totally creepy. Yet it made for an explanation of what Baranwen had done as nothing else did. Seona was the only person in her own time who would take magic seriously, and if she thought this was possible, even probable – well, Gerry had never yet known her great-aunt be wrong.

Her last thought was the worst one of all. This – thing, within the chalice – assuming it had spoken to, or communicated with, Baranwen. Had it at any point tried to reach her too?

Chapter Nine

Everyone knows the feeling: the few seconds when you wake up, before you remember. Then it all comes back, along with the guilt, grief, anger or whatever you'd so briefly been able to forget. When Gerry woke, she was hit first by overwhelming guilt about Seona, for all that her great-aunt had begun to accept the news that set a term to her life even before her visitor had left the house. Then Gerry reproached herself bitterly for thinking she could get round the prohibition on time travel, and for being so pleased with the solution she'd devised. She hadn't thought of the effect it might have on Seona when she turned up on the doorstep and introduced herself.

And after that pain came the memory of Ryan and Claudia: Claudia, who'd always refused to have visitors, smiling at Ryan, and inviting him to come back again in better weather. Claudia the ever-aloof looking so relaxed over the meal, talking easily about things she'd always kept to herself. And then Ryan's preoccupation as Gerry drove him back to Penzance afterwards. In the car he'd talked about nothing but Claudia, and then hurried off with barely a goodbye. Gerry might have expected this from Martin or from Justin, but not Ryan. It was worse that this had happened the very day after he'd told Gerry how he felt about her. Now she wondered if she'd been a fool to believe his every word. And if she was about to have her heart broken yet again, when she hadn't even really got over Justin.

By the time Gerry got up she was already feeling wretched. Claudia wasn't in the kitchen when she went down to get some coffee. Gerry was glad about that; she didn't know how she would react when she saw Claudia. Or how she would reply if her landlady said casually that Ryan "seemed a pleasant chap". Gerry took her coffee and a slice of toast up to her room, but left half the toast uneaten on the plate. She knew from past experience that if she didn't eat she would feel even more miserable, but logic didn't help the lump of unhappiness sitting in her stomach.

Gerry was so distracted at work that in the middle of the morning Lowenna took her into the manager's office. The manager was at a meeting, so they could talk there in private. Lowenna sat behind the desk and waved Gerry into the chair opposite.

'Gerry, I'm sorry to have to do this,' she said, 'but I've got to ask if there's anything wrong.'

Gerry looked at Lowenna, alarmed. She could feel her heart beginning to pound.

'Why?' she asked, though she was pretty sure she knew why. At least Lowenna was looking sympathetic rather than critical.

'Well, you've been a pretty useful member of staff all the time you've been here,' Lowenna said, 'at least up till now. Of course there's a lot of things you don't know, and you've made some mistakes, but everyone's been happy enough with your work. Plus you're reliable. And the customers like you.'

The last three statements were all news to Gerry, but she wasn't going to argue. She waited for the 'but' which she could feel coming.

'But this week,' Lowenna went on, leaning forward a little and resting her elbows on the table, 'you've not been yourself at all. You went sick for a day with no explanation either at the time or when you came back. You don't seem to be paying any attention to what you're doing. Mark had to go through all the early O.S. maps yesterday to get them back in order, and I had to get Graham to do half your print-out requests again. You did one whole batch from the Cornish Guardian instead of the Cornish Times, and from 1932 instead of 1942. There's obviously something wrong; do you want to tell me what it is?'

Gerry knew this was right, but felt obliged to point out that she had never been off sick before.

'No, that's true, you've a very good record,' Lowenna agreed. 'But I can't keep getting the others to redo what you've done wrong. We don't have enough staff for that.'

Gerry couldn't tell her, of course. Even part of the truth wouldn't do this time. She just muttered something about family problems, said she was sorry and would try to concentrate more. Family, relationship worries; you were supposed to put them to one side at work. Gerry added, curious, 'Do the customers like me? I didn't know.'

Unexpectedly, Lowenna smiled.

'Oh yes, you've got some fans,' she said. 'Mr. Trembath who's going through the Parish Records for Lanner, always asks for 'the wee Scottish lassie' if he doesn't see you. And Mr. Keast who's researching naval bases in Cornwall, he gets quite put out if it's your day off. I've seen you helping people, you've got a good manner with the public. I don't want to have to lose you, none of us do. If you don't want to talk about the problem, do you think you could try to put it aside while you're here?'

Gerry said she would try, and Lowenna sent her off early for her coffee break. This really was all Gerry needed. As she was a temp, they could ask for someone else if her work wasn't up to scratch, and she couldn't afford to lose her job. Perhaps Hilary would take her back at Penzance. But in the face of whatever Baranwen might be planning to do next, Gerry knew there were worse things that could happen than finding herself unemployed.

Gerry tried to concentrate for the rest of the morning. She went out at lunchtime, walking down Fore Street past the shops to the café where she usually bought a take-away sandwich. She always avoided the section of the road with the side turning to Alastair Fletcher's jewellery shop. Gerry had never passed him or Simon, his assistant, in the street, and she wanted to keep it that way. She had no way of knowing if Baranwen's assault on the two men in the summer had had any lasting effect on either of them. Mr Fletcher had tried to steal the sapphire, but Simon had simply been in the wrong place at the wrong time.

Worse than that was the case of Mr Trewartha, the kindly Penzance jeweller. Gerry thought of him whenever she was in Causewayhead where his shop was. She'd gone in there a month or so after Baranwen's attack. He wasn't there, so Gerry asked after him. The woman behind the counter had spoken vehemently and at some length about hooligans who struck down a frail old man. At last she said that Mr. Trewartha had more or less recovered his health, but was afraid to come back to work.

'He'd been putting off his retirement for years, but this wasn't how it should have happened,' the woman said indignantly. 'This shop was his life, I don't know what he'll find to do with himself. He'll just lose the will to live.'

So that was something else Baranwen was responsible for. Or, if Seona was right, the Kelegel itself was to blame. That was a concept Gerry was still struggling with. She could believe that Baranwen was evil, but the Chalice of the Rainbow? Gerry had never know Seona to be wrong, yet this seemed too fantastic to be possible.

Gerry was so lost in thought that she walked right past the café without noticing. She came to a halt at the bottom of Fore

101

Street, startled back to reality as she saw she'd almost stepped off the pavement into the road. The shock started her heart pounding again, and she moved back a few paces, trembling as she realised she would have walked right into the traffic before she knew it. At that moment her mobile sounded the set of notes that signified a text message.

It was from Ryan. He'd managed to get a good enough shot of the "stalker", and Debbie's guess had been right. The man was one of the Wasps. Then Gerry spotted the message that had come through with the picture. Ryan wrote, 'I've seen him at the library, with Monica'.

Which matched what Debbie had said; she'd seen Monica with a man who dressed like the Wasps. The only two Debbie had met were Cathno and Elwyn. The man in the picture wasn't Talan, the one member of the Gohi who was unaccounted for. It was Kenver.

'Kenver,' Gerry said aloud said in indignation, thinking of how the man had tormented Claudia for so many weeks. Kenver had seemed a nonentity, always in the shadow of Elwyn and Cathno. Now he was hanging out with Monica and making Claudia's life unbearable. Claudia had never done him any harm, she didn't even know who he was. Gerry might have expected it of either of the other two. She could believe anything of Elwyn and Cathno.

For the first time she wondered where, and how, they were living. And the answer came at once. To Gerry's astonishment, the ring on her finger gave a faint throb, and she saw a vivid mental image of a disused barn. The men had straw to sleep on, and it would be better than spending the nights outdoors, but they couldn't speak the language here and had no money. Had Baranwen simply abandoned them? Even if she had, they weren't Gerry's problem. Then Gerry found she could hear them too. As with the Museum and the car park in Penzance, the ring was giving her an overview of somewhere else.

Cathno was giving vent to a lengthy rant which, from Elwyn's expression, he had heard before, many times. It was something about a woman. Gerry's first thought was that he was complaining about the Guardian, then realised it was more likely to be Ysella. Meraud had said that after Baranwen disappeared, Ysella went back to her family to get married. Perhaps it had also been to escape a jealous and violent lover.

The clock up the street chimed the half hour. How long had Gerry been standing there on the street corner? She was going to be late back, and she mustn't be, not today, not after Lowenna's warning. Then her phone rang. It would be Ryan; he'd have expected her to call as soon as she got his text. At the same moment Gerry saw a tall young man in a black denim jacket among the people coming across the road. It was Mark, who was doing work experience in the library. He saw Gerry and stopped, looking at her in surprise.

'Are you all right?' he asked. His usual teasing manner had quite gone, and he looked concerned. 'You seem really dazed.'

'Oh,' Gerry said, caught unawares, 'I suppose - well, I was thinking about something just now and nearly walked out into the road without looking. I stopped just in time. Otherwise -' she indicated the stream of cars close by.

Mark looked horrified. 'You'd have been flattened? No wonder you look so shaky. Shall I walk back to the library with you? I was going to get a pasty, but that can wait.'

'I came out to get a sandwich myself,' Gerry said, remembering. 'But I'll be late.'

'Don't worry,' Mark said, 'I'll take you back and then pick up something for you to eat. I'll tell Lowenna what happened. Even she's got to accept nearly being knocked down as a reason for being five minutes late. I know she's been coming down heavy today, but we've all been bigging you up.'

103

'Thanks,' Gerry said, pleased but surprised, and embarrassed too. Did everyone in the library know what had happened?

Mark took Gerry's arm and steered her gently up the street and back to the library, where they found Lowenna at the desk. Mark was as good as his word, explaining what had happened then going off to get Gerry some lunch. He made it sound as if he had seen Gerry all but going under the wheels of a passing van. She knew he was exaggerating, and was grateful.

Lowenna's manner changed from severe to concerned on the spot. She put Graham, another assistant, on the desk, sat Gerry down in the staff room and made her a cup of tea.

'What a thing to happen,' she said, passing over the cup. 'Do you want to stay, or would you rather go home? Yes, I know what I said earlier, but this is different.'

Gerry thought for a moment.

'No, thanks,' she decided. She didn't want to be on her own at Windhaven, thinking about Seona, and Kenver. 'I'd rather stay here.'

'Okay, just sit in here for a bit,' Lowenna said. 'Mark's going to bring you back a pasty. Drink your tea while you wait, it'll do you good. Now, if you're all right, I ought to go back on the desk, Graham's due for his lunch break. Have your pasty, then come back out.'

Gerry sat in the staff room, trying not very successfully to keep her mind blank, till Mark came back with two pasties. Gerry wasn't sure she wanted one, but they did smell good. She bit into the one Mark handed her, and swallowed two more mouthfuls before stopping to say thank you. Mark laughed, eating just as eagerly himself. But Gerry was only halfway through her pasty when Lowenna came back.

'Gerry, there's a call for you from Penzance library,' she said. 'I think it's their computer man, anyway he definitely asked for you. Shall I put it through to the office?'

'Yes, please,' Gerry said, abandoning her plate and grateful that she wouldn't have to talk to Ryan on the main counter in front of all the staff and public. The gossip line here was probably as active as the Penzance one. Gerry went into the manager's office and picked up the phone on the desk.

'Hi.' She heard a click as the receiver was put down on the desk.

'Gerry?' Ryan's voice was sharp, worried. 'Did you get my text?'

'Yes, thanks,' she said. 'Sorry I didn't get back to you, I was in the middle of Fore Street and it was really noisy. And I was already late getting back from lunch.'

That needn't have stopped her texting back a word or two. Again it was the truth but not the whole truth. Gerry hated lying to Ryan, even by omission, but couldn't tell him about her vision of the Wasps in the barn.

'So do you know him? Was he one of that gang at the museum?'

Gerry sighed.

'Yes, he was,' she told him. 'But what I said's still true. I don't know where they live. Perhaps Monica does.' Then she could have kicked herself. 'No, Ryan, please don't ask her.'

'Yes, I can just see myself doing that,' Ryan said grimly. 'Hello Monica, did you know your boyfriend's a violent criminal? By the way what's his name and where does he live?'

There was a tone in his voice which Gerry couldn't relate to the Ryan she knew. She wondered if he was angry on her behalf or on Claudia's. Of course, as far as Ryan knew Claudia was more of a victim than Gerry was, and Gerry didn't want to disabuse him. She'd already decided, when she watched him walk away from her the evening before, that she didn't want him coming back to her out of a sense of chivalry.

105

'Look, let's talk about it later,' Gerry said. 'Where do you want to meet?'

They agreed to meet at the cinema, then said almost simultaneously that they ought to get back to work. Gerry came out of the office feeling depressed, and wishing she could tell Ryan the real truth. It would be so good to be able to share it all, but that was totally impossible.

She'd told Lowenna earlier that she would try to concentrate, but it took a massive effort. Paradoxically Gerry found it was easier to deal with a difficult enquiry about family history which took all her attention. When she went back to the routine shelving she found herself thinking, not of the Wasps, but about Seona again. Gerry was working in the reserve stock this time, shut away from the public, getting the books and leaflets in order. She promised herself she'd double check them this time before actually putting them away.

There must have been a good forty years between Gerry's visit to Seona and the time when, as a schoolgirl, she began to realise that the odd things which she'd always taken for granted didn't happen to the other children. That had given Seona all those years to come to terms with what she'd learned during Gerry's rash visit. Gerry remembered, when she was about ten years old, asking her mother if she believed in reading the future, or knowing what other people were thinking. Her mother had laughed, and carried on with peeling the potatoes.

'Not since I was a wee girl, and stopped believing in fairies,' she said. 'I was younger than you are now. Auntie Seona believes in things like that, but it's all nonsense, of course, though I wouldna say so to her face. Now, would you pass me that big black saucepan from over there?'

Gerry hadn't asked her mother again, but had gone to Seona instead, and continued to over the years. When she hit the problems that every girl faces growing up, she took those to

Seona too. Her great-aunt had never married; Gerry realised now that, absorbed in her own concerns like any child, she'd never even wondered why. But despite having no children of her own, Seona had always been the perfect confidante.

Gerry heard the door open, and another member of staff came in to the closed section, bringing her back to where she was and what she was meant to be doing. Gerry didn't look to see who it was, but grabbed the stack of leaflets, maps and brochures she was supposed to be putting into the subject boxes at the far end of the room, and hurried off to get on with it.

It was raining heavily in Penzance, and by the time Gerry had walked from her car, which was parked a few streets away, to the cinema, water was running off her hair and dripping all over her jacket. With the image of Seona's stricken face in front of her, Gerry hadn't thought to grab an umbrella or a waterproof that morning, or even to check the forecast. When she arrived at the cinema on Causewayhead, Ryan was standing on the steps of the foyer, sheltered from the rain. He was looking as grim as he'd sounded on the phone, and as Gerry walked up to him she hoped no-one from the library was around. Not only because it would send the gossips into overdrive, seeing them out together, but because of his expression. Gerry thought wistfully of how his face used to light up when she walked into the library staff room back in the summer.

The cinema had a bar upstairs and also served light meals. Pizzas seemed the easiest choice, and the two of them went through the business of deciding which ones they'd like, finding a free table, ordering a drink. Gerry opted for coffee. She was beyond tired, and didn't want to find herself nodding off during the film. That would just finish off what was beginning to look like a disaster date.

Ryan brought her coffee to their table, with a pint for himself. He tried the beer, then said he'd gone back to the gallery after work.

'There wasn't any sign of him,' Ryan said, 'but I stayed while Claudia finished up and locked the place. Then I walked back to her car with her, to be on the safe side.'

Gerry winced. She didn't think she was possessive, she never had been before. Ryan had walked Claudia back to her car, and that was all.

'If he was watching us, I didn't see him,' Ryan went on, 'but I'll keep this up for a week and see if he takes the hint. That's all I can do for now.'

'I hope it works,' Gerry said. 'I really do.'

'Well, we'll see,' Ryan said. He drank some more beer, and checked the time. 'I hope these pizzas don't take too long. Now, you're sure you don't want to change your mind about which film to see? The others aren't sold out, I've checked.'

'That was good of you,' Gerry said, thinking how typical of him that was, 'but let's stick with the one you've booked. If it's awful I'll grovel afterwards.'

At this point the pizzas arrived and they started eating. Gerry's chicken and vegetable one wasn't bad, though rather too hot for someone in a hurry. Ryan finished the first wedge of his double pepperoni while Gerry had only had a bit off the outer crust.

'Sorry,' Ryan said, 'I'm starving. I didn't get any lunch.'

Gerry thought of her half-finished pasty, and of Mark's unexpected kindness. Back to the present, she told herself, and screwed up her courage.

'I've not seen many sci-fi films,' she said. 'But I like some of the ideas. Like telepathy, or being able to use magic to get from one place to another.'

'Cheaper than petrol, specially at the price it is now,' Ryan said, finishing his second triangle of pizza. 'Though that sort of thing's fantasy more than sci-fi. Is your food all right?'

'Oh, yes, of course. I was just letting it cool down a bit.' Gerry ate a few mouthfuls and washed them down with coffee. She had to keep trying.

'It's – well, you know I've got Highland blood,' she said. 'Like the Celts in Cornwall. Are you "proper job" Cornish, as they say?'

'Oh yes,' Ryan said. 'My dad's Cornish, six generations back. My mum's family goes back even further, though they were originally from North Cornwall, I think, which makes them incomers here. She says my great-great-great-great-great-gran was the village witch. Probably means she sold fake love potions. Doesn't mean I ever thought of myself as Celtic.'

He wasn't making it easy, but what had she expected?

'There's still a lot of folk traditions in the Highlands,' Gerry persisted. 'Kelpies and selkies and sprites. And people still believe in the Sight. I had a great-aunt who was sure it existed.'

'People used to believe in vampires,' Ryan retorted, 'and there's more than enough books and films and series about them, but that doesn't mean they're real. Look, I don't want to rush you but the programme starts in about ten minutes.'

Gerry gave up, offered him a wedge of her pizza, and managed to more or less finish the rest. Then they joined the queue of people heading downstairs to the middle of the Savoy's three screens.

Ryan did take her hand once they were sitting down, which Gerry found ridiculously comforting. But she wished she could be certain he was thinking about her, or else the film, and not Claudia. Not that Gerry herself was paying the film much attention to begin with. After their evening at the Godolphin she had wondered about taking Ryan up to Chapel Carn Brea on Saturday morning, assuming he wasn't working, and showing

109

him the view with no roads, no airport and no monastery on the Mount. That wouldn't break her promise to herself; she wasn't going to visit the Gwenen or the Makers or anyone. Gerry could let the Bysow a'n gammneves find her a space of a few minutes when the place was deserted. There just wasn't any other way Ryan was going to believe the truth about where the Chalice, the Wasps and the Guardian came from. And while Gerry had been able to find enough reasonable part-truths for Claudia and Debbie, it was already getting harder to do that with Ryan. More than that, she longed to be able to try and find a way through her present troubles with the help of someone supportive, who truly understood her situation.

But Gerry had thought of that before she'd taken Ryan to meet Claudia. Now she'd have to wait and see if she and Ryan had a future at all before taking him to the past. Her abortive attempts over the meal had convinced her that nothing less would work. And she hadn't even mentioned time travel.

Gerry settled back in her seat, trying to ignore the crashing of popcorn from the couple in front. The film was pure sci-fi with no magic or anything, but the story turned out to be quite gripping. She was very aware of Ryan's hand over her own, and had to resist the urge to grip it tightly at a couple of exciting moments. He let go before they stood up at the end, and they left the cinema quite close together but not touching. Ryan walked with Gerry up the dark, semi-deserted streets to where she had parked, and they talked about the film as they went. When she got her car keys out, Ryan leaned forward and gave her a light kiss on the cheek.

'Drive carefully,' he said, then stood back to give Gerry room to get in. She drove off, still with no idea of how things stood between them.

It was quite late when she got back and Claudia was upstairs, but Gerry knew she couldn't keep avoiding her landlady.

She hoped that if she saw her in the morning she could talk with her just as she had been doing for the last three months. Living here was the one stable thing in Gerry's chaotic life. For an awful moment she pictured Ryan moving in with Claudia. Then there would be no need for a tenant to be in the house when Claudia was in London.

No, Gerry told herself firmly, she totally was letting her imagination run wild. She ought to be concentrating on something useful, like the Gohi. She got into bed and switched off the light. It wasn't Seona she was thinking of now, but Kenver. Gerry was furious with both him and Monica for their despicable hounding of Claudia.

Monica had blamed Claudia for Justin's death. Justin himself had hinted to Monica that Claudia was jealous. Gerry was certain that was purely Justin stirring up trouble; no way would her landlady be jealous of someone so plain and mean-spirited as Monica. Also, Monica had resented being forced to introduce Gerry to Claudia but it was Justin who'd made her do it, and Monica couldn't refuse Justin anything. Suddenly Gerry sat up in the dark and reached for the light switch. She should have seen this sooner. Gerry could believe that Monica had dreamed up the "stalking" scheme. She could believe that Monica had persuaded Kenver to carry it out. But what she could not believe was that it was coincidence that the man she'd chosen for the task was one of the Wasps. Nothing connected with the Tegennow had ever been coincidence. There was only one possible explanation. Baranwen was responsible.

So why, and how, had the Guardian brought Monica and Kenver together? What further devious scheme had she got in mind now?

Chapter Ten

At the Cornish Studies library the next day, Gerry felt self-conscious after the unexpected vote of confidence Mark had told her about, and simply tried to keep a low profile and get through the day as best she could. She called Ryan at lunchtime and told him she was really done in and could do with an early night. She hoped he might suggest she could stop for a quick drink with him in Penzance on her way home, but Ryan just said he'd thought she looked pretty shattered at the cinema. It was something, Gerry supposed, that he'd noticed how she looked. They agreed to meet in Penzance on Saturday morning and go for a coffee. At least Ryan said 'Take care,' before he said goodbye.

When she got back to Windhaven after work she found Claudia in the lounge, sitting on the leather sofa, the Tiffany-style standard lamp behind her shining onto her copper hair. Gerry stood in the doorway and said hello. Claudia had the news channel on the tv and was sorting through a pile of post, but looked up when Gerry spoke.

'Oh, hello,' she said. 'Not going out tonight?'

Gerry shook her head.

'No, I could do with a decent night's sleep.' She wondered if she dare ask if Ryan had gone to the gallery again, but didn't need to.

'Yes, you do look tired,' Claudia said. She dropped the letter she'd been looking at onto a small stack on the coffee table in front of her, and picked up a glossy magazine, slitting open the cellophane wrapper with an elegant paper knife. 'Your friend's been coming round twice a day as he suggested, it's very good of him.' She put the magazine aside to look at later, and dropped the next item, an advert, straight into the bin. 'He said he'd like to try it for a week and see if it does any good. I have to say I'm not sure it will, but I don't mind giving it a go.'

She turned her attention to what looked like a bill, and Gerry left her to it and went back to the kitchen. Claudia had spoken of Ryan in the same offhand tone that she would have used of a handyman who'd volunteered to come round on his day off to get a job finished, something Gerry had seen happen more than once. But Gerry did know her landlady well enough by now to be certain her casual mention of Ryan wasn't an act put on for Gerry's benefit. In all the weeks she'd lived at Windhaven, she'd never seen Claudia be anything but herself.

In the fridge Gerry found a ready meal lasagne she'd forgotten about, and put it in the microwave. That was one thing she and Claudia had in common; neither did proper cooking. Gerry had learned the basics at home from her mother, but it didn't seem worth the trouble for one person. She brought her laptop down to the conservatory table and caught up with emails and Facebook. There was nothing she wanted to watch on the iPlayer, and she looked without enthusiasm at a couple of library books. All she could think of was Ryan, Claudia, the Wasps, Baranwen – and Seona. Finally she went to bed, her mind still racing.

Yet despite everything, Gerry slept surprisingly well, and arrived in Penzance feeling quite positive. Once she'd parked, finding a space near her old home at the Angoves' house, she texted Ryan to ask where he was and got the reply that he was down by the Ross Bridge. She walked there along the front and found Ryan leaning on the pale blue painted railings looking at the 20-odd small boats rocking on the rising water. Gerry always liked the harbour, even at low tide when the boat keels were resting on the mud.

'If you don't mind, I'd like to go up to Chapel Street first,' Ryan said, 'just to call in at the gallery. There's a chance that man might be there, it's about that time of day. Then we can go for coffee afterwards.'

'I'd better not come with you,' Gerry said. 'He only saw me the once, but if he recognised me that would rather blow your cover.' When the Gohi had seen Gerry in that clearing in the woods, they thought she was a boy. Today she was wearing a mid-thigh length dress and thick tights with knee-high boots, not unlike tunic and leggings; her loose, shoulder-length hair also fitted that image.

'Yeah,' Ryan agreed, 'you're right. Well, there's a coffee place in Queens Square – do you know the one?'

Gerry nodded. 'I think so.'

'Okay,' Ryan said, 'suppose I meet you there in about twenty minutes?'

Gerry agreed, and Ryan set off, skirting the side of the inner basin of the harbour which led to the Dry Dock, making for the slope of the Abbey Slip which led up towards Chapel Street. She dawdled past the flower beds beside the end of the bridge then followed Ryan, slowly enough for him to get to the gallery well ahead of her.

Chapel Street had more unusual shops and buildings than any street in Penzance: the old Admiral Benbow pub with the life size model of a revenue officer lying on the roof watching for smugglers; the bookshop which had been an early post office, the Chocolate House, now a holiday let, the Egyptian House

114

with its remarkable facade. Gerry could stop and admire them on the way to the café; there was time enough.

Then as she turned the corner from the slipway into Chapel Street, any thoughts of strolling along vanished. Things you haven't been paying attention to always click into place suddenly. Gerry saw that a crowd had gathered further up the street, and the same instant registered that there had been a smell of smoke in the background all the time she'd been walking from the bridge. The emergency vehicles were already in place, blue lights flashing. There was a police car, two fire engines and an ambulance, though it didn't look as if anyone was hurt. A couple of uniformed officers were doing their best to keep people back, but it looked like they had their work cut out. Gerry spotted more than one person filming the scene on their phones. Then, forgetting about keeping out of sight, she began to run as she realised which building they were gathered round.

The firemen had been there long enough to contain the fire. It looked as if the blaze hadn't been a big one; there was no apparent damage to the shops on either side, and they seemed to have saved the upper floors of the building itself. But the showroom of Claudia's gallery had been completely destroyed.

Then Gerry saw Claudia herself. She had been forcibly held back but was still struggling, trying desperately to free herself and get back inside. There were no flames now, and the interior had been drenched by the hoses. Of course, all the paintings on show must be ruined; Claudia wouldn't be that frantic about rescuing her handbag, phone or computer.

Gerry pushed her way forward, trying to get nearer to Claudia, though with no idea what she could do to help. As she watched, Claudia suddenly gave up and stopped fighting, apparently recognising that it was too late now. And at that same moment someone ran up, said something to the man who had just let go of Claudia, and put his arms round her. Claudia seemed to fall against him and buried her head in his shoulder. Gerry guessed she was weeping, which was so unlike her landlady that it hurt to see it.

It was Ryan. He held Claudia, supporting her and letting her cry. And as if Gerry's thoughts had reached him he looked up and straight across to where she stood. Ryan's eyes met Gerry's across Claudia's slumped shoulder with a wordless apology. Although Gerry understood, she couldn't bear to look and, turning, walked slowly away up to Queens Square.

Of course Claudia was distraught, and anyone's instinct would be to give her a hug and let her cry, with reassuring pats on the shoulder. Gerry knew it, and would have done so herself if she'd got to Claudia first. She knew it was unreasonable, even childish, but she couldn't stand there and watch Ryan comforting Claudia.

The traffic here was in chaos: the entrance to Chapel Street was blocked by the fire engine, and Queen Street which met the top end of Chapel Street was no entry. The narrow street which went past the Acorn Theatre only led to dead ends. So drivers were trying to turn round in the constricted space of the small square where all the roads met, causing further gridlock. Gerry looked at the café where she'd been going to meet Ryan, and decided there wasn't any point in going there now. But she couldn't help turning back to look towards Ryan again, and as she did so she saw a familiar figure at the back of the mass of gaping onlookers.

Up till that moment Gerry had assumed that the fire was an accident. But she could see the expression on Kenver's face as he watched Claudia and Ryan, and knew that it had been deliberate. Gerry shouted, then saw at once that was a mistake. She should have gone up to Kenver unobtrusively then got others to help hold him, keep him from getting away. Kenver heard the shout, turned, and saw Gerry running towards him. It was obvious that she knew the truth. Kenver looked round in every direction but his escape route was barred. He couldn't force his way through the packed crowd round the gallery. Queens Square was a mass of vehicles, too jammed to dodge between. He took the nearest way out and raced towards the traffic coming up Queen Street, throwing a glance back over his shoulder in Gerry's direction. The next second, it seemed, she heard the prolonged blast of a horn and the squeal of brakes. Then someone screamed.

It felt like hours later, though it was only the beginning of the afternoon. Claudia, Gerry and Ryan were in the conservatory at Windhaven. Ryan had come back with Claudia; Gerry had driven back on her own. There was no food laid out this time; no-one wanted to eat. Nor were they seated round the table; they all seemed to be too restless to sit down. Claudia couldn't keep still for a moment, which was totally out of character.

'It's Andrew,' she said, pausing to face Gerry and Ryan. 'Andrew Dymond. He's only twenty-six, and it was his first show. That was three years' work destroyed, and besides, a quarter of the paintings had been sold already. And it was going on to a place in Exeter afterwards. I meant to get his name known.' Claudia walked to the end of the conservatory where she turned, facing them. 'That's what I can't bear. I can find somewhere for the next show, there's enough empty shops in Penzance even if the locations aren't as good. The insurance will take care of it, but no money can make up for this. Andrew will have to start all over again from the beginning.'

She started pacing again, and they both watched her in silence.

'What I can't understand,' Claudia went on, 'is how it started. Everything's fire tested regularly, all the equipment's safety checked, all the wiring. No one's ever been allowed to smoke anywhere in the building. It doesn't make sense.'

She and Gerry had made statements to the police, but Claudia had been so distraught that they'd only taken the minimum information from her. Someone would come to the house to see her later. Gerry had told the police that Kenver had been haunting the gallery, and that he'd run when he saw her watching him. No, she said, she didn't actually know him, she'd once met him with a friend of a friend.

If Claudia was tormented by the situation of the young painter, for Gerry it was the driver of the van. The man had stood on the pavement repeating over and over, 'He just ran straight into me, he wasn't even looking. There was nothing I could do. He ran straight into me.' There were witnesses who could confirm that it wasn't the driver's fault, but the man was still going to be haunted by it.

Of course Kenver had none of the traffic instinct natural even to someone who'd grown up in such a rural area as Gerry had, though he must have been given some basic lessons in survival in this century or he'd not have lasted a day. Justin himself had lived in the modern world long enough to learn to drive, and get involved in what Claudia had referred to as his "dodgy business dealings".

But it was different for the Wasps. From the glimpse Gerry had seen, the Guardian had left them holed up somewhere, presumably with some food but without resources. They couldn't shop or travel by themselves. The vision Gerry had seen of the three of them with the girls from the club must have been a "reward" for their help at the Museum. The Gohi were like penniless, homeless immigrants from a remote rural area who couldn't speak a word of English. Not even "like", that was exactly what they were. So how had Kenver managed to talk with Monica? Gerry had been able to talk to the Bees in their own century because the sapphire, and Seona's gold chain, had translated for her. She could only guess that Kenver had been introduced as a man who couldn't speak the language and didn't know his way around. That would have made Monica feel superior, and she had no doubt enjoyed getting him to harass Claudia. Which he seemed to have relished. But why, why had the Guardian done it? What could Baranwen possibly have against Claudia?

The morning's events would be on the evening news, and were probably headlines on the local radio stations already. Not because of the fire in a small gallery, even one in historic Chapel Street and belonging to the eminent Ms. Claudia Mainwaring, but because of the sudden violent death of the suspected arsonist, fleeing the scene of his crime. She had better tell Claudia about Kenver now before she heard it on the news.

'Claudia,' Gerry said nervously and Claudia stopped pacing to look at her. Gerry didn't want to do this. 'Claudia,' she began, 'it wasn't an accident. I saw that man, the one who's been watching you, in the crowd on the street. Ryan texted me his picture the other day in case I'd seen him before, so I knew who he was. He was looking so pleased with himself I just knew he'd started the fire.' Gerry had no idea how; she couldn't see Monica teaching Kenver to use matches. If the CCTV had survived the fire they might find out, but it didn't seem likely. 'He saw me looking at him, and ran. He just ran, he wasn't looking, and he ran straight into a van that was coming up Queen Street. The driver didn't stand a chance.'

Claudia had gone white. She gripped the back of a chair, then sat down so hard that Gerry heard the jar of her bones.

'Why?' she breathed. 'Who was he? What have I ever done to him?'

Ryan sat down too, clutching the side of the table.

'I can't answer the why,' he said, 'but I do know one thing

119

about him. I've seen him in the library and he's always been with Monica Fraser.'

Gerry would have stopped him from saying it if she could. From white, Claudia's face suddenly turned dusky pink with anger.

'That bitch.' Then she shook her head. 'Surely even she wouldn't dare.' She looked at Ryan. 'You wouldn't know, but there's a history between us.'

Before Gerry could stop him, Ryan proceeded to put his other foot in it. Of course, he couldn't know. Gerry wished now she'd told him enough to prevent this.

'Gerry knows something about him too. He was involved in a really nasty robbery last week.'

Inevitably Claudia turned back to Gerry. She was still standing, looking helplessly at them both, but came to sit down at the table too, facing Claudia.

'Do you remember that chalice I showed you,' she said, 'the one I gave to the museum?'

'Yes,' Claudia said, surprised at the apparent change of subject, but turning her thoughts back to Gerry's early days at Windhaven. 'That was the one that Justin wanted. He made you help him get hold of it.'

Gerry might as well get this out as well. She gave up trying not to see Ryan's expression, and looked at him too.

'Justin took two of his mates round to Deb's house and held her at knife point,' she said. 'That was how he forced me to help him. But those two were also involved in the robbery.'

Claudia looked bewildered.

'What robbery?' she asked. Gerry sighed.

'The chalice was stolen from the museum in Truro on Tuesday,' she said. 'It was all pretty violent and a lot of people got hurt.'

'Yes,' Claudia said. 'I heard something about it, but I'd no idea that was your chalice.'

'Well,' Gerry said, 'there were three men involved. Two of those three were the two who went to Debbie's house, and the third was your man from the gallery. They knew the chalice, and wanted it as much as Justin did.'

Claudia suddenly put her head in her hands.

'I really can't cope with all this,' she said. 'I think I need to be on my own for a bit. Would you mind?' She looked at Gerry. 'Will you take Ryan back?'

'Of course,' she said, and got up, glancing at Ryan. He looked so stricken that Gerry wanted to put her arms round him, just to comfort him. Of course that was exactly what he'd done for Claudia earlier; she could see that properly now. Ryan got up and followed her out, with just a brief word to Claudia. As he got into the car, fastening the seat belt automatically, Gerry remembered the first time she'd driven him, from the Long Rock car park to the Godolphin Arms in Marazion. Things had been simpler then.

Ryan didn't say a word as they drove up the lane, and he looked so wretched that Gerry couldn't bear it. She decided that, even if it was because he'd had to leave Claudia rather than staying to help her come to terms with what had happened, it was better to know.

At the junction of Trewellard Hill and the North Road there was a parking area for a few vehicles. On the far side of this a gate led onto the area of moorland called Woon Gumpus. There were footpaths from the gate leading in several directions; dog walkers came here a lot, as did other locals, ramblers and holidaymakers. As usual there were half a dozen cars and vans parked on the rough gravel surface. Gerry took a space next to the gate, switched off the engine, got out and walked round to the passenger side to open Ryan's door.

'Come on,' she said, 'out.'

Ryan seemed too stunned to protest, and got out dutifully. Gerry stopped at the granite post beside the gate. Ryan came and stood next to her, one hand on the top of the gate. She didn't look at him, and kept her eyes fixed on the moor in front of her.

'Tell me,' she said. 'Please. What is it?' Ryan still didn't say anything, and Gerry went on, desperately. 'Ryan, I really want to know. Perhaps I can help?'

She thought he too was staring away across the moor, but carefully avoided looking at him. Gerry waited as patiently as she could, trying not to rush him. When Ryan did speak, it wasn't what she expected. He sounded defeated.

'It's all my fault,' he said. 'I should never have tried to help. He'd have got tired of it in the end, hanging around there, but because I came along, he decided he had to do something more drastic. Now Claudia's work's ruined, all those years she's built that place up, and then there's that lad Andrew that she's so upset about. I thought it was such a good idea, and look at what's happened.'

Gerry was so dismayed that she forgot caution. She put her arms round Ryan's shoulders and held him as tight as she could. She knew so well how he was feeling; she'd felt just like this herself after she'd gone to see Seona. She'd thought she was being so clever and it had blown up in her face.

'You mustn't blame yourself,' Gerry said. 'You couldn't possibly have known he'd do this.' She knew the words couldn't help; she only hoped Ryan could feel the sympathy she was trying to convey. 'I do understand,' Gerry told him. 'If I hadn't shouted when I saw Kenver, he'd not have run into that van. The poor driver feels like a murderer, and that's my fault.'

That shocked Ryan. 'You shouldn't think like that,' he said. 'You're not to blame for it.'

'Maybe, but it wouldn't have happened if I hadn't been there,' Gerry said.

Ryan pulled away at that, and looked at her.

'You told me it would be dangerous to get close to you,' he said sadly. 'I didn't believe you. I thought you were trying to put me off, that you didn't want to get involved. Now I'm starting to understand what you meant.'

Gerry couldn't think of an answer to that. Instead she said, 'Claudia's a lot tougher than she looks. She's been through worse than this and survived. Besides, didn't she say the insurance would sort things out?'

'Yeah,' he agreed. 'Once the smell of burning's gone, however long that takes, they can fit the Chapel Street place out again, and like she said there's plenty of empty shops in Penzance. It's not that; it's not even that artist. There's something about Claudia – though perhaps I shouldn't say this to you.'

'No, please do,' Gerry said, though she felt her stomach muscles tense. This was the moment she'd been dreading.

Ryan hesitated, then said, 'Well, she doesn't invite sympathy, does she? I mean, she's in this desperate situation. If I ever saw anyone who really needs an understanding friend, it's her, but she's completely walled up behind all these "keep off" signs. I'm glad she's got you there.'

Gerry had never dreamt this was what Ryan had been thinking.

'She puts the "keep off" signs up for me too,' she told him. 'There's only ever been a couple of times I've seen Claudia drop her guard.' Gerry wondered what she could say without feeling she was breaking confidentiality. 'I think she feels people only want to know her because she's rich. Or because of how she looks.'

'Yeah, I can believe that,' Ryan said. 'But even so – I mean, you said she was beautiful, and I suppose she is, but it's a – well,

I'd have to say a distant kind of beauty. I'm not trying to be rude, specially as you're her friend, but I can't imagine any man feeling he couldn't keep his hands off her. Not like you.'

'What?' Gerry was so astounded that she thought she must have misheard him. 'You can't mean that.'

It was Ryan's turn to be surprised.

'Of course I do,' he said. 'Don't you know how hard it's been, seeing you this week and not doing anything? Surely you -' he stopped, and started again. 'After that first day, I didn't want to try to rush anything. Besides, you've been kind of closed off yourself.'

Ouch, Gerry thought. Seeing Seona, introducing Ryan to Claudia, then finding Kenver was Claudia's "stalker".

'Yeah,' Gerry admitted, 'I've had a lot going on.'

But suddenly she felt ridiculously happy. At last Ryan started to really smile at her. The smile spread across every bit of his face, and Gerry could feel herself returning it.

'You can't imagine what it was like, sitting next to you in the dark at the pictures and just holding your hand. But, I'd already told you how I felt – didn't you believe me?'

'No,' Gerry confessed. 'I couldn't.'

'You've had a bad time around men, haven't you?' Ryan said more quietly. 'I won't enjoy hearing it, but I think I ought to know.'

Before Gerry could answer, an estate car pulled in on the left hand side of the gate. A tall thin woman with long grey hair, in old jeans and a green gilet over a light sweatshirt, climbed out and opened the rear door. Three excited dogs leaped out, barking, jumping and running around. There were two black labradors, and a springer spaniel which bounded up to Ryan. The woman whistled and it ran back to her.

'Okay, I'll try and tell you,' Gerry agreed. 'But not here.' To her embarrassment her stomach gave a loud rumble, and they both laughed.

'Look, I'll tell you what,' she said. 'There's cafés in St. Just, let's go and get take-away coffees and sandwiches. Then we'll go somewhere a bit quieter where we can talk.'

Ryan agreed, and they got back in the car, both much more relaxed. At St. Just they picked up a ham sandwich and a cheese one along with a couple of coffees. Ryan suggested going to a place called Cot Valley, and directed Gerry to a narrow road at the far end of the town centre.

'I haven't been here for years,' he said, 'but I remember it pretty well. If you haven't been here before I promise you'll like it.'

He was using both hands to keep the coffees balanced on his knees; Seona's car didn't have cup holders. Gerry followed the turns of the road, trying not to send the drinks flying. Soon they were going through a stretch of road with a mass of trees and bushes on each side, more green and luxuriant than anywhere else at this rugged end of Cornwall. Then the road opened out and she saw they were heading down towards the sea, with the land rising away on each side. At the end the road widened out and there was space for half a dozen cars to park. Gerry pulled in, stopped, and relieved Ryan of one of the cups.

'Shall we eat in the car or on the beach?' Gerry asked.

'Beach,' Ryan said firmly. He took Gerry's coffee back as she took out her bag and the sandwiches and locked both doors, then led her down to the beach. To her surprise, it was not a sandy beach but made up entirely of large rounded oval stones.

'That's just how I remembered it,' Ryan said. He waved his free arm up at the cliff. 'Look, you can see there's even some round stones sticking out up there.'

They sat down on a large flat slab of stone by the path above the beach, and divided the food. Gerry gave Ryan half of the ham and most of the cheese sandwich. She'd begun to feel nervous again, but did feel a bit braver once she'd eaten a little. Then she took the lid off her coffee and tried it. It wasn't hot any longer, but it was warm enough and she drank about half of it before turning to Ryan to ask, 'So, what do you want to know?'

Gerry found he was watching her, his food hardly touched. He smiled again.

'Don't mind me,' he said, 'I just like looking at you. Watching your hair blowing back from your face, watching how you sit, how you hold your cup. It's so good to be able to do this without having to hide it. Why, what's the matter?'

Gerry found there were tears in her eyes.

'I'm not used to this,' she said, hunting in her bag for a tissue.

'Not used to what?' Ryan asked, surprised. 'Being looked at?'

'Having someone say nice things to me,' Gerry said. She blew her nose and drank the rest of her coffee.

Ryan looked really angry for a moment, then it changed back to concern.

'You poor girl,' he said. 'Just as well he's not around now or I might have to have a few words with him.'

That really was just as well, Gerry thought. The idea of Ryan confronting Justin made her shiver.

'It wasn't only Justin,' she said. 'There was a man in London when I was a student there. He really blew me away – he was the best-looking guy around. I was, well, I couldn't believe my luck when he asked me out. You see, the boys at school never noticed me. I was always the quiet one, getting on with my school work, going round to my great-auntie's house. And it was the same when I went to London. Men never looked at me.'

'They must have been blind,' Ryan said. He was so indignant that Gerry laughed.

'Well, I had my head in the clouds for a month,' she went on, 'then Martin began cancelling dates, making excuses. In the end he told me his girlfriend was back and he wouldn't be seeing me any more. He'd only been with me because she'd been away for a while. I was heartbroken, I'd fallen for him in a big way.' Looking back Gerry had trouble believing it, but she remembered those nights when she'd cried so much she had to dry her pillowcase out every day. 'But what really finished me was finding that everyone else knew - they'd known all along. I felt they'd all been laughing at me. I don't know if they really had, but I just couldn't face them.'

Ryan made a movement as if he wanted to hug her, but stopped himself.

'It seems a long time ago,' Gerry told him. 'I'm well over that now. I ought to have gone back to Scotland, but everyone there had said I'd hate London and I was too badly hurt to face going home and being told they'd all warned me.'

'Would they have done that?' Ryan was incredulous.

'Oh, probably not,' Gerry admitted. 'Not to my face anyway, but they'd've been thinking it. So I thought, where could I go that would be as far as possible from London and from Lochallaig? Land's End seemed the end of the world.'

'It is,' Ryan said with feeling. 'You really don't want to go there. Well, for my sake I'm glad you decided to come to "bonnie Cornwall". Those people in London sound awful, though I expect really the women were jealous of you.'

Gerry doubted it, but didn't want to start on that track again.

Ryan took a bite out of his sandwich, swallowed it, then said, 'So, what can you tell me about Justin? It sounds like he was involved around everything – Claudia, the chalice, these three men. It won't be easy for either of us, but I need to know, and I didn't feel I could ask Claudia.'

Claudia doesn't know the half of it anyway.

Gerry decided to take a risk, though she was beginning to get fluttery feelings in her stomach. Ryan's honesty was one of the best things about him, and she had to know this, even if she was afraid of the answer. Gerry knew whatever he told her would be the truth.

'Tell me something first,' she said. 'You remember when I took you to the house the other evening?'

'Mmm, of course,' he said through a mouthful of bread and ham. He hastily finished it. 'My memory's not that bad.'

'Well,' she said, 'in the car on the way back, you were all quiet and didn't speak to me, not even when you got out.'

Ryan put down the rest of his sandwich.

'I know,' he said. 'I'm sorry, I didn't mean to be rude, but I was worrying about what I'd let myself in for. I did say to you, didn't I, that I wouldn't have dreamed of telling Claudia my idea if I'd ever seen her before. But aside from that I really was concerned about her. She looks so efficient and capable, but she's so vulnerable.' Ryan shook his head. 'Look, you were going to tell me about Justin.'

'Yeah.' Gerry had to try. 'Look, bits of it might not make sense but I just want to cover the basics for now.'

Gerry stared out to sea, where two little humped islands called the Brisons stuck up on the horizon, then began.

'I met Justin the same day as I met Claudia,' she said. 'In fact I'd seen them having a row. I was in Penlee Park with Debs and we both saw it. Then Monica turned up and told me Claudia was looking for someone to rent a room. Monica knew Claudia a bit and she introduced us. I said I'd go to her house later. I had some time to spare so I went up to Chapel Carn Brea – do you know it?'

Ryan shook his head.

'No' he said. 'I might have heard the name.'

'Well,' Gerry said, 'I went there and walked up to the top and Justin was there. Then that evening I saw him again and he told me he was looking for this chalice.' Gerry had skipped most of the story, and the coincidences sounded fantastic, but she'd have to leave that for now. 'I'd already met the women it belonged to. He asked me to help him and – oh, he wasn't someone you say no to. That was the evening of the fireworks.'

Ryan interrupted, looking puzzled.

'But how did -' he began, but Gerry stopped him, putting her hand on his arm.

'After work next day,' she said, 'I went to the place where I knew the chalice was kept, and the woman agreed I could take it. She knew someone was trying to steal it. I gave it to someone else to look after – I'd twigged by then that Justin had no right to have it. Anyway Justin came up to the house the day after that. Claudia was away, and I wouldn't tell him where it was. That was when I broke my rib.'

'Did he do that?' Ryan looked furious, and Gerry hastened to answer.

'Not exactly,' she said. 'Justin startled me when I was standing at the top of the stairs, so I fell, and that was how it happened, but I'm sure he did it on purpose. Anyway because I wouldn't tell him, next morning he and his friends went to Debbie's house, like I told you.'

Just the bare bones of the story sounded appalling, put like this, and Gerry hadn't even mentioned Wylmet, or the two jewellers. Ryan, horrified, was listening intently. A gull swooped down suddenly, making a dive for the remaining food. Ryan swept a hand at it and it flew off, squawking noisily.

'To save Deb,' Gerry went on, 'I had to take Justin to the people I'd left the chalice with. They weren't happy, but he threatened them and the village where they lived. Afterwards I went back to see that Debs was all right, then went home. Justin came back there, it seems that after all that the chalice wasn't what he thought it would be, wasn't old enough or something. Claudia found him attacking me and told him to get out, and, amazingly, he did. He was really nasty to her first, though.'

Gerry looked at Ryan to see if he was still following, then continued.

'The next morning at breakfast time Monica came roaring up to the house and told us Justin was dead. Someone had found his body at the foot of a cliff. He might have fallen off or he might have been pushed. Or else he was already dead when he went over. They couldn't tell.'

Ryan's brows were furrowed.

'But I don't see what Monica had to do with that?' he said.

'Ah, that's part of the whole thing. It's all so complicated.' Gerry groaned. 'Look, I'll have to beg you not to let on that you know this, and not to tell anyone at the library. Monica had been seeing Justin as well.'

'She had been – are you serious?'

'Oh yes,' Gerry said. 'I'm serious. Monica was kind of hysterical when she came to the house. She actually accused Claudia of paying someone to do away with Justin because she was jealous of Monica. As if.'

'Monica – I – oh,' Ryan tailed off. 'I don't know what to say. You'll be telling me next that Hilary was involved too.'

'No.' Gerry had to smile at the thought of the formidable library manager mixed up in this affair. 'No, no-one else you know has anything to do with it.'

'Well,' Ryan said, 'no wonder Monica had it in for you. And you were going through all that and I had no idea. But who -'

Gerry put her finger across Ryan's lips to stop him.

'No,' she said. 'No more now. Are you free tomorrow morning?'

'For you, yes,' he said. 'But I won't have wheels.'

'That's all right,' Gerry said. 'I'll pick you up. There's something I want to show you and then it may all start to make sense. But no more for now.'

Ryan was reluctant to accept that, but Gerry refused to change her mind, and besides, she thought she'd given him enough to think about for one day.

'Okay,' Ryan said at last. 'It's hard to believe so much was going on with you, and you came into work and didn't say a word. And when you wouldn't go to the gig with me, was that because of this?'

'Oh,' Gerry sighed, 'it was all of them. My rib of course, Justin, the chalice, and something else I'll explain in the morning.'

And when I do, you may never want to see me again.

'All right, I'll leave it,' Ryan said. 'But what do you want to do now?'

'I don't know,' Gerry said. 'I suppose we could go back to St. Just and have a drink.'

They went to the Kings Arms in the square, and got a seat at a table outside. Gerry talked to Ryan about her family, though she only mentioned Seona in passing. She told him about Lochallaig, the mountains and the moors, the lochs, and her brothers taking her fishing in her school holidays. It was easy, except that it was so vivid in her mind because of her visit to Seona.

131

When Gerry drove home at last after dropping Ryan back to Penzance, she was trying to remember as many details of the evening as she could. It might well be the last day she would spend with Ryan, and that would really hurt. But she had to tell him more of the real truth, and there was only way to do that. Ryan would never believe her unless she took him to Chapel Carn Brea and into the past.

Chapter Eleven

Gerry decided she wouldn't begin till they were out of Penzance. She would allow herself just a few last minutes to enjoy things as they were, for however this morning turned out, nothing could be the same between the two of them afterwards.

Ryan had suggested Gerry should pick him up at his house mid-morning, but she'd said she'd do that next time. She didn't want to meet the brother and his friend till she knew if she and Ryan had a future. Instead she texted him when she got to the end of the road. It was one of a network of streets of small terraced houses at the lower end of the town, near the station. Gerry had parked near here on Mazey Day, and after her unexpected talk with Baranwen in the café, she'd come back to find Justin standing beside her car. Penzance was full of memories like that: the churchyard of St. Mary's where she'd sat next to Justin on the bench by the steps, the promenade where they'd watched the fireworks. But it was disturbing to find one of these memories so near Ryan's home.

Gerry looked up and saw Ryan coming. He looked relaxed and happy, and swung rather than climbed into the car. Then he leaned over to give her a kiss on the cheek. It was a warm kiss, and Gerry could still feel it after Ryan had sat back in his seat. She drove down towards the station and round past the car park where she had "seen" the Wasps on her visit to Hedra.

133

As they went along the front Gerry was very aware of Ryan sitting there, close enough for her to touch his knee when she changed gear. Then he said, 'Did you know there's a rattling noise under your car?'

Gerry pulled a face.

'Yeah, but I don't dare take it into the garage,' she said. 'They'd probably find half a dozen other things that need fixing and I can't afford it.'

'Do you know when your MOT's due?' Ryan asked.

Gerry slowed down as the road narrowed at the swing bridge by the Dry Dock, where they'd met the previous morning.

'No, not off the top of my head,' she said, 'though it must be nearly a year since the last one.'

'You might find it's going to cost more than the car's worth to get the repairs done,' Ryan pointed out.

'You sound like my brothers,' Gerry grumbled. 'I can't buy another car.' What was it with men and machines? 'Besides, it belonged to Seona. You know, my great-aunt, I mentioned her last night. She meant a lot to me, and I want to hang on to her car as long as it's got four wheels and a roof.'

'Okay,' Ryan said, 'but I don't like the idea of you driving around in something that's not safe.'

Gerry had no answer to that. Besides she wasn't sure if he was being caring, which she might like, or blokey and bossy, which she wouldn't. She drove the full length of the front, glad that the roads were more peaceful now that the summer visitors had gone. Gerry knew this road very well by now: the right turn after the bridge at Newlyn and the awkward crossroads at the A30 which led to a tree-lined road past the Trereife estate. The end of that road joined the one from Penzance to St. Just, and once Gerry had turned onto it she felt she ought to begin.

'Um.' No, that wasn't a good start. 'Ryan, you know we were talking about sci-fi the other night?

'Oh, yeah,' he said. 'You said it would be good to get around without needing cars.'

Not quite, but at least he remembered that.

'Right,' she said. 'But I kind of noticed that when I said some people believe in the Sight, you were,' oh shit, this was difficult, 'you don't go for that, like it's only hippies or weirdos who would.'

'Or those people who dance round the standing stones at Midsummer,' he agreed. 'There's a crowd of them in St. Just.'

This wasn't going well.

'Mmm. And if I told you that I believe in it – that I've got it myself?'

Ryan didn't say anything. Gerry plunged on.

'It started when I was quite young,' she said. 'I found I always knew if someone was coming to the house, even if no-one else knew. And wherever I was, I knew if someone was going to speak to me. As I got older I'd find I was thinking about someone and then within a few minutes they'd call me or text.' Gerry kept her eyes on the road and didn't look at Ryan. 'I asked my mum once and she said it's a lot of nonsense. But once in a while I ring her, and she almost always says, that's funny, I was just thinking about you.' Then she added, 'Don't you and your brother ever find one of you starts saying something and the other was just going to say the same thing?'

This was a bit of a long shot, but it was worth trying. Ryan sounded surprised, then annoyed.

'Yeah, we do sometimes.' He hurriedly qualified that. 'Of course, we grew up together, we think the same sort of things quite a lot. But that doesn't make us spooky.'

He was obviously uncomfortable with the whole subject, but there was more Gerry had to say. After that she'd wait till she could actually show him.

'Okay' she said. 'I told you my mum thought it was a load of rubbish and so did almost everyone else in the family. There was only one who took it seriously. My great-aunt had the Sight herself, though I didn't know that as a kid. All I knew was she understood what I was talking about when no-one else would. Seona,' she added, in case he had missed it. 'The one who left me this car.'

Gerry wanted to see how Ryan reacted to this and was tempted to pull in and look at him, but was afraid that if she did he might jump out of the car and hitch a lift back to Penzance. She kept driving.

'Remember yesterday morning in Chapel Street when you went to help Claudia?' she asked instead. 'I'd just got there, and I saw you. There was a pretty massive crowd by that time, but out of all those people you just looked straight at me. No looking around, no hesitating. Like you'd felt me watching you.'

'No, but that was -' Ryan began, but Gerry cut across him.

'And if I said I believed in time travel,' she went on, 'then you're going to suddenly remember something really important that you'd promised to do this morning. And you'd get a bus back from St. Just because you don't really want to be sitting in the same car as me.'

Ryan didn't deny it, and Gerry could feel her insides turning over, but she had to stay calm.

'I'm not a mind reader,' Ryan said angrily. 'Those things you said, stuff like that happens with people you know really well. And time travel – that's just Dr. Who and movies. Where is it we're going, anyway? You said you wanted to show me something.'

Gerry held up her hand, then slapped it back on the steering wheel. They were coming to a bend.

'Ryan, will you give me just one hour?' she asked. 'Set the timer on your phone if you like. I promise that when the pinger

136

goes off, then if you still want me to I'll drive you to the bus stop in St. Just and say goodbye.' However much that hurt. 'I won't blame you if you never want to see me again. I did try to tell you I wasn't the person you thought I was.'

'Right,' Ryan said, but he didn't sound happy. 'One hour it is.' And he set the timer like Gerry had suggested. She knew then that she had hoped he might trust her, but after all, how could he? Now he thought she was like people who think Elvis is still alive. Gerry was certain Ryan was wishing he'd never asked her out, never bumped into her outside the library on Tuesday, and been left with his dream – or illusion.

They passed the turn-off to Pendeen and Trewellard, the road which led to Windhaven, and went on towards St. Just. Gerry felt Ryan shift position. Intentionally or not, he'd moved a little away from her.

Gerry wished passionately that she didn't have to do this. He was the best man she'd met and they could have had a good relationship, the one that had started to grow between them. But it would have been based on a lie, and sooner or later something would happen which would explode it. And the closer they got, the worse that would be. It would probably be sooner rather than later; you couldn't live with someone who had the Sight and not notice. Gerry would have spent every day dreading that moment when something would happen that would blow it all open. Could this be this why Seona had never married?

'We're going towards St. Just,' Gerry said, 'but I'm not taking you to the bus stop yet. We're going to Chapel Carn Brea, out near the airport.' *And to Chapel Carn Brea when there's no airport.*

Ryan didn't question or argue, just sat on in silence. There were more bends and a steep hill, so Gerry had to concentrate, but it wasn't much further to the left turn which would take them towards the airport. She'd already used several precious minutes of her hour, and prayed they wouldn't meet any hold-ups on the road, or one of those tractors that go along the road at 10 miles an hour. She got to the Chapel Carn Brea car park as fast as she could, wishing she'd thought of waiting till then before starting the hour's timing. But within a few minutes Ryan would either be in the past, or this would all have been pointless anyway.

There was a dusty brown van and an old VW Beetle in the car park. Gerry hoped they wouldn't find the drivers, and maybe their dogs, at the top of the hill. That could make things very difficult. She wondered what she'd have done if there had been a circle of mist on the hillside like there had been that first time. It was essential they could see clearly as far as Mounts Bay.

'So, what did you want to show me?' Ryan asked, breaking the silence at last.

'We need to go up there,' Gerry waved her arm towards the top of the hill. 'You have to see the view.'

Ryan looked incredulous.

'You brought me here to show me a view? Gerry, I don't think I'm -'

Gerry stopped him.

'No, of course not,' she said. 'It's 'cos this is where I first heard about the chalice. Plus there's a cave at the top where the chalice was hidden, that's where I found it.'

'Are you telling me,' he asked, 'that you brought me here to show me a view and a cave?'

By now Gerry couldn't tell if it was disbelief, irritation or impatience that was uppermost in his voice.

'No!' She tried to be reasonable. 'But come up there first. It's the only place where I can explain. You'll see why in a few minutes.'

Ryan looked at her, then took out his phone and pointedly checked the time remaining on the alarm button. It was such a dismissive gesture that Gerry was suddenly angry. She turned on her heel and marched to the gate without another word, sliding the catch open.

Ryan followed her through the gate and as they walked up the first bit of the slope he gave another glance at his phone.

Seething, Gerry set off uphill. She marched on as fast as she could, but Ryan kept pace effortlessly. Gerry stopped at the top by the direction stone, and found her heart was thumping. Now, she would show him.

'Right,' Gerry said. 'Look all round you. That's the airport down there, and there's the road.' She put her hand on Ryan's shoulder, with nothing of affection in the touch, and gave him a quarter turn. 'You can see that farm down there, and then that way,' she pointed, 'that's St. Michael's Mount. You can more or less make out the castle on top. Or monastery or whatever.' It had been both in its time.

'Yes, of course I can,' Ryan said. 'There's nothing wrong with my eyesight.'

It wasn't supposed to happen like this. Gerry had planned, so far as she had planned anything at all, to do this gently. To show Ryan these crucial reference points: the tiny planes at the airport near the foot of the hill, the road on the Land's End side with toy size cars, the cows like a child's farm set, everything as it was here now and had not been in the past. Then to tell him how she had first come up here and walked through the mist on the hillside to find herself in a different world.

'Okay, this is the last thing,' Gerry said. She stepped over to the stone plinth with the bronze plate on top. 'This tells you what you're looking at, in every direction. And, just over there, you see that path?' Even now, the sight of that dark entrance brought a shiver. 'Under those rocks, that's the entrance to the cave.'

Ryan was standing by the plinth. His reply was cool.

'Yeah, I can see all that' he said. 'I thought you said you had something you wanted to explain.'

His coldness really hurt. Did it matter so much that he should know the truth? Should Gerry say that it was all a mistake and just go back to the car? No, he would still have her marked down in his mind alongside the people who believe in UFOs, or say they've been abducted by aliens. No, it was too late to wish she'd never started. Too late to draw back.

'Right.' Gerry laid her right hand on his arm and felt him flinch, but she closed her fingers tightly round his wrist. 'Shut your eyes for a minute. And whatever you do, don't take your arm away.'

Something about her voice made Ryan look up, startled, questioning. Then he said grimly, 'Okay. But then I'm going home.'

'Fine,' Gerry agreed. 'But now, please shut your eyes.'

He did. Gerry brought her left hand down on top of her right one, laid two fingertips over her ring and held her breath. She barely had time to give the ring any reference points, only asking it to take them more or less to the time of her last visit to Hedra, and to have the hillside bare of people. Nothing happened for a few seconds. They stretched out and gave her time to panic. This just had to work. Then she was in the familiar darkness and felt Ryan shift beside her as he realised that something was happening.

'Don't let go of me,' Gerry shouted, clutching his wrist as tight as she could. She had no idea what would happen if they got separated here, in the space between times. She didn't know if Ryan could even hear her. If he was saying anything, she certainly couldn't hear him.

Then it stopped. Gerry opened her eyes and looked around quickly. This was definitely the past, though she'd need to check if it was the time of the Bees, the Makers, or some other that she'd not been to before. She'd never given such hasty directions and could only trust the Rainbow Ring could read her mind. She kept hold of Ryan's arm and said, 'Right, you can open your eyes now.' She saw he had them screwed up tightly like a child. 'You can open them,' she repeated.

Gerry watched Ryan's face as he began to take in their surroundings, and the anger she'd been feeling vanished. He was trying to keep his face cold, but she could see the panic in his eyes. He pulled his arm away, looked round in every direction, then cried out, 'What did you do? What's happened?'

Gerry went to him and took his arm again, afraid he might run from her. She couldn't lose him here, or let him meet anyone.

'Please,' Gerry said, 'I would have explained first, but you wouldn't listen. We're still on the hilltop, but that stone thing's gone. You can see those two little islands just off the coast there, but if you look down there's no roads or airport or farm or anything. And look this way.' She swivelled him round; for the moment he wasn't resisting. 'There's St. Michael's Mount. Look at the top – there's no building on it. Ryan, we're in the past.'

Ryan stared at the Mount, but Gerry wasn't sure he'd heard a word she'd said. She expected him to say he didn't believe it, but he seemed too shocked to say anything. She remembered how Justin had been impatient when she refused to accept that she'd moved in time. Gerry didn't want to be like Justin. She pulled Ryan over to the side of the hill. If there was a village near the top, this was the Makers' time. If the villagers had moved their homes down the hill to the better farming lands there, then it should be the time of the Gwenen. If it was neither.. She reached the edge, looked over, and gave a sigh of relief. It was the Bees' village. She pointed to the woods beyond the village.

'Do you see those trees over there?' she asked. 'There's another village and that's where those three men come from. That's why I couldn't go to the police about them like you wanted me to. Didn't you notice anything odd about Kenver's clothes? I had to bring you here, to show you.'

Ryan had gone white. He seemed too dazed to speak, so Gerry pushed on as fast as she could and hoped he really was listening.

'Justin was from the past too,' she said, 'but Claudia didn't know.' Ryan's face had changed at the mention of Claudia's name and for a moment Gerry's earlier fear came back. Then she understood. 'Did you think we were in this together? Of course she doesn't know, can you imagine me trying to tell her? I mean, like, you're actually here and you still don't believe it.'

It was autumn, as it had been in their own time; the air was slightly cool, and the first wash of gold leaves lay across the woods. There was a breeze off the sea and though the village was sheltered, the smoke from the hearth fires in the houses, which rose out through the tops of the roofs, blew about with the wind. Gerry recognised the sounds and was startled at how familiar they seemed: the lowing of a cow near to the village, the bleating of sheep on the far side of the hill, the voice of a woman calling to her children. Further off came a metallic clang which must come from the forge at the Wasps' village. A dog barked and she drew back, not wanting anyone to look up and see them.

Ryan had come forward as far as the edge of the hilltop and was standing looking down at the courtyard buildings below him. Gerry pulled him back to stand beside her.

'Please,' Ryan said, and now he was so scared that it wrenched her heart. 'Please tell me I'm dreaming. Tell me we're not really here. Wake me up, take me back, do something, anything!'

'I'll take you back,' Gerry told him. 'I'll take you to St. Just, like I promised. You can get the bus home.' The mention of something as ordinary as a bus didn't seem to help. 'I shouldn't be here anyway,' she said, 'I wasn't supposed to come back, but there wasn't any other way to make you understand. I'm in deep

142

shit here. I wanted to tell you about that, but we'd better go back first. I can't risk hanging about and meeting anyone.'

Gerry had meant to tell him this before they came here. Why had she let herself lose her temper?

Then Ryan caught her arm and gripped it.

'You said you shouldn't meet anyone,' he breathed. 'I think we just did.'

Heart hammering, Gerry spun round. Ryan was looking at the path from the fogou and she saw what he had seen. Someone was coming out from the dark entrance. A woman in a plain gown, apparently alone. Gerry knew who it was at once; there was no mistaking the halting walk.

'Hedra,' she whispered.

'You know her?' Ryan was incredulous.

'Yes.' Gerry wondered if there was any chance of the teacher not seeing them. If Hedra went down the hill to her home, if she didn't look round - but they weren't going to be that lucky. Unlike her, Ryan hadn't whispered his last words, and Hedra had heard him. She turned at the sound of his voice and saw the two standing above her. Gerry could have taken the two of them back then, but she didn't believe Hedra would harm them. And perhaps the teacher could help to convince Ryan.

'Gerralda.' Hedra's greeting was so neutral that Gerry couldn't guess if she was pleased to see her, or angry. They both waited in silence until Hedra reached them at her dragging pace, while Gerry worried about how to introduce Ryan. She'd probably broken another time rule by bringing him here at all.

'Gerralda,' Hedra repeated when she stopped in front of them. 'Do you feel you need someone to protect you now? Have you acquired a bodyguard for yourself?'

Gerry glanced sideways at Ryan, who was looking nothing like a bodyguard, then understood that Hedra was being ironic.

'No,' Gerry said, wishing suddenly that she could take Ryan's hand. 'He, oh, he said he wanted to be part of my life. And I felt I shouldn't agree unless he understood what it was he was asking to be part of.'

'And he does now?' Hedra was still sardonic, as she took in Ryan's bewilderment.

Before Gerry could answer, Ryan cut in.

'Gerry, I can't understand a word you and she,' he nodded at Hedra, 'are saying.'

'Oh, sorry, I forgot.' Gerry took his hand and rested it on hers. 'Look, keep your fingers here, just make sure you're touching this ring. Then you should be okay.' She had to trust that the ring would work for Ryan if she asked it to.

Ryan was beyond surprise now. Gerry hoped he'd settled for believing this was all a nightmare. Hedra looked at the ring.

'It does that for you?' she asked curiously. 'And what of the time before you had it?'

'It was this,' Gerry told her, pulling out the gold chain from below the neckline of her dress. 'This chain, it was a gift from my great-aunt. Baranwen told me she was a wise woman.'

'Baranwen.' An odd expression crossed Hedra's face. 'Have you seen her again?'

Gerry looked at Ryan before she replied. 'Can you follow us now?' she asked. He nodded, so she added, 'You're not going to like this.'

Gerry had decided she'd done so much already she might as well do the lot, and turned back to Hedra.

'I haven't seen Baranwen myself,' she said, 'but she's done some terrible things.'

Gerry told Hedra briefly about Mr. Trewartha, the elderly jeweller, then what Baranwen had done to Colenso, Rosenwyn and Keyna.

'I didn't tell those three,' she finished, 'but I did think that if Baranwen had done it just using the Kelegel, then perhaps if it was destroyed like you said, then maybe I could use my ring to heal them. They didn't deserve what she did.'

Hedra looked at Gerry, who couldn't read her expression.

'You still want to right the wrongs of the world, then?' she asked.

'Hold on, there's more yet.' Gerry felt Ryan's hand clench over her fingers. 'No, wait.' She moved his hand, pulled off the Rainbow Ring and offered it to him. 'See if you can put this on, it ought to fit one of your fingers. Then see if it still works. I've got my chain.' Worrying if Ryan could understand what she was saying to Hedra was distracting her too much.

'Well,' she went on, 'you know I told you that Justin was responsible for poisoning the flagon of wine, but used four men from the village to do the job for him?'

Gerry had meant to tell Ryan about Wylmet later, but still wasn't sure if there would be a "later" when she could talk to him. She felt him give a start at the mention of poison; this was totally new to him. So Seona's ring was translating for him. Ryan had said his great, great, lots of greats-grandmother was supposed to be a witch. Perhaps he'd inherited something as Gerry had herself. But she was certain the ring would only obey her – Seona had made it to respond to her. She sure was it wouldn't take Ryan back to his own time without her. Besides, he no longer looked scared or angry, but appeared to be concentrating hard. Perhaps he'd decided that whether he was mad or dreaming, he might as well go along with this.

'Well, Baranwen brought Elwyn, Cathno and Kenver into our time to help her take the Chalice,' Gerry went on, including Ryan in the phrase "our time", 'but I've not seen anything of Talan. Tell me, has he come back here?'

'Talan?' Hedra wrinkled her brow. 'No, no one has seen him or Kenver for a long time. The other two vanished a few days ago. It is a cause of great distress to their families, and hardship too. There has been trouble with the harvest, I know. Do you have any news of them?'

'Well, Kenver won't be coming back.' That was a bit blunt, but Gerry felt very bitter about him. 'He died in an accident after causing a load of grief to someone he didn't even know. I suppose Baranwen pushed him into it, though I don't understand why. I don't know what's happened to Talan; he wasn't with the three who helped steal the Kelegel. Now the others are holed up somewhere and can't come back without Baranwen. But that's not all.'

'Are you thinking of bringing them back yourself, then? It seems that you are able to.' Hedra glanced towards Ryan to emphasise her point.

'You must be joking,' Gerry muttered. That was one idea that had never occurred to her. Ryan still hadn't said anything, and Gerry wondered how he was fitting what she'd told him about the chalice and the Wasps against what he was hearing now.

'Gerralda,' Hedra said. Something in her voice jolted Gerry out of her own thoughts.

'I saw Baranwen here, two days ago,' Hedra said quietly. 'She looked strange, haunted. She did not stay long.' Hedra rubbed her forehead with the back of her hand, remembering. 'I think she wanted to speak to me but was unable to. If it were anyone but she I would say she was being controlled.'

'The Kelegel,' Gerry muttered. 'That's just what Seona said.'

'Seona?' Ryan asked. 'But, I thought,' he stopped.

Hedra gave Gerry a penetrating look.

'Tell us,' she said.

Gerry wished they could sit down or move or something. Standing here on the exposed top of the hill didn't feel good.

She groaned. 'All right,' she said, reluctantly. 'I wanted to talk to someone who would understand. Seona always understood. I knew, I'd been told, I must never go back into my own past. So I decided I could jump back to at least thirty years before I was born. I didn't see how that could do any harm.'

'But it did,' Hedra said. It wasn't a question. After her long years of teaching she was an expert in reading body language.

'What happened?' Ryan asked. 'What went wrong?' Gerry wondered if he noticed that this time he had spoken as if the concept of time travel was quite normal. Gerry totally didn't want to tell them, these two of all people. But she had to.

'I found Seona, obviously a much younger Seona than the one I knew,' she began. 'I told her about the Chalice and the Guardians and coming back to your time.' She nodded at Hedra. 'And the Makers, that's Colenso and the others. Then about what Baranwen had done. Seona said it sounded as if Baranwen was no longer making the decisions, but the Chalice itself. She believed that there was some power in it that had, like, got in there from the magic the Makers used, but they didn't know about it so they hadn't wiped it out like the rest. But then,' Gerry hesitated. Even remembering this bit was painful. 'Well, she knew I was family, but just thought I'd come from another part of the country. She hadn't realised that I was from the future, her future. When she understood at last, oh, it was horrible. I hadn't thought..'

'Thought what?' Ryan asked. He hadn't seen it coming either, and Gerry was glad. It made her feel a bit less crass. Hedra raised her eyebrows in a question.

'I explained that her niece was my mother,' she said, 'Seona had already clocked that I was there because I'd grown up coming to her for advice. And,' Gerry's voice shook, 'that if she'd still been alive when all this happened I'd have come to her then. So she knew she was going to die before I was twenty.'

'What did she do?' Ryan asked. He moved closer and reached for Gerry's other hand. He seemed genuinely concerned, and also hadn't questioned that she'd been talking to a relative who'd been dead for three years. Would this acceptance last once he was back in his own surroundings? Might he still think this was a ghastly dream?

'Seona kind of crumpled up,' Gerry said. 'She looked terrible and I couldn't understand why until she told me. Then I felt so awful, you can't imagine. Everything she'd done, all the support she'd always given me, and in return I'd done that to her. I swore to myself I'd never go back into the past again.'

'An oath which you broke as soon as it suited you to do so.'

Hedra's words stung; Gerry knew they were true. She looked at Ryan.

'You'd never have believed me if I hadn't brought you here.'

'I'm not sure I believe it now,' he muttered, but quietly.

Hedra, however, seemed to have had a completely new idea. For the first time she spoke to Ryan directly.

'It grieves me beyond words that our revered Chalice has been so misused,' she said, 'but the evil cannot now be undone. Those who first created it tried to so and failed. It has to be physically destroyed, and Gerralda cannot do this. She is bound to the Jewels and they would prevent her from ever harming them. But you could do it. You are the only person who knows of the Chalice but has no personal loyalty to it. The Kelegel would have no influence over you.'

To Gerry's astonishment, Ryan gave this suggestion serious consideration.

148

'Would that mean that Gerry – Gerralda – could go back to leading a normal life?' he asked Hedra.

She shook her head.

'No,' she replied. 'It would mean that the ills Baranwen has wrought could be combatted in part, and most importantly no new ones could arise. But Gerralda has experienced too much to return to being what you would call a normal person ever again. Knowing that, would you still help to put an end to the Kelegel?'

Ryan surprised Gerry even more.

'What's it made of, your chalice?' he asked.

Men, Gerry thought, thinking of her brothers again. Give them a technical problem and they're happy. Then she did a double-take as she saw why Ryan had asked. He was going to try it.

'It's made of gold and of gemstones,' Hedra told him. 'The same as on that ring of Gerralda's that you are wearing. Garnet, topaz, sapphire and amethyst. Why?'

Ryan was frowning, but with concentration, not annoyance.

'Connor works in a body shop,' he said. 'They've got welding tools and stuff. I could probably swing it.'

Gerry was open-mouthed.

'Hang on just a minute,' she interrupted. 'What are we saying here?'

'I'll tell you what I'm saying.' The determination on Ryan's face would have made his resolution apparent to anyone. 'It sound like someone's got to put a stop to this thing before it does any more harm. I'm not making myself out to be a hero, but I should think a welding arc would do the job.'

Hedra stepped closer and looked at Ryan intently.

'You are saying that you know of a tool that could do this – that could cut through the materials? And that you could use it? You have such powers?'

'It's engineering, not powers,' Ryan said. 'Where my brother works they work with metal, and gold is a lot softer than what they have to cut.'

Please don't start talking about cars, Gerry thought. Of all things.

Ryan looked at the ring more carefully.

'How big are the jewels?' he asked. 'I might be able to cut some of them but I know sapphire's near as hard as diamond.'

'That is not important,' Hedra assured him. 'If you can break down the gold and split even one or two of the stones, the chalice would lose any power that remains within it. The stones are about this size.' She held up her thumb and forefinger about two centimetres apart.

Ryan frowned.

'Sounds like it'd be worth a bundle,' he said. 'I don't want to be arrested for wrecking someone else's valuables.'

'It belongs to us, the Gwenen,' Hedra, said and her voice changed as if she were making a formal pronouncement. 'In the absence of the Guardians, I invest you with the authority to destroy the Kelegel a'n gammneves by any means known to you.'

Gerry felt it was time she got a word in.

'Fine,' she said. 'Now all we have to do is get hold of Baranwen and take the Chalice off her. Have either of you any ideas how we might do that?'

Chapter Twelve

'Do you really mean you're going to do it?' Gerry asked.

'Yeah, if you're sure all that really happened,' Ryan replied.

They had said the same things over and over, all the way back from Chapel Carn Brea. From time to time Ryan put his hand to his head as if it hurt him, but mostly he just sat, still looking dazed. He had started asking questions as soon as they got back to the car.

'And Debs?' This too Ryan had already asked. 'You said those men came to her house, didn't she think they were -'

'No,' Gerry interrupted. 'No, of course not. She knew they were talking a different language, but just thought they came from Eastern Europe, thought they were flower pickers or something. They'd grabbed her the day before, at the Quay Fair, but let her go when I came along. She found Justin was running them when he took them to her house, but that was all.'

'So Debs met Justin?' Ryan asked 'I can't believe she never said anything either. And all this was, when, in the summer?'

'It was in June, in Golowan week,' Gerry told him. 'Debs wouldn't've talked about it, she just wanted to put it behind her. And I was too wrecked after what happened to the Chalice, and then Justin getting killed. Look, we're nearly there, then I can tell you properly, from the beginning. If you've got time.'

'I've got time,' Ryan said. 'Oh yes.'

Gerry turned off the bypass and into the Treneere estate, coincidentally not far from Debbie's house. It wasn't a grey, forbidding concrete jungle like some London estates. The roads were wide, some with grass borders. There were terraces of small plain houses, cream and white, or grey pebble-dash, with little front gardens. The route she wanted went left, then right, and up a hill. Gerry followed the curves of the road past a maze of little side turnings till she reached the highest point of the estate. From here the road led down into the body of Penzance, seen as a mass of roofs above its rows of granite grey buildings. Gerry parked just past the top and led Ryan across the road to a large wooden gate where a sign proclaimed "Lescudjack Castle Hill Fort".

'We should be okay to talk here,' Gerry said. She'd discovered this place by chance at the end of the summer. Once the schools went back it was a peaceful spot to go to on her day off to sit and think, or just stare down at the bay and not think at all.

Gerry opened the catch on the gate and Ryan followed her through to a footpath which led upwards through overgrown grass. Some of the grass had been cut short to form green paths, and they followed one of these. This area was enclosed by shrubs and trees, edged by the backs of the surrounding houses. The path led to an open space at the top. Standing on the highest point they could look out across a foreshortened Penzance to the sea and the Newlyn harbour wall. Ryan stood still and stared round.

'I've not been here since I was a kid,' he said. 'I used to climb over the gate after dark with my mates to, well, to do lads' stuff. I know it's an old place.' Suddenly he looked alarmed. 'This isn't another of your -' he stopped, not knowing what word to use. 'Portals?' he hazarded.

152

Ryan, a computer trainer, would be more used to the portals used as links on the internet than for the time travel he'd been so sceptical about. It seemed an appropriate word.

'Oh no, it's not that,' Gerry said. 'I just wouldn't've felt safe talking that near to the fogou - just in case we got drawn back there again. I don't know if that would really happen; I've no idea how it works. I mean, I suppose I could go into the past from anywhere; I've gone from Claudia's house a few times. But I'll be happier telling you here.'

Being Sunday, they didn't have the hilltop to themselves. There were a couple of the ubiquitous dog walkers, a dad playing with a toddler, and three teenage girls with long hair, hooded tops and long legs in denim shorts and warm black tights. They had shed the world-weary expression teenagers wear when they're out with their parents, and were giggling over some smartphone pictures, probably last night's party. In the nearby houses people would be cooking dinner or watching football; ordinary families at home.

Gerry walked along, with Ryan beside her, to where the ground began to slope down again. What looked like a tree trunk trimmed of branches and cut in half lengthways was set in the grass on short wooden rests to make a bench. From this lower level they could see less of the town but could still see the sea. The high straight tower of St. Mary's church and the round dome of the Lloyds Bank building stood out above the lines of slate, windows and chimneys.

'You're all right to sit here?' Gerry asked. 'Oh, and can I have my ring back?'

Ryan looked down at his hands, startled. The Rainbow Ring was sitting snugly on the ring finger of his left hand. Gerry found it weird seeing someone else wearing it. Ryan pulled off the ring and gave it back. It was a bright morning, and the jewels caught the sun.

153

'Look,' Gerry said, putting the ring back into its usual place on the middle finger of her right hand. 'Can you see anything?'

Unlike the Kelegel, the Bysow a'n gammneves didn't need water to function. Gerry called up the beams of light from the gemstones, and as they overlapped, the tiny rainbow stretched across the back of her hand, down to the wrist.

Ryan blinked.

'Just for a second, I thought – no, I must've imagined it.'

So he was still unconvinced? Gerry let it go for now.

'Okay,' she said, and was about to begin, but just then a short sequence of music came from Ryan's pocket. He pulled out his phone which gave three short buzzing notes. He looked at it, first puzzled, then, as he remembered, in disbelief.

'An hour,' Ryan said. 'I set that an hour ago. How long were we – there?' He wasn't going to say 'in the past'. Gerry let that go too.

'I can't say,' she told him. 'Sometimes you come back at the moment you left, sometimes the same length of time later, like if you'd been gone an hour you find you've missed an hour. But I've known it be two or three hours longer. I don't know how to control that. Anyway, now I can tell you properly from the beginning.'

And she did, starting with how she'd bought the sapphire and gone to Mr Trewartha's shop. 'He's the one I told Hedra about, but I'll get to that later. He said he thought the stone and the setting were old, except it was in surprisingly good condition. Of course I know now that's because it'd come forward about thirteen hundred years.'

Gerry went on: meeting Debbie in the park and seeing Claudia and Justin, Monica introducing her to Claudia and then her first trip to Chapel Carn Brea. As she talked, details came back which she hadn't thought about in nearly three months, and they all fitted into the pattern of events in a way she couldn't have seen at the time.

As the story progressed, Gerry couldn't believe how good it felt to tell all this to someone in her own time. She'd carried it alone for so long. She'd told Ryan a little the previous day, but leaving out so much that it probably hadn't made sense. She tried to skip how Justin had persuaded her to help him, though the memory of his hand resting on her shoulder, pulling her towards him, came back too sharply for comfort. Like sitting close to him on the bench in the churchyard; and what he'd done on Claudia's sofa. Ryan probably guessed; Gerry would have if their situations had been reversed. But she did tell Ryan about Justin's brother, the real reason he wanted the chalice, and why it had been so vital to keep it from him. She repeated that Claudia knew nothing, nothing at all, except that Justin had been hounding Gerry for the Kelegel. Claudia had once said that Justin was "like a mind reader", but obviously she had no idea that it was literally true.

Gerry cut the dreary weeks between giving away the chalice and receiving the ring from Seona down to a couple of sentences. Then she asked, 'Do you remember you said you saw me in the street and thought I wouldn't know who you were? Can you understand it now?'

Ryan hadn't said anything all the time Gerry had been speaking, just listened intently. She didn't know how long she'd talked for. Ryan had taken her hand when she told him about Wylmet's death, and held it more tightly as she described taking the Makers to the fogou where they had been ambushed by the Guardians and Kerenza. Gerry looked round and saw that the girls, the father and child, and the dogs had gone. Two boys were knocking a football about, and as she raised her head one of the boys kicked it straight at them. Ryan caught the ball and lobbed it back with both speed and accuracy.

'Good shot,' Gerry said. 'So, shall I tell you what happened this week?'

Ryan stood up.

'Yeah, but I think we need to move.'

'Okay,' Gerry agreed. 'Let's get out of range of those kids. We can go out down there.'

There was another gate below them leading out into a lane and down to the street below Lescudjack. Gerry unlatched the gate and they crossed the lane, then went down a steep path between two garages. This led to a bright, open street of white houses with gardens sloping to low granite walls, their beds still filled with colourful flowers. The road was quiet, with cars parked outside many of the houses. The harbour lay below, looking much nearer from here. Gerry walked to the end of the close where they could see St. Michael's Mount. Ryan stood still, just staring at it.

'I can't get my head round it,' he said at last. 'Did I really see that without -' he waved at the castle.

'Yeah, you did,' Gerry said. 'Of course you can't get your head round it. I had enough trouble and I was used to things you couldn't explain. But that was why I wanted to show you the farm and the airport and the stone thing first so you'd see the contrast. Only, well, I got wound up and skipped the explanations.'

She looked at Ryan and thought how honest and straightforward he was. Justin had been devious, calculating and cruel, but even knowing that she'd still been under his spell. Ryan she could trust. And he wasn't shrinking away from her any longer, even if he still had doubts about what had happened.

'Let me tell you about this week,' Gerry said. 'You know quite a lot of it already.' She told him as they stood there, both gazing at the Mount which stood out sharply in the gap between the last two houses. Now Gerry could explain how, while she sat in Morrab Gardens, she'd actually watched Baranwen take the chalice. How she'd visited Meraud, Hedra, and the Makers, plus seeing Seona, which he already knew about. 'And that's it, really.'

'That's it,' he said, and suddenly laughed. 'Except that you kept trying to warn me off. Have you got anything else up your sleeve? What's going to happen next?'

'I don't know,' Gerry said. 'Right now all I want is to get hold of the Kelegel so you can deal with it. Perhaps if I got it off Baranwen, the Wasps would simply go back to their own village, just like that. I wish I could lend you something like this ring so we could keep in touch. I don't suppose I could text you if I had to go back into the past after Baranwen.'

'This is the woman you were just talking about, the one in the cave waving that axe about?' Ryan asked. 'The one who smashed the glass in the museum?'

'Yeah, that one.'

Ryan shook his head.

'I don't know if you're the bravest person I ever met, or just plain stupid,' he said. 'Going to rescue Deb at the fair, confronting those men at her house, and now this.'

That wasn't how it had felt when it was happening. Gerry laughed, but didn't feel she deserved any praise.

'I honestly don't believe I've had much choice,' she said. 'It's like I've got to do it, every time. And it's been easier since I've had this.'

She patted the ring. Ryan frowned.

'Your present from your great-aunt?' he asked. 'But didn't it ever strike you that -' he stopped and gave her a questioning look.

'What?' Gerry asked. 'Did what strike me?'

'Oh, nothing,' he said. 'I'll tell you tomorrow. I feel like Claudia did yesterday, I need to be on my own for a bit. It's a lot to take in.' He gave her a quick hug. 'I'll go down to the harbour and walk home from there. I'll call you later. I need to talk to Conn, but not till I've got this cup. He'll have to do the actual cutting, there's no way I'd be allowed to use their tools. Even if I do just happen to know how to use the blowtorch.' Ryan smiled. 'I'm going to tell him it's an old stage prop I picked up. If the jewels are that big no-one'll believe they're real. So I'll say I want the gold melted down to make a bracelet or something for you.'

Gerry stared at him, appalled.

'Ryan, listen to me,' she said. 'You can't just do it like that. You've got no idea how dangerous this thing is. It's not going to just sit there and let you cut it in half.'

Ryan frowned.

'What do you mean, it's not going to let me?' he said. 'It's only a chalice, a cup thing. Anyway, I've got to get rid of it. Otherwise you'll never be free to live your own life. It feels like you can hardly stop thinking about it.'

'But it's alive,' Gerry pleaded. 'Don't you understand, you could be risking your brother's life! You've got to believe me. At least let me come with you. I might be able to help shield him.' This was so frustrating, but Gerry didn't see what more she could say to convince Ryan. She would bet everything she owned, including the gold chain, that she was right. 'Okay, just don't do it unless I'm there with you. Promise me. Tell him I want to see the gold for this bracelet. It's a good story, if you think he'll believe it.'

'He won't be bothered,' Ryan said. 'Don't worry so much. Come on.'

They walked back together along the road to the car. They reached the corner, and Ryan gave her a quick kiss on the lips. Then he stepped back to make sure she didn't mind. Gerry didn't mind, but it was better to take things slowly. What she was feeling mostly was overwhelming gratitude that Ryan was still with her. She had told him everything, the entire unbelievable story, and he was still standing here beside her. She wished, though, that she could convince him of the very real danger.

'You be careful,' Ryan said, and pressed Gerry's hand between both of his. Then he went off down the hill, looking back once to the corner where she was still standing, watching him go. Ryan smiled, raised his hand, then disappeared down the road into the town.

Gerry walked slowly back to the Volvo, missing him already and feeling very alone. Ryan was ready to help to destroy the Kelegel, but first she had to find it for him. She reached the car and got in, already wrestling with the problem of how to contact Baranwen. That was ironic, after all the time she'd spent hoping she'd never see the Guardian again. Then she realised how simple the answer was. Baranwen had come to Penzance and Redruth when she believed the Jewels were in danger; she had summoned the Makers when Colenso had announced she would take the magic from the chalice. It was miraculous that Baranwen hadn't materialised when Hedra charged Ryan with the task of destroying the Kelegel. Or when she and Ryan had talked about it just now.

Gerry drove back through Treneere and round the Penzance bypass. She turned right at the Mount Misery roundabout. She had read that it got its name because in the old days the fishermen's wives would stand there, waiting to see if their men had come back alive from their fishing trips.

Gerry glanced in the rear view mirror once she'd joined the St. Just road, and got the shock of her life. Baranwen was sitting behind her. In the back seat of Seona's car.

Chapter Thirteen

Sunday September 14th continued

Gerry nearly ran the Volvo into the hedge, but by sheer luck kept it straight. She jammed on the brakes, pulling in to the side by pure instinct. The engine stalled and the driver behind hooted furiously, but Gerry barely noticed. She swung round to face the Guardian, and saw at once what Hedra had meant. Baranwen was struggling to speak, her face contorted. She was hardly recognisable as the woman who had so triumphantly freed the Kelegel from its glass prison. She lifted her hand slowly, and then reluctantly, as if compelled, pushed something towards Gerry.

'Take it,' Baranwen said roughly, the words dragging out as if forced from her lips. She sounded like someone who'd had a stroke. Gerry reached out, then gasped in disbelief. Baranwen had handed her the Kelegel a'n gammneves.

'Why?' Gerry breathed, then, coming to her senses, grabbed the chalice and tucked it into the diagonal of her seat belt, the base resting on her lap. 'Why?' she repeated.

'It – made – me,' the hoarse voice said, each syllable palpably an effort. 'In – danger. Don't – stop.'

Obediently Gerry turned the key and restarted the engine. Just up the road from here there was a wide gravel area where she could pull off and park. She looked in the rear view mirror. There was a van coming off the roundabout but she had enough room to get going ahead of it.

Gerry signalled and took off up the hill, wanting to reach the place where she could talk to Baranwen in safety. Before she got there, there was a road on the right, but Gerry never went that way so she didn't give it a glance. Then, as she came level with it, a large black car shot at terrifying speed out of the side road and straight into the Volvo. It just missed Gerry but ploughed right into where Baranwen was sitting. The impact spun the Volvo round. The van coming up behind tried to swerve but slammed into the back of the Volvo as it veered, still pointing uphill, and stopped. The black car came to a halt diagonally across the road. And at the same time a blue hatchback, heading down the hill towards Penzance, collided with it. The driver of the hatchback had a few seconds' warning and braked desperately, but couldn't stop. The hatchback slid inexorably into the black car which was completely blocking his side of the road. It had all happened in about a minute.

The driver of the blue hatchback was unhurt. He got out and came over to Gerry. The driver of the van climbed down from his cab, and made his way round the vehicles with some difficulty to reach her too.

'Are you all right, luv?' the van driver asked.

That was a stupid question. Of course Gerry wasn't all right. But she was still alive. A woman passenger got out of the blue car and walked down to join them, talking urgently on her phone.

'Maniac,' said the driver of the hatchback, a middle-aged man with thinning hair, wearing a grey V-neck sweater. 'Where did he go? Did you see him?'

The van driver shook his head. He was already on his phone too. Gerry couldn't speak, and couldn't look behind her.

161

There was no sign of the driver who'd caused the accident.

'Wasn't looking where he was going, coming out at that speed onto a main road, what was he playing at? Look at my car!' The middle-aged man was furious.

The woman on the mobile stopped talking for a moment and came up to Gerry. She tried to open the driver's door but it had been damaged by the collision and was jammed. She gestured to her companion to go and try the front passenger door, and called to Gerry, 'Can you open your window? Are you hurt?' Gerry just looked at her. 'The police and the ambulance are on their way,' the woman said, trying to be reassuring. 'They'll be here very soon.' The man had opened the passenger door so Gerry could get out, but it seemed too much effort even to undo her seat belt. Baranwen had not been wearing one.

That was when the woman realised there was someone else in the Volvo. She called across to tell the man, and he leaned over to look into the back seat. He stepped back so fast that he banged his head, then gestured to the woman to move away before she could see what was there. Gerry knew, had known from the second of the impact, that she could do nothing for Baranwen. That car had been deliberately aimed at the Guardian.

Reluctantly Gerry clambered over the gear stick and out of the far door. She could move, though her ribs felt bruised. There had been no airbag to protect her in Seona's old car. It had meant so much to her and now it would be a write-off. Ryan'll be pleased, she thought, he reckoned it wasn't safe to drive. And at that Gerry nearly wept. The tears were so close, but she couldn't give in to them. The woman who'd called the police came to where Gerry was standing and put an arm round her shoulders. Gerry clutched her bag; she'd pushed the chalice into it before climbing out. She could feel the Jewels pulsing inside, but she ignored them. Right now the Tegennow a'n gammneves were not, for once, uppermost in her mind.

162

The helpful woman had been right. Two police cars were there in minutes, followed almost at once by an ambulance and a fire engine. The roads were quiet, and none of them had far to come. The firemen got to work at once to try to cut what was left of Baranwen out of the car. The police from the second car began to set up traffic cones, and a cameraman walked all round, looking at the different cars, the angles of impact and the tyre marks on the road surface. A policewoman and two paramedics came over to Gerry.

'I think she must be in shock,' the woman told them. 'She hasn't said a word. I don't know if she's hurt, but she climbed out of her car okay.' The driver of the blue hatchback was talking non-stop, complaining to everyone about the lunatic who had raced out from the side road.

'I couldn't stop,' he said, 'no-one could've with no warning. And he'd run off before I even got out. What am I supposed to do without my car? Who knows how long they'll take to fix it? And that'll be off my insurance.'

'They'll give you a hire car,' his companion said sensibly, but the man went on grumbling. A young policeman was patiently taking details. The van driver said that Gerry had been parked at the roadside, he'd seen her pull out and start off up the hill. Then the black car came out of nowhere and collided with the Volvo. As yet, then, they didn't need to ask Gerry what had happened, but the WPC kept asking her gently for her name and address. The paramedics in their dark green uniforms wanted to check her out, to make sure there were no internal injuries before she was allowed so much as a cup of tea. They wanted to take her to the hospital and examine her properly but Gerry refused point blank. She would be all right, but she had to go home.

At that point Gerry understood that she would need to tell the WPC where she lived. She offered Claudia's number and said she was sure her landlady would come and get her, but the policewoman said no.

'I'll take you back myself,' she said, 'but I'll ring her first and see if she'll be there when you arrive.'

After she'd spoken to Claudia the WPC called to a colleague to get a car sent to the road on the northbound side of the accident. She couldn't drive to Claudia's house from here, she explained. Nothing was to be touched, and no-one was going anywhere up this stretch of road till the police had all their information, measurements and pictures. There had been a fatality and they'd need the information for the coroner. Gerry listened but without interest.

'The car will be here in a few minutes,' the WPC said. 'While we're waiting, is there anything else you can tell me? Who was your passenger?'

At that question Gerry's brain spun back into life.

'Her name's – was – Baranwen,' she said. 'I'd met her a few times but I don't know her surname or where she lives. Lived.'

Gerry was so well versed in these half-truths that by now she hardly had to think what she could say and what she couldn't. She began to register that other things were going on: talk about road closures, details of witnesses, how long it was likely to be before the cars could be moved. The police had already established that the black car had been reported stolen that morning.

'Joy riding,' the middle-aged man said in disgust. His companion was back on her phone, explaining their delay to whoever they'd been on their way to see.

It was all just noise to Gerry. All she cared about was getting home to talk to Claudia. And to Ryan.

It wasn't long before the third police car arrived, coming down from the next road up. The driver turned it and handed the keys to the WPC after she and Gerry had picked their way through the debris, skirting the damaged vehicles. Gerry gave directions, and though the short journey seemed to take forever, at last they were driving down the lane to Windhaven. Gerry's heart lifted as she saw a grubby white van parked outside. Claudia had had the sense to ring Ryan. Ryan had given Claudia his number earlier in the week in case she needed to call him about the gallery. He'd have known how to get here and bypass the crash scene, so that he could be waiting for her.

Claudia and Ryan were both were at the door of the police car before Gerry had even got out. Claudia looked concerned, but Ryan was frantic. Heedless of the others, he put his arms round Gerry, as if to be sure she was really safe and unhurt.

The policewoman gave Claudia a few details of the accident and said she'd call later.

'I'll need a proper statement later when Gerry's recovered a bit,' she said. She gave Gerry a card with her number. 'My name's Frances,' she said. 'Ring me when you're feeling better, or I'll get in touch if I haven't heard from you.'

At last she left and the three of them could go inside. Ryan still had one arm round Gerry as they walked into the kitchen.

'When Claudia said you'd been in an accident, I –' he began, but Gerry interrupted. She was too desperate to explain to be polite. She'd been holding this back ever since the moment of impact.

'It wasn't an accident,' she said. 'It was deliberate. I couldn't tell them. I don't want to believe it, but I saw him. It was Justin.'

Claudia gave a cry. Ryan just stared at Gerry, his brow furrowing.

'I thought you told me he was dead,' he said.

'He faked it,' Gerry said bitterly, pulling away from Ryan so she could look at them both. 'There's a man called Talan who's been missing ever since the time of that supposed cliff fall. A friend of Kenver's. Talan's the one I asked Hedra about,' she added to Ryan. 'He was close to Justin's height, and had fair hair.' Then, to Claudia, 'Do you remember what Monica said?

165

That the face was so damaged she couldn't tell if it was him? She could only be sure of his clothes and his phone. Justin told Monica his life had been threatened. Monica was stupid enough, or biased enough, to believe the body was the man she expected to see.' Gerry paused for breath, then went on. 'Justin dressed Talan in his clothes, and stuck his phone in the pocket. He must have bashed Talan's face in so it would be unrecognisable. They didn't look like each other. That's why he had to stage it, to make it seem like he'd fallen onto rocks.'

'But,' Ryan queried, 'surely they wouldn't have just taken Monica's word for it?'

'No one else to ask.' Gerry had thought it all through while everyone round her had been talking about cars and police, damage and insurance. 'He didn't have any family to contact.' *You know why, Ryan. Justin's family are five or six hundred years away.* 'And none of the people he knew, drug dealers or whoever they were, would be likely to come forward. However he made his money, it wasn't anything legal.'

Claudia's hand had gone to her throat.

'Are you quite sure it was him?' she asked. It was barely a whisper.

'Yes.' Yes, Gerry was sure. She couldn't bring herself to say it to Ryan or Claudia, but she had turned unthinkingly to stare at the car that had run into hers, and seen his face. Justin had looked straight back at her with that smile which she remembered so well. And he hadn't run off like the other drivers assumed; he'd simply disappeared.

'It explains why you got targeted,' Gerry told Claudia. 'I never understood that, I couldn't see any reason for it. Justin was behind that. I suppose he never forgave you for finishing with him. No one ever did that to him. Kenver used to work for him. Justin must have thought it was very funny, setting Kenver up with Monica.'

'So,' Claudia said slowly, 'he's been in hiding all this time. But then why's he come back now? Why drive into your car – if it really was on purpose.'

'It was on purpose all right.' Gerry could feel herself shaking as she let loose the feelings she'd been keeping in check since having that brief glimpse of Justin. She looked back to Ryan.

'After I left you I was on my way back here when I – saw Baranwen. The woman who stole the chalice from the museum,' she explained to Claudia. 'She got into my car.'

'You let her?' Ryan was horrified.

'Yeah,' Gerry said. 'She was in a terrible state, she could hardly move or even speak. Did you hear what Hedra said about her? She wasn't going to hurt me. But Justin knew. He always had ways of finding things out.'

'Are you saying,' Ryan asked, 'he waited in a side road till you just happened to come past?'

Gerry shot Ryan a warning look. She didn't want Claudia thinking that one through. Now he could begin to see what it had been like for her, having to censor stuff all the time.

'But why?' Claudia asked. 'Why should he?'

'Because of this.' Gerry reached into her bag and pulled out the Kelegel. 'Baranwen gave it to me. She said there was danger. I'll never know if she meant danger to me, to her, or the Chalice.'

Gerry had a pretty good idea, however. If Seona was right, the Kelegel had its own agenda. It had forced Baranwen to hand it over. 'It made me,' she had told Gerry. No wonder the Guardian had found it so difficult to utter the words. She had plotted for so much of her long life to get her hands on the chalice, and must have fought against the command with all the considerable power she possessed – and lost. The chalice had used Baranwen to free it from the museum, and now appeared to have no more use for her. Instead it now wanted – what?

'I'm afraid Baranwen was right about the danger,' Gerry said. 'I'm really sorry, but you both have to know. Justin got it wrong, I think, there were too many people around. They were all over the place as soon as it happened. He didn't get a chance to raid my car. But he got Baranwen. They'd both wanted the chalice for, oh, for years.'

Gerry thought of the car Seona had left her, like leaving her great-niece a piece of herself, and felt another rush of misery, but she hadn't finished the bad news.

'I'm sorry,' she told Ryan and Claudia, 'but he's not going to stop now. Next thing is, Justin'll turn up here.'

Chapter Fourteen

For perhaps a minute there was absolute silence. Then Claudia slammed her hand down on the work surface with such violence that it rocked a glass of water standing nearby. Gerry just managed to catch the glass before it tipped over.

'That's it,' Claudia said, 'I'm out of here.' Her voice was tense with anger, her eyes blazing. For that moment her unfaltering self-control had totally gone. The blow must have hurt her hand a lot but she ignored it.

'Out of here?' Ryan asked. The simple question seemed to bring Claudia down to earth, the sudden rage fading. She looked rueful, another expression Gerry hadn't seen before.

'Sorry,' Claudia said. 'Oh, let's sit down and be grown-up about this. Though I admit I feel more like shouting and breaking things.'

Ryan looked at Gerry, and they went into the conservatory where they sat down side by side. Gerry was still holding the Kelegel, and put it down on the table in front of her. Claudia sat down too, facing the two of them.

'Right,' Claudia said. 'I was going to talk to you about this anyway, Gerry. And to you,' she added to Ryan. 'I've been thinking about it ever since I knew the gallery was deliberately torched. I need a break, need to get completely away. I'd more or less worked it out. I could set up temporary premises for the

169

next exhibitions, arrange the repairs for the gallery. I'd have got it sorted by the end of the week, and after that I could Skype Ethan and keep up to date with what's happening. I don't need to be here in person to make decisions.'

'So where would you go?' Gerry asked. It sounded like Claudia had it all planned.

'Buenos Aires,' she replied. 'I've got a cousin who's quite high up in the Embassy there.' That was so like Claudia, Gerry thought, and felt herself smile despite the gravity of the situation. 'He's been pestering me for years to go out and visit him, and I was going to email as soon as I'd discussed it with you. But now – I'm not sure that waiting's a good idea. Not with that murdering bastard around.'

'Hang on,' Ryan said, getting in before Gerry could. 'If you disappear off out of the country, what happens here? Are you suggesting Gerry stays here alone at the house with Justin liable to turn up when he feels like it?'

'No, of course I'm not,' Claudia said. 'That's why I wanted to see you. I'd like to be away for a good month, to really put some distance between myself and all of this. But no, I don't want Gerry here by herself. This isn't like when I go up to London at weekends. What I'm asking is if it would be all right for you to stay here too. I'm not making any assumptions,' she added quickly. 'I had the third bedroom converted into what's now Gerry's bathroom, but there's a very good sofa bed in the lounge and you can sleep there. I'd feel a lot happier if I knew you were here too. I know you're trustworthy.'

Ryan didn't answer. Gerry could see he was thinking about it. Claudia went on, 'I know it's asking a lot. This isn't like just calling in to the gallery. I've no idea what might happen, but I can't stay and face it myself. I just can't. I never thought I was a coward, but I've been through too much already.'

It was asking a lot more than Claudia realised, Gerry

thought. Claudia knew only part of what Justin was capable of. But with the chalice here at Windhaven as bait, at least he wasn't likely to materialise in Buenos Aires to persecute Claudia further.

Ryan looked at Gerry first, then at Claudia, and said, 'Of course I'll do it. I'd have offered to help even if you weren't going away. I feel it was my fault, what happened at the gallery, because I interfered. Otherwise he wouldn't have done it.'

Gerry could see this hadn't occurred to Claudia. Whether or not she agreed, she didn't pursue it.

'Thank you,' Claudia told Ryan, and some of the tension began to leave her body. 'That's really good of you. Of course there's things we'll need to sort out. I was awake half the night thinking it through. Not problems, just stuff you need to know. Oh, and transport. I know you don't have your own car, and you'll need one. It's not like being in Penzance where you can walk everywhere. I'll ring my insurance people in the morning and get you put down as a named driver for the Skoda.'

She was reverting by the minute to the usual brisk, practical Claudia. Then she turned to Gerry.

'As your car's a write-off,' she said, 'I'll put you down for the Audi. You're used to a big car.'

Gerry didn't know what to say. All she could manage was, 'Are you sure?'

'Of course I'm sure,' Claudia replied. 'My god, if it was Justin who wrecked your car, it's the least I can do.'

Gerry could feel her voice trembling as she replied.

'That was my great-aunt's old car. She left it to me. I feel as if I've let her down, after what's happened to it.'

'Of course you haven't,' Claudia began, but Gerry went on, 'Oh, I can tell myself that, but I can't help feeling awful about it.'

Gerry touched the gold chain at her neck. She still had that gift from Seona. And the Rainbow Ring.

Claudia stood up, giving Gerry a reassuring smile.

'I'll go and ring my cousin Vivian now,' she said. 'If it's all right with him I want to try to get a flight out tomorrow evening.' She looked at Ryan. 'Either way, can you stay here tonight? After what Gerry's told us I think we'd both be glad to have you here.'

Ryan didn't have to think this time. He'd already decided.

'Yep,' he said, 'I'm okay with that.'

'Good,' Claudia said, and swept off to the lounge to try her cousin's number. Before Ryan could speak, Gerry hurried into the kitchen to get the glass of water which had nearly tumbled over when Claudia had banged her hand down. She brought it back to the table.

'Quick,' Gerry said. 'Before she comes back.'

The sun was lower in the sky than it had been in summer, and the roof of the main building blocked part of its direct light now, but the end of the conservatory still had some autumn sunlight.

'Just give me a minute,' she said, 'I need to try something.'

Gerry tipped some of the water from the glass into the chalice and held it in the full beams of the sun. She needed to be careful; she didn't want a rainbow stretching from here halfway across the garden.

Just across the table.

And it came. The beams from the gemstones began to rise, small but pure and clear, and the sun broke into prisms within the rock crystals. Then the droplets of water moved up into the four lines of colour. They overlapped and the rainbow began.

'What the hell are you doing?'

Ryan's voice came as a shock; Gerry was wholly absorbed in the beauty of the glowing object that she held.

'Can't you see anything?' she asked.

'Only you holding that sodding cup,' was the blunt reply. 'Here, you're dripping water.'

172

Ryan took the water glass. At his words, the rainbow had vanished.

'You didn't see it?' Gerry didn't know if she was gutted or grateful. 'Oh, I'll tell you another time.' If Ryan hadn't seen, or refused to see, the rainbow she'd made, he had a better chance of resisting the lure of the Kelegel a'n gammneves. And if that was so, a better chance of being able to carve it into pieces, whatever it might do to try to stop him. Gerry put the chalice back on the table.

'Ryan, I'm so grateful you'll be here, you can't imagine. I'd no idea Claudia would go overboard like that.'

'She's too bottled up,' Ryan said shrewdly. 'Now Connor and Jez'll think I'm moving in with you, but they can think what they like. What do you reckon this man will do?'

'Turn up here,' Gerry said at once. 'Probably with the remaining Wasps, Elwyn and Cathno. Cathno's the one who was holding Debs at knifepoint. Elwyn was going to cut my throat when I saw them poisoning the wine.'

Ryan winced. 'Nice friends he's got.'

'Oh, they're lovely,' Gerry agreed. 'Plus, I'm pretty sure Cathno was screwing Ysella, one of the Guardians. But it seems she found someone else, and he's been threatening to slash them both.'

Ryan drew his eyebrows together. Gerry was beginning to recognise the expression.

'Wasn't she the one you said reminded you of Monica?' he asked.

'That's her, except she's better looking,' Gerry answered. 'Meraud told me Ysella went back to her family to get married. I'd lay money it was to get away from Cathno too. And she might've been pregnant. Anyway that's not our problem.'

'No,' Ryan agreed, though he was still looking thoughtful. Then his eye fell on an official looking brown window envelope lying on the table. The addressee was Ms. G.M. Hamilton. 'M?' he asked. 'What's your middle name?'

'Melinda. It was going to be Belinda,' Gerry explained. 'Luckily my dad spotted in time what initials that would give me.' The comparative lightness of heart she'd been feeling since Ryan had agreed to stay overnight was starting to fade. 'Perhaps he should have left it as it was. As for my first name, it was Seona who talked my mother into calling me Gerralda. I never found out why.'

'I think I know,' Ryan said. 'It's what I was going to say before.'

Something in his voice made Gerry uneasy. She changed the subject.

'Look, I can't tell Claudia this, 'cos she changed all the locks after Justin's last visit here and she thinks the place is secure. You and I know that wouldn't keep Justin out. He can simply appear in the house. You could wake up in the night and find him standing beside you. Probably laughing. Or else sneering.'

'I hope he does,' Ryan said. 'I want to meet him. He won't bully me like he did Claudia. And you.'

'Yes, but Ryan,' Gerry began.

'What's the problem?' he asked, and he sounded seriously annoyed. 'Do you think I can't stand up to him?'

'No, of course it's not that.' Oh fuck, Gerry thought, something she hadn't needed to allow for before. Male pride. 'But remember he's just mown down Baranwen. And assuming I'm right about Talan, I don't suppose he just happened to conveniently fall down dead when Justin was planning his own bogus death. I bet it suited Justin to disappear, I'm sure he had people after him in Penzance. Claudia thought he did.'

'You are totally certain it was Justin?' Ryan asked. 'I mean, you only saw the guy for a minute.'

Gerry shuddered. 'It was Justin,' she said. 'Besides, he vanished. One second he was there and the next he wasn't. I've not met anyone else who can do that. And it's the only thing that makes sense. Why Talan's missing, who taught Kenver how to set fire to a building, why it was Claudia's gallery.'

'Look, Gerry,' Ryan said, 'I did listen to everything you told me this morning. I'm not shedding any tears for Baranwen. As for Justin, I'd like to run into him when I had a welding torch in my hand. He's a coward, bullies always are. Didn't you notice that up till his supposed death he never did any of the dirty work himself, just got the others to do it. Unless it involved a woman.'

He was right, though Gerry hadn't seen it. 'But that's not true any longer,' she said. 'He smashed in Talan's face before he pushed him off the cliff. He must have stolen that car himself, and rammed it into mine.'

'But none of those meant actually standing up to someone, facing them down,' Ryan pointed out.

Gerry felt it was better not to argue. Besides, she'd just thought of something else.

'I don't think he will come here yet, at least not appearing inside the house in the middle of the night,' she said. 'He never did anything like that when Claudia was here, only while she was away. How could he have explained it?' That had better still be right. It would depend how desperate Justin was to get his hands on the Kelegel. Was it still just to get back at his brother, or had it now become an end in itself? She reached inside the neckline of her smock.

'You should have my gold chain,' she told Ryan. 'It may offer some sort of protection, and it wouldn't show under your t-shirt.'

'Are you sure,' he asked, 'that your ring isn't linked to the Chalice? If it is, it could make some sort of connection between you and the Kelegel. And the chalice always had an influence over you, even before you saw it. You told me that too.'

It was totally unbelievable to have Ryan standing there giving Gerry advice about the ring and the chalice. So unbelievable that she could have laughed. Or hugged him. Then the door from the lounge opened and Claudia appeared, the heels of her shoes clicking as she walked smartly across the tiled kitchen floor.

'That's sorted,' she said. 'I'll go and book the ticket now. Ryan, if you haven't changed your mind, do you want to go home and get some overnight things?'

'Nope, I've not changed my mind.' Ryan was definite. 'I wouldn't dream of leaving Gerry here by herself after what she's just been through. But Jez needs his van in the morning for work, I'll have to leave it back at the house.' He turned to Gerry. 'If you drive behind me then we could come back together. Your own insurance should cover you to drive the car with Claudia's permission.'

Gerry was taken aback, but it made sense. They say if you fall off a horse you should get straight back on. She didn't want to get back in a car yet, but she'd have to soon anyway. Besides the only other option was for Claudia to follow Ryan, leaving Gerry at the house. Alone.

'Okay,' she said, 'but Ryan, I think you should take the chalice. Keep it with you all the time, don't leave it for a minute. If Claudia can give you a bag you can take it into the house without the others seeing it. I don't want Claudia left here with it.'

'Absolutely not,' Claudia agreed.

Soon afterwards Gerry was driving gingerly up the lane in Claudia's saloon car, with Ryan following in the van. If Ryan went first, Gerry might have trouble keeping up with him, and she didn't want him out of her sight at any time. For now all she wanted was to get to Penzance in one piece and let Ryan drive the Audi back to Windhaven. He wouldn't be fazed by it.

Since she passed her test Gerry had never driven any car but Seona's, but she seemed to be managing all right. She turned from North Road onto the road to Penzance, checking the mirror to make sure Ryan was still in view behind her. She was just beginning to feel more comfortable when she reached the parking area where she had intended to talk to Baranwen. Gerry's heart began thumping and she knew that once she rounded the corner she would be on the long straight stretch which ran down to the actual scene of the crash. She slowed down, but made herself keep going. Nothing would happen to her, the police would still be here collecting their evidence and directing drivers off down the side road which led to the crossroads with the road to Newlyn.

When Gerry did get to that turning she managed not to look towards the Volvo. She felt she couldn't bear to see the car that had been Seona's with its side and back smashed in. The recovery lorries were waiting at the side to remove the cars and van as soon as the investigations here were completed. Gerry turned right, away from the sight. Ryan would drive them back and she could keep her eyes closed round here. She guessed she would feel jumpy every time she drove down to or back from Penzance for a long time. Maybe always.

Gerry reached the bypass and drove round towards the network of streets where Ryan lived. At the end of his road she pulled in where she'd waited for him that same morning. Back when he thought her claim to time travel was as likely as saying that she'd been Cleopatra or Joan of Arc in a previous life. Ryan parked the van on the other side of the road and came over.

'Do you want to come in with me?' he asked.

This would hardly be the best time to meet Connor and Jez, if they were in, but if Gerry stayed here alone she would spend every minute dreading the sudden appearance of a slender, fair-haired man at the door of the car. Or, like Baranwen, inside it. No contest.

'I'll come in,' she said.

They walked together to the door of Ryan's house. All these terraced houses faced straight onto the street, without even the smallest of front gardens. There were no lights on in the house, no sound of music or tv. Ryan unlocked the door.

'They're both out,' he said. 'Good, that'll save a lot of hassle. I'll message them later.'

The door led straight into the front room. Inside, there was a flight of stairs directly opposite the door and Ryan went up them, holding the bag with the chalice in it and calling, 'Shan't be long.'

Gerry looked round. The small room contained an old sofa, two rather battered armchairs, a large tv and a phenomenal amount of clutter. It looked like the set for a scene in a soap labelled "three lads sharing a house". Dishes on the floor, empty beer cans, a precarious stack of old CDs in a corner, items of clothing scattered around and assorted motoring magazines lying open on the sofa. It reminded Gerry of her brothers' rooms when they were still living at home, though her mother never let them get as bad as this. She remembered that Ryan had said his mother complained when she came round. Gerry could hear music coming through the wall on one side, and the sound of voices as a couple walked down the street past the front window. It came to her with a shock that she had been spoiled by living at Windhaven. Without noticing it, she had come to take the silence for granted along with the open space, lack of neighbours, and a house kept spotless by Claudia's twice-weekly cleaner.

Ryan came downstairs with a rucksack on his shoulder. He dropped the keys of the van into a jug beside the tv.

'I'll come back tomorrow and pick up more stuff,' he said.

'I won't offer you a cup of tea here, perhaps we can stop for a drink on the way.'

'No,' Gerry said, 'let's just get straight back. Claudia's there on her own and I'm worried about her.'

Ryan smiled.

'You two do look out for each other, don't you?' he said. 'I think she was more worried about you after the crash than she let on. Okay, let's go before anyone gets back here. I don't want to have to start explaining now.'

Gerry remembered how protective she'd felt towards Claudia after she broke down on hearing of Justin's death. Supposed death. As Ryan put down his rucksack and locked the front door of the house, Gerry offered to carry the bag with the chalice, but he said no.

'I'm keeping it,' Ryan insisted.

'But we're in the same car,' Gerry protested. 'That's not a problem now.'

'I'm keeping it,' he repeated. 'Once we're back and we know Claudia's all right, I'll tell you what I'd like to do tomorrow.'

Tomorrow. Was this about torching the Kelegel?

'Ryan, just a minute.' Gerry pleaded. 'Can't we talk now, on the way back?'

'No,' he said, with a grim determination in his voice that shook her. What had happened to her light-hearted colleague from the library staff room? Gerry felt like he was changing in front of her. Oh Ryan, she thought, what have I done to you?

Ryan touched her hand as he started the car.

'Don't worry, we'll sort it out,' he said. 'But first we both want to be sure Claudia's all right.'

Gerry watched him drive, envying the ease with which he handled the unfamiliar controls. Perhaps it was just another bloke thing. The morning after she had gone to the fireworks with Justin, Claudia had said that Gerry didn't know much about men. That had stung, though it wasn't said unkindly, just as a statement of fact. Now Gerry was beginning to see how right Claudia was. Justin had run rings round her, but he was an expert in the field. Ryan had seemed so straightforward that Gerry had felt she could tell him anything. Perhaps she had been wrong.

Ryan looked at Gerry as he drove up the bypass.

'You're very quiet,' he commented. 'What are you thinking about?'

'You,' Gerry said, then wasn't sure if she should have said it.

'Oh,' he answered. 'You looked very serious. I hope it wasn't bad.'

Gerry didn't know what to say. They came to the Mount Misery roundabout where the road to St. Just began. The St. Just road was still coned off, and yellow diversion signs directed drivers to the next turning. Gerry felt Ryan look at her again, but he didn't repeat his question.

The diversion was straightforward, and Gerry was glad when they rejoined the St. Just road past the scene of the crash. She was just starting to relax a little when she felt small darts in her middle finger where she wore the Rainbow Ring. Last time that happened it had signalled Baranwen's theft of the Chalice. What was it this time? Gerry turned to look through the gap between the driver's and the passenger's seats, to where the Chalice of the Rainbow lay in the bag Claudia had given Ryan before they left. A glossy dark blue carrier bag with gold lettering; the colours of the sapphire and its mounting that had started everything. Gerry could see the lump that should be the Kelegel, but, feeling uneasy, she reached a hand through the gap to touch the bag. At once Ryan's left hand fastened on her wrist.

'Don't,' he said. 'It's all right, it's still inside the bag. I checked when I put it in the car.'

180

Gerry tried to free her wrist but couldn't. Ryan's grip was too strong.

'But I've just had a warning,' she said. 'Something's happening, something wrong.'

Ryan didn't try to contradict this, or ask how she knew. He just said, 'If anything's wrong, it'll be at Windhaven. We should get there fast, but I can't change gear if I've got to hold you back all the way there. Would it be easier for you if I put the chalice in the boot where you wouldn't be tempted to try and get it?'

'No,' Gerry said, 'that'd be worse.'

Ryan gave her a searching look.

'Then promise me you won't try to pick it up,' he said.

Gerry nodded, but it got harder every minute. The Kelegel wanted her to hold it, she could tell. Gerry tried sitting on her hands, but that didn't help much. She bit her lip hard, then held her breath as Ryan speeded up, taking the curves of the road a lot faster than she would have herself. He did seem to be in complete control of the car, though Gerry was glad when they reached the lane to Windhaven. It had been a short but nerve-racking journey, and she had been reliving the moment of collision, that terrible bang of metal on metal at high speed. It had at least taken her thoughts away from the chalice.

Ryan slowed to walking pace along the bumps of the bridle path.

'Sorry if I scared you,' he said, 'but I think you were right about getting back here.'

Ryan was wearing Seona's chain, but was it helping him to sense things? Or was it linking up with her ring? They crossed the cattle grid. Now Claudia would get an alert from the hidden camera and would know they were almost there.

'There's no other car here,' Ryan said, looking ahead to the parking area. 'Only Claudia's Skoda.'

'Justin doesn't need a car,' Gerry reminded him. 'Last time he just materialised in the lounge when I was in there on my own.'

'We'll know in a minute,' Ryan said. He ran the car down the last bit of the lane and hit the brakes as he pulled in beside the Skoda. 'Come on.'

Leaving his rucksack, he grabbed the blue and gold bag with the Kelegel in it and dashed over to the courtyard. Slinging her own bag over her shoulder, Gerry raced after him. Then Ryan stopped dead and threw an arm out to stop her too. Claudia was standing on the step of the kitchen door, blocking the way into the house. Facing her, with his back to the newcomers, was Justin.

There was no mistaking the hair, pale but filled with light, the lean back and arrogant stance. Justin must have heard the car arrive, its tyres crunching across the gravel of the parking space, and the hurrying footsteps as the two of them came up to the gate, but he kept his back turned through a whole long minute. Then he turned very slowly and deliberately, and looked at the pair as if they were two children who had kicked a football and broken a pane of glass.

Ryan had said he wanted to meet Justin. He hadn't meant to be panting and jolted when it happened, but he had one supreme advantage here. He was carrying the Kelegel. Justin knew it and his eyes had fixed on the bag.

Gerry looked first at Claudia, hoping she was all right. Claudia had told her on her first visit to this house that Justin would never try to force his way in but would use persuasion. That must still hold, for if he wanted to he could have pushed her out of the way in seconds. He would know, though, that the Kelegel wasn't in the house; he was always tuned to its presence.

Claudia looked strained, and Gerry hoped she'd already booked her ticket to Buenos Aires before Justin got here. That ought to give her something to cling onto, knowing that by this time tomorrow she'd be on her way to another continent.

Then Gerry realised that Justin had changed. The fair hair had lost some of its gleaming soft shine, and the fine cheekbones were more pronounced. Justin could never look scruffy but his clothes were less perfect than before. Wherever he had been, in the past or the present, since his presumed death, he had not been doing as well as he was accustomed to. Yet some of the old magic still held. Not so long ago Gerry had wanted this man more than anything, and that doesn't go away, no matter how much you might want it to. Gerry couldn't bear the contempt in Justin's eyes as he looked at her. Then he turned the same look onto Ryan.

Gerry didn't move, didn't glance sideways at him. She expected to feel Ryan tense, but instead he seemed to relax. He stood there in an old t-shirt, denim jacket, jeans and trainers, as assured as if he were a magistrate and Justin was a sneak thief brought in front of him for sentencing.

'I might have expected to find you harassing a woman,' Ryan said, and the scorn in his voice was deeper than the disdain in Justin's eyes. 'Fits with everything I've been told about you.'

Justin's eyes raked Ryan again, then that smile Gerry knew so well spread over his face. She squirmed inside, but managed to keep motionless and silent.

'That's funny,' Justin said. 'I haven't heard anything at all about you.'

His voice was one long sneer, but Ryan didn't rise to it, just returned look for look. Justin moved forward, and as he left the entrance, Gerry willed Claudia to get inside and shut the door, but her landlady stayed put, as if dazed. Justin held out his hand towards the bag Ryan was carrying. The Chalice was pulsing inside it now, and Gerry wondered if the chain enabled Ryan to feel it too.

'You've got something there which I want,' Justin said. He came a little nearer, and with every step it got harder for Gerry to keep still. Justin appeared to be ignoring her for now, but he knew she was there. 'I'll take it now. Perhaps I'll even say thank you for looking after it for me.'

'Oh, I don't think so,' Ryan said. 'This doesn't belong to you.'

Their eyes were locked now, brown onto grey. Then Justin took another step. He was near enough now to lean forward and snatch the bag, but that was never his style. This close, Gerry could see lines round his eyes that hadn't been there before. Ryan didn't draw back or try to move the Kelegel to safety. He just stood doing what he'd said Justin never could, facing him down.

And then, without knowing what she was going to say, Gerry cried out, 'No!' She reached out to take the bag from Ryan, but he moved it to his other hand so she couldn't reach it.

'No,' Gerry said again, 'you don't understand. Nor did I, till now. I have to have it. Baranwen gave me the chalice. She knew she was finished. Morvoren's drowned, and Ysella's left the Gwenen for good. There's no-one else left.' With Claudia still there, Gerry couldn't say that she was sure the Chalice itself had told her.

'It's me,' she said instead. 'I'm to be the next Guardian. Guardian of the Jewels of the Rainbow.'

Chapter Fifteen

Sunday September 14th continued

Ryan didn't look at Gerry, or answer her. Instead he called across the courtyard, 'Claudia, this man's wanted on a charge of causing death by dangerous driving. Or deliberate murder. Why don't you go and ring the police and say he's at your house, though you'd best say we can't be sure of holding him till they get here.'

For a minute, Claudia didn't seem to understand. Then she said 'Oh, right,' and disappeared into the kitchen, closing the door firmly behind her.

Well done Ryan, Gerry thought. Then she saw that Justin was looking at her, and his expression was thoughtful, appraising; very different from the disdain he'd shown when they arrived. But it was Ryan he spoke to first.

'So, the lady does what you tell her?' he said. 'Interesting. I thought it was our Gerralda you were with, but maybe not. Or do you have both of them? In turn perhaps? Any man would enjoy that.'

Gerry had forgotten what a bastard Justin could be. That shot had been too close to the fear she hadn't yet fully overcome, and she felt her heart thumping. Ryan, however, ignored Justin and spoke to her as if they were alone.

'Gerry, you know you can't become a Guardian,' he said. 'It wouldn't happen like that. The chalice has been working on you, that's obvious. Probably since Baranwen took it from the

185

Museum. You're open to it, vulnerable, and you can't see what this is really about.'

And since when did Ryan believe the Kelegel could act for itself? He'd refused to accept that when Gerry suggested it earlier. What had happened to "It can't think"?

'You're wrong,' she said. 'The chalice needs me, I can feel it.'

'Oh, I agree it needs you,' Ryan said, 'but look at what it does to the people who serve it. Baranwen smashed to pieces, Morvoren drowned, Delenyk tortured to death. And it didn't save that girl from being poisoned.'

'But I'm not -' Gerry began, but Ryan put his hand on her shoulder.

'Gerry, you mustn't believe this,' he said.

Gerry pulled abruptly away, so that Ryan's hand fell to his side, and she heard a soft laugh from Justin.

'Lovers' tiff?' he asked mockingly.

'Get stuffed,' Gerry muttered. Annoyance and discomfort were making her temperature rise.

Ryan hadn't finished.

'I'm sorry,' he said, 'but I can see what's really happening here, and you can't. You're too close to it.'

Close to what? What was he talking about? Ryan came nearer to Gerry and spoke in a low, urgent tone.

'Have you forgotten what we agreed with Hedra?' he asked. He tried to hold her gaze, look into her eyes, but she wasn't having it.

'Yes, but that was before I knew I was going to be Guardian.'

Gerry shifted position, trying again to get round Ryan and reach the bag, but he twisted sideways and stopped her. As he moved, the carriage lamps on the side of the house came on, activated by the motion sensors positioned on the thick granite walls which formed the two sides of the courtyard. In the growing dusk the sudden lamplight changed all the colours, made the sky darker and floodlit the ceramic flower pots arranged in clusters near the gate and the kitchen windows. They were filled with the last of the geraniums and lobelia, bright rose-red and blue. The fuchsia bush still carried a fine display of its deep crimson hanging flowers, but the flower bed had little left in it compared with the colourful blaze of summer.

Lights began to come on in the house as Claudia moved around inside. Seen through the kitchen window, the strip lights glowed below the wall units. They illuminated the rows of herb and spice jars on the work surface, which looked decorative but were rarely if ever used. A softer light through the lounge window showed that Claudia had switched on the side lamps. Had she finished on the phone? How soon could the police be here? It couldn't be too soon.

From the house Gerry would occasionally hear a siren a mile away on the North Road, speeding down to the village, but it was a rare sound, unlike London where they were racing around all the time. She was more likely to hear the noise of the rescue helicopter as it beat its way along the coast, searching the cliffs, or else the air ambulance, but neither happened often. Of course if the roads were quiet the police car might not need a siren, but Justin could still disappear as they came down the drive. Would he do it if Claudia came back outside? But surely she wouldn't.

No, Gerry thought, forget the police, forget Justin, the only thing that mattered was that she had to stop Ryan from harming the Kelegel. Earlier in her ignorance she had agreed it was the only thing to do. Now the notion was unthinkable. She actually considered telling Justin what Ryan was planning to do, seriously contemplated allying with Justin against Ryan. He would know how to prevent this sacrilege. It was nothing less.

She remembered Baranwen threatening the Gohi in the fogou, felt herself drop into the formal old-style speech of the age of the Gwenen.

'No man can have the Kelegel a'n gammneves,' she pronounced. 'Time was when it was death for a man even to touch it. It was made to aid the work of the Goddess and has been blessed by Her.'

'Well, listen to you,' Justin said softly.

Gerry didn't reply. Where had that come from? She didn't talk like that. Ryan tried again to meet her eyes.

'Gerry,' he said, 'I know the chalice was made with the highest ideals but it lost them centuries ago. I thought you'd accepted that. Look what it did to the women who actually created it.'

Justin was alert at once. 'What did it do to them?' he asked. 'Whatever it was, they deserved it.' He was so eager to hear that Gerry's allegiance wavered. She didn't like that look of malicious satisfaction.

'Just because they stopped you from using it,' she snapped. 'They were quite right, they knew you were up to no good.'

'The women were mutilated,' Ryan said without elaboration. He really had remembered everything Gerry had told him at Lescudjack. 'And they didn't deserve it.'

Ryan was right not to give Justin the details to gloat over. But he was wrong, terribly wrong, about the Kelegel being at fault.

'Give it back to me,' Gerry said. 'I'll show you what a miracle the Chalice really is.'

'It won't work on me,' Ryan said. 'Like whatever you were trying to do with it and the water in the conservatory.'

Shit, she'd forgotten that. Perhaps men just couldn't see it. No, Justin had seen the rainbow, even brought it to life himself in the time of the Makers before he returned to this century to find the cup rendered lifeless. Now Justin put his hand on her wrist, and he was quivering with excitement.

'Can you bring it alive now, here?' he asked. 'Is that what he means? Has that really changed?'

Gerry had forgotten the effect Justin's slightest touch could have on her. Perhaps if she hadn't been at odds with Ryan, she could have resisted better. As it was it reminded her too vividly that at one time they had worked together for a shared goal. Gerry didn't try to remove Justin's hand from her wrist.

'It worked,' she said. 'Only on a small scale, but that was enough. I can call the rainbow.'

Gerry looked at Ryan, and it began as defiance, but she saw his face as he looked at Justin's hand on her arm. She shook herself free, embarrassed. Justin laughed again.

'You still haven't learned to guard your thoughts, Gerralda,' he said. 'So the two of you were planning to destroy the Kelegel? You needn't worry, I won't let him do that.'

Gerry put her hand out and gripped the top of the white wooden courtyard gate to steady herself. She had totally forgotten that Justin could follow what she was thinking. And when Justin touched her he would have picked up her response.

'You can't stop me, you know,' Ryan said. 'Neither of you. I'm going to make an end of this menace, whether you like it or not. As for you,' he said to Justin, 'I'll give you a word of advice. I wouldn't try to make use of your Wasps again. If you do – well, just remember I warned you.'

'Why not?' Gerry asked. 'What do you mean?'

It was Ryan's turn to smile.

'Remember,' he said, 'you told me that Ysella reminded you of Monica?'

'What are you on about?' Gerry said. 'I don't understand.'

'Good,' said Ryan. 'If you don't then he won't either.'

Gerry was about to reply when she heard a noise and,

stepping away from the gate, saw headlights coming down the lane. There was no way the police could have got here from Penzance so fast. They must have had a patrol car in St. Just, three miles away, maybe keeping a lookout for weekend drinkers who'd been at it since lunchtime.

'Bitch,' said Justin, but he meant Claudia, not Gerry. 'I'll see you both tomorrow.' He gave a last sardonic smile and disappeared. Ryan had never seen this before. Gerry had, but she'd never got used to it. Ryan was staring at the spot where Justin had been, only seconds before, when Claudia burst out of the front door.

'They're coming, I saw the lights from upstairs.' She ran over to the two by the gate, looking all round, then her face fell.

'He's gone,' she said, her voice flat with disappointment.

'We, uh, couldn't stop him,' Ryan said, adopting Gerry's rule of "the truth and nothing but the truth but no way the whole truth".

When the car stopped and two men in uniform got out, Gerry was happy to leave everything to Ryan and Claudia. Ryan explained to the thwarted officers how he and Gerry had arrived at Windhaven to find Justin at the door, and had distracted him to give Claudia a chance to get away and call for help. Gerry confirmed that Justin was the man she'd seen at the wheel of the car that rammed hers. She could swear to that.

'Let's hope you don't have to,' Ryan muttered to her as Claudia ushered them all into the kitchen, directed everyone to chairs in the conservatory, provided coffee. 'If it went to court, Justin would make things unspeakable for both you and Claudia. But they'd never be able to hold him in a cell, would they?' He looked back to where Justin had vanished right in front of him. Only the day before he'd never have believed it possible.

Claudia gave her own statement regarding Justin but could tell them surprisingly little about the man, given how long she'd

190

known him. Moreover Justin had been confirmed as dead three months earlier, and that would now have to be looked into afresh. Ryan made a good job of saying everything that was reasonable, and Gerry was glad of that. She could easily have fallen asleep where she sat, the day had exhausted her, but she wasn't to be allowed to. Five minutes later another car arrived. Frances, the WPC of the afternoon, had learned about Justin being at Windhaven and had turned up to ask Gerry some more of the questions she hadn't answered earlier.

It all felt tedious and unnecessary. Gerry longed desperately for the enquiries to be over and the three officers to go away and leave them, particularly her, alone. For all she knew her answers were wandering off in any direction, as she found it impossible to concentrate. Ryan had kept the Kelegel beside him in its bag and had taken the seat furthest from Gerry. She fantasised for a moment about accusing Ryan of having stolen the chalice from the Royal Cornwall Museum. They'd only have to look in the bag to find the evidence, but then they'd take away not only Ryan but the Kelegel too.

Gerry came back to herself and realised the policewoman, Frances, had asked if she was sure about the driver being Justin. She'd already gone through this with the two men, and wanted to snap with frustration.

Ryan paused mid-sentence, alerted by something in Gerry's voice, and looked at her. 'Gerry's half asleep,' he said to Frances. 'Are you going to be much longer?'

'No, we're nearly done,' she said. 'But where there's been a fatality we need every bit of evidence, for the Coroner's court and for any other authorities who might get involved. This Justin Chancellor might have a record somewhere else.'

He ought to, but Gerry couldn't see Justin letting that happen. She was sure he could wipe out evidence against him, as Baranwen had.

191

Finally the officers left, repeating that if any of the three thought of anything else, anything at all that might help, they should get in touch.

'I thought they'd never go,' Claudia said. She went to the fridge, took out a bottle of her preferred chilled white wine and poured three glasses, handing one to Gerry. The stem of the glass was so fine that Gerry was afraid it would snap if she touched it.

'It's a dry wine, which is what I like,' Claudia said, passing the other glass over to Ryan. 'I expect Gerry would prefer something medium, but this one's open and we could all do with a drink.' She brought some Stilton from the fridge and a pack of Bath Oliver biscuits from a tin with a Wedgwood pattern. 'The cheese ought to be at room temperature but there isn't time for that, I've got to go and do my packing.'

She put plates and knives on the table, and they all sat down, moving aside the chairs the police had used. Gerry sipped her wine and found Claudia had been right on both counts. She didn't like the taste, but was glad all the same to have a drink. Ryan, who she guessed would prefer beer, drank his wine politely.

'I know Gerry doesn't usually work Mondays, but I expect you do,' Claudia said to Ryan, cutting neat slices of the cheese and offering round the biscuits. Gerry hadn't had any lunch, and bit into one. She found she didn't like Bath Olivers any more than the dry wine, and would have been happier with a thick slice of toast, but any food was welcome.

'I just wanted to run a few things past you,' Claudia said. 'When Gerry moved in, I asked her not to bring other people up here. I know that's an imposition, especially as you're doing me a massive favour, but, could you see your way to it?'

Ryan nodded.

'Okay,' he said. 'You don't want any wild parties here, even though there's no neighbours to annoy. Not even any polite tea

192

parties.' He understood that what Claudia didn't want was spilled beer and muddy boots, broken china and pervasive cigarette smoke. 'I can live with that,' he agreed. 'Oh, and in case I don't see you in the morning, I'd suggest you don't answer the door to anyone before you leave. The press could get hold of this, someone might spot a link between your gallery fire, an arsonist getting run over, and a fatal car crash involving your tenant and your former,' he stopped. "Partner" seemed the wrong word, "lover" or "boyfriend" even more so. 'Whatever.'

Claudia shuddered.

'Heaven forbid. If anyone in the Jermyn Street galleries picked that one up it would be all over London as fast as you can tweet. Okay. Gerry can show you where everything is, and there's a list of emergency numbers on the inside of that cupboard door.' She waved a hand to show Ryan which one. 'Everything from the electrician and the plumber to the AA and the Skoda place. The weather'll be getting cooler soon. The heating controls are in the utility room, just round there on the left. I expect you can find your way round anything electronic?'

Gerry couldn't believe this. She'd always known Claudia was an organised person, but why was she going on about plumbers and heating now? Couldn't Claudia leave them alone? She desperately needed to talk to Ryan about the Chalice.

'I've booked a cab for the morning,' Claudia finished. 'I'm flying to London from Newquay to pick up my plane to Argentina.' She gave Ryan a piece of paper. 'That's my phone and email, and the numbers for the safe and alarm. Memorise those two then shred them. Or eat them, like they used to in old spy films. I ought to have written them on rice paper.'

That was the closest thing to a joke Gerry had ever heard from her landlady. Claudia rose, picking up her glass and plate. 'I don't know how to thank you,' she said to Ryan. 'Get in touch at once if there's anything – any problems, any questions.'

'That's all fine,' Ryan said, 'I'm okay with it. I can deal with practical stuff.'

'Good,' said Claudia, giving Gerry an unexpectedly warm smile, 'because Gerry can't. Perhaps you could show her how to use the controls on the washing machine?' With that she went through at last to the lounge to go upstairs to her room, but before Gerry could begin, she reappeared. 'I'll put the bedding out for you on the sofa bed in the lounge,' she said to Ryan. 'That's through this door. There's a cloakroom just beyond the door at the far end. And if I don't see you in the morning, I'll be in touch soon.'

Then she had gone, leaving them together. Justin had gone, the police had gone. There was only Ryan and Gerry, and the Kelegel.

Ryan forestalled Gerry.

'I'm not going to talk about the chalice,' he said. 'Not tonight. I want to talk to you about Seona.'

'Why Seona?' Gerry asked. What did he mean? Whatever it was it couldn't be as important as the Kelegel.

'You said,' Ryan replied, 'correct me if I'm wrong, that no one else in the family's called Gerralda, that you didn't know where the name came from or why you were called that. I think I can tell you.'

That didn't make sense.

'How could you?' Gerry asked, pushing her plate away. Without noticing, she'd finished everything on it, down to the last crumb. Her glass seemed to be empty too.

She looked at Ryan and was surprised to see he was looking wretched.

'I think I can tell you,' he said, 'and about your ring and chain too, but I'm afraid you're going to hate me for it.'

This was alarming. What could he conceivably know about Seona that she didn't? It wasn't as if he knew any of her family.

Ryan finished his own glass of wine.

'D'you think Claudia would mind if I had some more?' he asked.

'Oh, the rule's simple here,' Gerry said. 'You can use anything as long as you replace it like for like. I don't touch Claudia's food, I can't afford to buy the brands that she does. Except when she goes away, then I can use up anything she's left behind that won't keep.'

Now she was the one talking practicalities. Ryan had taken out the wine bottle and was looking at the label.

'I'd better put this back then,' he said. 'No, she offered us this, she's off on holiday and it won't keep either. I'll buy myself some food tomorrow and bring it back with me after work.'

He refilled his glass and Gerry's, then sat down opposite her.

'I'm putting this off,' he said with his characteristic frankness. 'Gerry, I'm afraid that if I upset you it'll drive you straight back to Justin.' It had been only too apparent that Gerry was still drawn to Justin. 'It's no use me telling you he's evil. You already know that and it doesn't seem to change anything.'

Gerry's heart had begun to beat faster. What did Ryan have to tell her that could hurt her so badly? Who had she been named after?

'Tell me,' she said, her voice barely above a whisper.

'You did it yourself,' Ryan said, his hands catching at the edge of the table, 'when you went to visit Seona. You told her you were called Gerralda. Didn't you say Seona pushed your mum into giving you that name, against all her objections? It was because she knew her great-niece would be called Gerralda. Because she'd already met you.'

'Yeah, that was why my mum wanted me to have a middle name,' Gerry said, picking up on the easy bit. 'In case I thought "Gerralda" was a stupid name.' Then she took in the rest.

For a minute she thought her head was going to explode.

'No,' she said, then, 'no,' again. She put her hand over her mouth, then put both hands over her eyes, pressing the fingers against her eyelids. 'You're saying,' she could hardly get the words out, 'you're saying that I'm called Gerralda because I went back to see Seona and told her I was called Gerralda.' It was like those halls of mirrors where they keep reflecting each other into infinity. 'But – what if I hadn't gone back to see her?'

'But you did go.' And Seona had lived all those years waiting for Gerry to be born. Waiting after the birth of each of her three elder brothers, for the girl she had known would come. 'Because you told her your story, she knew she had to prepare you, to help you understand that thing you were born with – ESP, the Sight, whatever you call it. And to create the tools that would help you.' He leaned across the table and touched the ring. 'This, and the gold chain.'

Gerry removed her hands from her eyes and looked at him, incredulous. She could hardly speak.

'You can't mean that.' She had to force the words out. 'How could she know about them?'

'You were wearing them,' Ryan said simply. 'You said they told you – Baranwen, Colenso – that Seona had powers. Even if the chain was hidden under your clothes, even if you'd put the ring in your pocket, which I don't suppose you did, they'd have shouted to her. You don't seem to appreciate half what these two can do, especially when they're working together.' He paused, and gave an embarrassed laugh. 'Listen to me. I'm such an expert now. Perhaps I did inherit something from my great-great-great-great-great gran, the one who was sup- posed to be a witch. But why d'you think I didn't yell my head off when Justin just vanished like that, right in front of me? I'm wearing the chain. I think it functions like a sort of tran- quilliser.' Ryan touched the chain lightly with his fingertips, as Gerry herself had done so many times. 'Just think of some of the things you've been through yourself. Anybody would've been wrecked by just one or two of them, and you've had one after another. I'm sure they've helped you survive without having a nervous breakdown. You've been just accepting what they did. Your Seona spent more than half her life working on them for you.'

A succession of memories began flashing through Gerry's brain. The ring, the Bysow a'n gammneves, challenging Baranwen in the very moment of her triumph. The chain calling to the Guardian when Gerry was walking innocently up Causewayhead on that very first day. The ring obligingly taking her to see Hedra, and Seona, carefully picking the best time and place for each. Even simply showing Gerry where the Wasps were when she was wondering about them. Colenso telling her that she underestimated the gold chain.

'Are you saying,' Gerry asked, through the throbbing that had begun in her head, 'that if I hadn't gone back to see Seona, none of this would have happened?'

'They warned you,' Ryan said, and his face and voice were shot through with pain, 'not to tamper with your time line.'

This time Gerry buried her whole face in her hands. Colenso had warned her against going back to see Seona, in case her great-aunt died from the shock before she had ever given Gerry the gold chain which she had used to get there. There were sci-fi stories about people who'd gone back in time and unknowingly killed their own parents, or done something which changed the future of the world. It would have been easy to tell herself Ryan was wrong; but if she believed that, she wouldn't be feeling so dreadful now.

Ryan stood up, walked round the table to stand behind her, and put his hands on her shoulders. It was a simple but surprisingly comforting gesture.

197

'Please, Gerry,' he said quietly, 'don't shut me out.'

Gerry stood up, shook him off.

'Leave me alone,' she said, then, savagely, 'and give me that chain back.'

'Keep your voice down.' Ryan said, glancing towards the open door of the lounge.

Gerry didn't care about Claudia. 'Give it back!' she repeated.

'I'll give it back tomorrow,' Ryan said. 'I might need it tonight.'

Gerry didn't ask what he meant. She wasn't interested any more. In that moment the fight had gone out of her and she felt drained.

'I'm going to bed,' she said. It was too early, and she didn't know if she stood any chance of sleep with all this turmoil in her head, but she needed to be alone. 'I might see you in the morning.'

Gerry walked away without looking back at Ryan, down the length of the kitchen, past the door to the courtyard, and into the lounge. Claudia would be down soon to check that all the doors were locked and bolted, and Gerry didn't feel up to talking to her again this evening. To get to her bedroom she had to turn left out of the lounge, go through Claudia's office and upstairs from there. She stopped at the lounge door, knowing Ryan was still standing in the conservatory, alone and desolate. Part of her wanted to go back and hug him, forgive him, tell him he'd been brave to explain. But Gerry was too shocked by what Ryan had told her to accept that he'd done the right thing. She walked through to the office, closed the lounge door behind her and went upstairs to her room.

Chapter Sixteen

Usually when Gerry went upstairs the first thing she did was to sit on the bed and open her laptop, but tonight the world of emails, Facebook, Twitter and Google seemed to belong to another reality. She didn't feel like listening to any music, and couldn't have read a word of a book. Too much had happened since she was last in this room, from the morning's painful drive with Ryan to Chapel Carn Brea through to the final revelation about Seona.

Gerry had been first impressed, then astounded, by how much detail Ryan had taken in of her lengthy tale at Lescudjack. Moreover he'd not only remembered but analysed it too. This was even more amazing as until he'd been into the past himself he'd have refused to accept a word of it. It occurred to Gerry that perhaps Seona's chain had been at work again. Was Ryan right about it shielding him, and herself before that, against successive shocks? Before, Ryan had been so sceptical, even scornful; now he was giving her advice about time travel. In her heart she knew he was trying to help, in the same way as she suspected he was right about Seona; otherwise she wouldn't have felt so distraught. She couldn't face thinking through what he'd said. Gerry wished now that she'd never let him wear the gold chain, or the Rainbow Ring, in the first place.

Yet Ryan's explanation of her name was so reasonable that she could have thought of it herself. But why would she? And

199

did it really matter so much? It had only hurt when she tried to think of what would have happened if she'd never gone back to see Seona. She'd not have been called Gerralda; not have had the ring or the chain. Yet Seona would still have answered her questions when she was a schoolgirl, because it was in both of their natures. So, was it so terrible? Yes, because she'd set a term to Seona's life.

Gerry walked round her room, shutting the curtains against the dark outside. She was so used by now to being there that she no longer noticed the quality of the furniture, the gleaming wood floor with the two thick colourful rugs, one on each side of the bed, which were so comfortable to step onto with bare feet. Gerry found herself looking at it all now, as if trying to fix her mind on anything other than her pain. She slid back the curtain of the window at the top of the stairs. From here she could see the street lights at the far end of the village where it extended out past the foot of the hill. Further along the coast road the headlamps of a car shone out and upwards in the darkness as it followed the bends of the road towards Morvah, the next village.

Gerry couldn't see into the conservatory, as the roof of the utility room blocked it from sight at this angle, but she could tell the standard lamp was still on from the way the light beamed across towards the garden, picking out the branches of the line of trees which protected this side of the house from the east winds. Ryan had stayed on alone in the conservatory, then, rather than going into the lounge. She had a clear mental picture of him standing by the table, staring at nothing, his mind running through everything they had said, over and over. Gerry slammed her hands down hard on the windowsill. It hurt, specially as she caught the edge of her wrists against the wood. There would probably be bruises there tomorrow but it had done what she wanted. The image of Ryan had gone.

She was too restless to get undressed and into bed, and in the end just took off her shoes and lay down on top of the bedspread, still fully dressed. When she switched off the light and shut her eyes, Gerry found herself thinking of Justin. How he had taunted Ryan, and his unexpected change of attitude towards herself. The feel of his hand on her arm, and his casual assurance that he wouldn't let Ryan harm the Chalice. At that Gerry sat up in a panic. Ryan would be going to his brother's workshop tomorrow to ask about the blowlamp, or whatever it was. She had to stop him. But then she made herself lie down again. She couldn't do anything right now. She would have to wait for the morning.

Gerry had known, as she and Ryan stood confronting Justin, that she was to be Guardian. The knowledge had slid into her mind, simple and obvious, and that knowledge must have come from the Kelegel itself. There was no other explanation possible. It had felt so good. The plan she and Ryan had made with Hedra had been based on ignorance, of course. Ryan had said the Kelegel didn't protect its servants; but he hadn't felt the reassurance the chalice had put into her. She knew she was going to be all right.

Much later Gerry woke to darkness and silence. There was no moon, and no lights anywhere in the house. She had a lingering impression of a dream where she had been wandering through a large building, along corridors, up and down staircases, in and out of rooms. She was shivering; the night had turned cold. She checked the time and found it was two in the morning. At the other end of the house Claudia would be asleep now with her packing efficiently completed barring any last minute items. Ryan would be lying on the sofa bed downstairs. He probably had the Chalice clutched in one hand or tucked under his arm.

201

Gerry wanted to go down to the lounge and take it, but didn't think she could get it without waking him, and didn't fancy her chances in a tug-of-war.

Gerry pulled off her outer clothes and slid under the duvet. This time when she closed her eyes she didn't go back to sleep. Instead she found herself watching Cathno and Elwyn as if she were floating above them. It was like when she had been in Redruth and "seen" the two Wasps in the barn; or when she had "seen" them at Penzance station with the girls. This time they were trudging along a road that ran across open moorland. It was evening and nearly dark. On the horizon Gerry could see the orange glow in the sky that was Penzance, and the two men were heading towards it; they must be within a few miles of the town. Gerry could follow what they were saying, courtesy of the Rainbow Ring, which also translated the liberally-used expletives into modern equivalents.

Elwyn was well into a long and monotonous grievance against the Guardian who had brought them to this time and place then abandoned them with no food, no women or means of transport. Finally Cathno snapped that he was tired of hearing about how hungry his companion was.

'Don't you ever think about anything but your belly?' he grumbled.

'Don't you ever think about anything but your dick?' was the angry reply.

That set Cathno off on his own rant about how his woman had cheated on him, and what he would do if he ever got his hands on her and/or her lover. He too became repetitive, and Gerry was wondering how she could get away and leave them to their mutual complaints when she saw headlamps coming down the road from behind the men. It looked like a farm lorry, the sort she sometimes got stuck behind on the A30 when they were stacked high with potatoes and going at 15 m.p.h. At this end of the day it looked to be empty. Cathno and Elwyn had turned at the approaching noise, then stumbled, dazzled by the blaze of light. The high-set headlamps on the lorry's front were shining straight into their eyes. They staggered backwards; like Kenver, they had no inbuilt awareness around modern vehicles.

The driver pulled up beside them, wound down his window and leaned out to shout to them, waving an arm in the general direction of the lights of Penzance. Even if they didn't understand a word, the gestures and the offer were self-explanatory. Like Debbie at the Quay Fair, he probably assumed they were a couple of the numerous local farm workers from eastern Europe. He indicated they should get onto the back of the truck, but they still looked bewildered. In the end the man climbed down out of his cab and gave them a hand up onto the empty storage space. There seemed to be some sort of sacking they could sit on, and poles at the side which they could hang onto. Gerry thought she saw Elwyn grab a stray vegetable which had caught in the sacking, rub it against his sleeve and sink his teeth into it, raw though it was.

It was a good thing the Wasps couldn't drive, she thought, as the driver got back into his cab and started up the engine, the sound roaring out in the silent emptiness of the moor. If they'd known how to get the truck to Penzance themselves he'd be lying by the roadside, with a sore head if he was lucky, or worse if he tried to stop them hijacking his lorry.

Gerry couldn't see her hand and was certain that she wasn't there in body at all, but she was sure she was still in contact with her ring.

Please get me away from here, she said to it, then *Hang on.* She didn't want another vision of Ryan. *What's Justin up to?*

Immediately Gerry was in another location, as different from the bleak, dark moor as could be imagined. She found herself looking at a wide, light room with pale walls and carpet, furnished as a lounge. It had floor length curtains with an abstract pattern in deep blue and black on a cream background. These stood on either side of a huge picture window, and were folded so stiffly they couldn't ever be closed. Gerry's first thought was that it looked like the sort of flat Claudia would have had when she lived in London.

Gerry could see the pinkish-orange glow of streetlights outside but the room must be on the second floor as it was above the tops of the lights and the traffic passed below out of sight, the noise well muffled. There was a wide dark space opposite and after a puzzled minute or two she realised she was looking across a river. Her viewpoint shifted slightly to include a bridge. The upright columns and the lines of iron wires radiating down from them were defined by the light of hundreds of bulbs strung along them. She recognised the unmistakable shape of the Albert Bridge, which at night looked more like something from a fairy story than a modern structure. So this was London, the Chelsea Embankment. Gerry had done a lot of exploring during her empty weekends in the city and knew this was one of the prettiest areas, as well as one of the most expensive.

Justin was relaxing on a wide, deep sofa which faced the picture window. The pale blue sofa had big cushions in the same deep blue as the pattern on the curtains. There was one large abstract picture on the side wall and it looked like an original. Living in Claudia's house, Gerry had absorbed a little about art. The door of the room was open and judging by the sounds that came through it a woman was cooking, and talking at the same time. For a moment Gerry thought she'd landed in another time paradox, and that Justin had gone back to Claudia, to the time when she was still living in London. Gerry listened hard, and found it wasn't Claudia's voice. The woman was chattering cheerfully and didn't seem to notice she wasn't getting any response. But Gerry could see Justin's face and he looked, quite simply, bored to death.

So, he had gone to wait in the anonymity of the capital. Of course he couldn't draw on any of his accounts as he was supposed to be dead. And even Justin's powers didn't extend to making money by magic. He might have time jumped after his staged death and skipped most of the weeks in between, but perhaps having no money of his own accounted for the indefinable difference Gerry had seen in him. Still, trust Justin to survive by taking shelter with another rich woman, who was providing food and a roof, probably even ironing his shirts.

Then to Gerry's dismay Justin gave a sudden soft laugh and turned his head towards the point where she was, as it were, viewing him from. Too late, she remembered that Baranwen had addressed her as she watched the Guardian seize the Kelegel from the Royal Cornwall Museum in Truro, although she had actually been forty miles away sitting in a park in Penzance. Baranwen had known Gerry could see her. Something comparable had happened here. Justin stood up slowly and began deliberately to walk to her side of the room. Alarmed, Gerry tried to fling herself back to Windhaven, but couldn't do it. Justin laughed again.

'So, you can't keep away?' he said, cold amusement lighting his grey eyes. He began to raise his hand. Gerry struggled but she was helpless, caught and held as firmly as if Justin was physically gripping her wrist. Then there was a clatter at the door of the lounge, and she had a glimpse of a woman coming in, holding a heavily laden tray. She had a sleek curtain of honey-coloured hair, large eyes which were beautifully made up and long legs showing below a short silky wrap.

'Darling, can you hold this while I move the table out?' she asked, and Justin loosed his hold on Gerry as he went to take the tray. Gerry would have bet a month's salary that he didn't call this woman "darling" in return.

He couldn't play his games with anyone else present. Gerry managed to wrench herself back to her room at Windhaven, and found she was shaking. That had been too close. Justin could have trapped her there for as long as it amused him to.

Gerry badly wanted to go downstairs and make a cup of tea, but she couldn't get to the kitchen without going through the end of the lounge where Ryan was sleeping, and had to make do with a glass of water. She didn't think the Rainbow Ring would be able to change it into a hot drink; it wasn't a magic wand.

Gerry drank the water, thinking about where she stood now. Everything seemed to be against her; she had never felt so alone in her life. She had lost Seona for good; her living family were six hundred miles away, and anyway none of them could have assisted her in this. Debbie couldn't help, and Gerry wouldn't have asked her; her friend had been through enough already. The Wasps at least she had always known were enemies. But Justin – he was such a twisted bastard. If he was helping to protect the Kelegel, he'd do it for himself, not for Gerry. Ryan was meant to be on her side, yet he wanted to destroy the chalice. The gold chain, Seona's treasured gift, now looked to be helping Ryan as well as, if not instead of, her. That was the worst betrayal of all. She couldn't even trust the Rainbow Ring now. It had led her almost literally into Justin's hands.

Gerry had to get some sleep. She would need all her wits about her the next day. So she pulled off the ring, for the first time since she had taken it out of its box nearly a week ago. She got into bed, put the ring under her pillow, switched off the light and fell fast asleep.

Chapter Seventeen

When Gerry woke it was full daylight. She looked at the time and found it was after eight. She hadn't slept that long in weeks. Or even months. She sat up, then remembered she wasn't wearing the Rainbow Ring. She reached under the pillow for it – and it wasn't there.

Gerry went into major panic mode. She looked under the pillows, down the side of the bed, between the top end of the mattress and the headboard. She got on her knees and, using the torch Claudia had left on the bedside table in case of power cuts, she searched everywhere under the bed. At last she found it by pure chance, while she was rummaging frantically through the pillows again. Instead of putting it under the pillow as she had meant to, she had inadvertently pushed it inside the opening of the lower pillowcase.

Gerry gripped the ring as tightly as if it might grow miniature feet or wings and walk or fly out of the room. This was totally not a good start to the day. She looked round to see where her clothes had landed when she threw them off in the night, then heard the familiar sound of the hatchback going up the lane. She hurried to the window beside the bed and pushed back the curtains far enough to see the small crimson car going over the cattle grid. For a few seconds she was confused; Claudia never left as early as this. Then all the things she would have remembered on waking if she hadn't been in a state of panic about the ring came rushing back. Claudia was going away. It was Ryan who was driving the Skoda. It only took ten minutes to drive to Penzance, and Ryan wouldn't need to leave for work this early, so he must be going home first. He'd said yesterday that he'd call by the house to pick up some more things today. If things had been as simple as Ryan acting bodyguard for Gerry, and for Claudia's house too, they could have laughed together about what Connor and Jez would be thinking.

But now, nothing was simple. Ryan wasn't just going to collect some more clothes and toiletries. He was going to talk to his brother Connor about using his welding torch. In the face of that, Gerry's distress about Seona and her own name had slid during the night to the lowest rung of her worries. She put the ring back on, wondering as she did so if taking it off had helped her sleep better. She picked up her phone and found she had a missed call, a message and a text. She took it off silent, but didn't look at them yet. It was more urgent to get some coffee, and as Ryan was out of the house it was okay to go downstairs in her dressing-gown.

Gerry brought the mug of coffee back upstairs and flung everything she'd been wearing the day before into the laundry basket in her bathroom. It was full, and looking in her wardrobe and chest of drawers for something to wear, she knew she needed to do some washing very soon. Claudia had suggested Ryan could explain the machine's programming. Gerry could have had fun letting him show her the way round the elaborate control panel. Now she didn't see how they could ever get back to how relaxed they had been together the night they went to the Godolphin.

Gerry treated herself to a lengthy soak in the big bath, something she hadn't done for a while. She usually had a hurried shower in the morning. When she finally came downstairs she felt clean all over, hair brushed and shining, make up applied with unusual care. Gerry felt as if she was arraying herself for a momentous occasion. Her choice of clothes had been severely limited, and she had ended up wearing a calf length waisted green dress with a scoop neck, and green tights. The finishing touch was a pair of copper earrings and a copper coloured necklace. Gerry had bought them on impulse during the summer, but had never yet worn them. The green garments and the copper jewellery brought her about as close as she could get to how Baranwen had looked the first time Gerry saw her. It was pure chance that they were almost the only clean things she had. Of course it was.

Gerry found Claudia in the kitchen checking up on last minute things and ticking them off on a list. She stopped when Gerry came in and looked at her critically.

'Are you sure you'll be all right, Gerry?' she asked. 'You should be fine with Ryan here, he seems quite capable of seeing Justin off. I don't want anything else to happen to you. Yesterday was enough for anyone in one lifetime.'

'I'll be okay,' Gerry said, trying to sound sincere. *I'll be okay once today is over.*

Claudia didn't look convinced.

'I don't know,' she said. 'It's just that you seem kind of, well, fragile these days.'

Gerry wasn't used to Claudia being so penetrating, or touching on anything so personal. She tried to shift the emphasis away from herself.

'That's funny,' she said. 'That's how I felt about you after Jus – after the day Monica came here.'

'Heavens, did you?' Claudia said. 'I never knew that.'

For that brief moment they felt like friends. Then Claudia reverted to the competent woman Gerry was used to.

'Okay then,' she said. 'My cab's due in twenty minutes.

Now, you've got my only spare key, but I'm sure you and Ryan can sort out your comings and goings between you. It's one of those keys you can only get a copy with written permission from the householder and that's not me, it's my father. I talked to Ryan for a while last night, and I have to say I've no worries about him.'

What had they talked about? The house? Justin? Herself? Gerry didn't ask. Claudia went off to finish ticking her check list, and Gerry found some cereal and the end slice of her last loaf. It seemed important to have something to eat before she went to tackle – whatever was facing her.

Over her second cup of coffee she looked at her phone again. There was nothing new. The text was from Ryan, asking her to call him. Gerry expected that the message was from Ryan too, but before she could check, Claudia came in with a large wheeled suitcase and a medium size overnight bag. Gerry stood up, putting her phone down again.

'Do you want a hand bringing things down?' she asked Claudia.

'Thanks, but this is all I'm taking,' Claudia said. 'I'll get more clothes once I'm there and I've a better idea of what the climate's like. Now, I'll just get my laptop.'

Claudia returned in a couple of minutes with the laptop in its carrying case. Other than her shoulder bag, that was it. Her phone rang, and in a minute Gerry heard her giving directions on how to find the house. Then Claudia turned to her.

'He'll be here in a few minutes,' she said. 'I'll just give Ethan a quick call. I emailed him last night to tell him what's happening.'

Gerry looked at her phone as Claudia began talking. Ryan's text had simply said "Please call me" and she assumed the message would be the same. At least he hadn't used the hackneyed "We need to talk". Perhaps he wanted to speak to her before his first lesson of the morning. Gerry pressed the view key, and her heart began to thump. The missed call wasn't from Ryan; it was registered as "number unknown".

This had happened before. Once on the day before Mazey Day when Justin had left the cryptic message that he'd see her at the fireworks. The other time was at the Quay Fair when he left no message, only the implication that he knew where she was. He'd done that to Debbie too. Gerry pressed the message button and held the phone close to her ear to hear Justin's cultivated voice. He said only 'I'll see you later,' then, after a brief but deliberate pause, 'darling'.

He'd picked that from Gerry's mind in the fraction of time before she had forced herself back to her bedroom. Where had he learned to do all these things? Or was he just born knowing it all? He'd implied that it ran in his family but needed training. She remembered he'd said his brother was too lazy to practise.

Gerry put the phone down on the nearest work surface. Her hand was trembling, and the confidence she'd been so carefully building up had evaporated. More than anything else she wanted to see Ryan, because he alone was totally dependable. Gerry refused to accept what he'd said about the chalice using her, though she knew he believed it. But Ryan had never undermined her, never lied to or mocked her. Yet he was not as ordinary or predictable as he looked. Each time they met she was seeing new sides to him. Her thoughts were swinging between wanting reassurance from Ryan, and knowing he intended to destroy the chalice. The two couldn't be reconciled.

Claudia came back to the kitchen, putting her phone away, just as a car horn tooted outside. Claudia opened the kitchen door, and Gerry got up to help with the cases. She was surprised to see that the driver had got out and was coming over to take them himself. She had once booked a cab in London and when it arrived the driver simply texted to say he was outside.

The cab driver wheeled the suitcase out the door, taking the overnight bag on his shoulder. Claudia picked up her handbag and laptop, said goodbye and followed the driver to the car where he was already stowing the case in the boot. Gerry stood on the step and watched the driver holding the car door open for Claudia. They waved to each other and Gerry watched as the cab disappeared up the lane. Then she heard the sound of a message arriving on her phone, and rushed over to it. It was from Ryan, and very brief.

"I'll call you about 10."

She sent back "Ok", but nothing more. He must be working, but at least he'd sent another message as she'd not replied to his first one. Ryan was too scrupulous to cancel or rebook the customers he was expecting this morning. Not even today, when he was planning to destroy the Kelegel. Gerry hadn't worked out a way to stop him, but was sure that the chalice itself would tell her.

Thinking about the chalice had reminded Gerry of Baranwen. Baranwen had had her moments of triumph, taking the Kelegel from the impious cage that had held it, then crushing the Makers. But after that? When Hedra had seen her the Guardian hardly seemed to know what she was doing. What had happened to Baranwen? Gerry didn't want to think about that. Ryan would have blamed the chalice, but that couldn't be right.

Gerry had to distract herself. How was she going to get through the day? She was in no mood to browse the shops, and with the wind rising it would be too cold to sit in Penlee Park or Morrab Gardens. If she went for a walk that would leave her mind too free to think. She had to do something. Gerry brought her laptop down to the conservatory, set it up on the table and tried to lose herself online. She went to Ryan's page on Facebook and saw he hadn't added anything in the days since they'd met outside the library. Gerry looked at his cover photo. The laughing face had probably been caught on someone's tablet, in the house to judge by the background. It looked wrong, as if the lines of the face should be firmer, the mouth and jaw more set, the eyes filled with a new determination. Gerry checked the timeline; the picture had only been posted a month ago. But if Ryan really had changed and she wasn't imagining it, the changes would have come about in the past week.

She was answering some family emails when her phone rang. It was Ryan, sounding harassed.

'I've not got long,' he said. 'I've rearranged all the bookings I had tomorrow, and had to fit in a couple of them today. I'm only getting half a lunch break, and I'll need that to speak to Conn. I missed him this morning.'

Gerry couldn't think what to say. She wanted to ask Ryan what he was going to do with the Kelegel and could she have the gold chain back. But this was her own fault. He'd asked her to ring him and she had ignored the message for over an hour. Now she couldn't connect this harried-sounding man with the Ryan who'd stood up to Justin, talked about Seona and slept in Claudia's lounge last night. There was one thing Gerry could ask, though.

'Why did you change your appointments for tomorrow? Wouldn't it have been better to put off today's lot?'

'I can't do anything till after half five this evening when Conn finishes work, and I thought you might need me around tomorrow,' Ryan told her. His voice sounded sad as he said the last part, then returned to the hurried tone he had started with. 'Look, I've got to go. I'll see you later.'

What on earth did he mean about tomorrow? And how was she going to get through the day till half five?

Gerry went round the house, checking the doors and windows and thinking how glad she was, despite everything, that Ryan would be there later. The house felt very different when she was alone in the daytime and Claudia was at work from how it felt when Claudia was in London and Gerry was on her own at night. She was getting jumpy and could feel her heart beating hard again. She got her shoulder bag and jacket, and left. There was no-one outside with press cameras asking for an interview. There would be something newer by now than a gallery fire two days ago or yesterday's pile-up by Lesingey Lane. It looked like no-one had made the connection between the two, and by the time the "Cornishman" came out on Thursday they would both be forgotten. Except by those involved.

Gerry drove to Penzance, still not knowing what she would do, ideas chasing around her brain. This time she hardly noticed that she was driving an unfamiliar car, and passed Lesingey Lane without thinking, not even connecting it with the accident till after she reached the roundabout. She went automatically to Alexandra Road and went to Penlee House for coffee, drinking it indoors for the first time there. It was no day for sitting outside. Gerry wished she could time jump to five o'clock, but if she got it wrong she might miss the crucial time. She was about to get up and leave when her phone rang. She pressed the green button automatically, then held it away from her ear to check the number. To her relief it was Claudia. That had been careless; it might easily have been Justin.

'I had to hang around in the airport lounge,' Claudia said, 'so I rang my car insurance people and gave them all your details. You and Ryan are completely covered now. I left a message on the landline in case, but you can ignore that.'

Gerry hadn't even thought about checking the landline. Another thing for her to remember.

'How do I do that?' Gerry asked. She could hear a lot of noise in the background, and a chiming sound.

'1571,' Claudia replied. 'Oh, typical, now they've decided to call the flight. I have to go, I'll speak to you soon.'

The car – that was the answer. She wanted to get away from Penzance anyway; last time she'd "seen" Cathno and Elwyn they'd been heading this way, and she certainly didn't want to meet them. Gerry walked back through Penlee Park to the Audi, and drove along the front to the east side of the town. From there she took a road she'd only driven a couple of times, the coast road to Helston and the Lizard.

This was the south coast, and it was very different from the granite and gorse of the north side. The houses in the villages Gerry passed through had flower-filled gardens, and at some places along the route there were wide stretches of the waters of Mounts Bay visible on the right. The sea was grey today, reflecting the clouds overhead, the waves ridged with white tips whipped up by the wind.

Gerry had gone several miles before she spotted a brown sign pointing to Porthleven. She'd never been there, so she turned right and after a few minutes found herself at a small grey harbour. The wind was lashing waves up by the harbour wall, and the road was all but empty of people. There was a pub, a café and an art gallery along the harbour side, and she could see what looked like more shops and cafés up a side street.

It looked like a place to come back to on a better day; Gerry didn't think this was the time to explore it. For now, she was well away from Penzance and any temptation to go and badger Ryan at work. She drove round some of the back streets till she found a space where she could park. The street was narrow, and she manoeuvred the Audi in with a nervous care she'd never shown to Seona's well-used Volvo. Claudia had mentioned, among numerous things about the Audi, that the wing mirrors could tilt down to help with parking. Gerry knew she ought to check that out. But not today. She undid the seat belt, slid the seat backwards and stretched out her legs. Rain was now bouncing on the car's roof, but she was quite comfortable inside. It would be best to stay here for a while. Gerry was tired, despite waking late that morning. She'd not slept much for days, and on top of that she was emotionally battered from the repeated shocks of the weekend. She tilted the seat back at an angle, closed her eyes and tried to relax.

The next thing Gerry was aware of was that the rain had stopped. So she had been asleep. She felt stupid now in the green clothes and copper jewellery. What had she been thinking of when she got dressed that morning? Two women were walking past the car carrying plastic carrier bags with the Costcutter logo, and talking loudly. Their voices must have woken her. What time was it? She turned the ignition key and the figures 16.30 lit up on the dashboard. It couldn't be. She was miles from Penzance, it would be rush hour and she had to get back to Long Rock. Ryan had said that was where Connor worked. She needed to get there before Ryan did.

But first she needed a better idea of where she was going. Gerry shut her eyes and touched the ring, voicing a question in her head. A picture came in front of her eyes. It was the inside of a workshop. There were a couple of cars or vans up on the ramps, and three men in overalls busy at different jobs round them. One was standing below a 4x4, holding something to the underside of the vehicle. He turned to call to someone out of sight, and Gerry saw his face. This would be Connor. He was a lot like his brother: the face, the eyes, the smile. Gerry's heart gave a lurch which she ignored. She was sure she could find the place now.

She returned westward through the succession of villages, with the bay on the left this time, the water calmer as the wind had dropped. It wasn't hard to find the small industrial estate; it was opposite the level crossing and the car park where she had met up with Ryan nearly a week before. They had gone for a drink and Gerry warned him it could be dangerous to get close to her. Ryan had chosen to ignore that advice, and now he was heading into who knew what.

Gerry checked the time; Ryan wouldn't be there for at least twenty minutes. She didn't need the plan at the entrance of the estate to guide her to the workshop; she could tell where it was as easily as if a floodlit beam was shining over the front doorway. This was the place where she had to be. She parked the Audi where she could see the entrance but not be noticed by anyone coming or going from it. Two of the men she'd "seen" earlier came out. They were now minus their overalls, dressed in jeans and work boots, with jackets ready to zip up as the evening became cooler. One stopped, pulled out a pre-prepared roll-up, and lit it while his companion waited. A woman followed them, wearing tight jeans, knee-high boots and a leather jacket. She strolled to a small car close to the door, and the men watched as she swung her legs inside. Then she drove off with a toot of the horn and a brief wave. Assuming she was the receptionist, did that mean Connor was inside on his own now?

Gerry was determined to stay calm, but this got harder as the minutes ticked by. She supposed Connor had said he was staying on to finish some piece of work. He must have done this before so it would be plausible. Then Gerry saw him come out to the front, look around and begin to slide the folding doors across their rails. He looked round again, then went back inside through the small opening he had left. Now they were both waiting for Ryan.

Gerry knew that they wouldn't have long to wait. She could feel the Kelegel, and it was getting closer. Close enough for her to track its progress and to be out of her car and waiting as Ryan drew up. She stood by the door of the workshop, trying to block the entrance and not succeeding very well. Gerry watched

Ryan intently as he came up to her, but even the Rainbow Ring couldn't tell her what he was thinking. She put her hand out – to touch his arm, to try and catch hold of him, she didn't know. Ryan removed it, gently but firmly, and stepped past.

'Don't, Gerry,' he said quietly. 'I did tell you, you won't stop me doing this.' Then he raised his voice. 'Hi, Conn, I'm here.'

Gerry followed Ryan inside, certain there must be something she could do. She just needed inspiration. Connor, still in his overalls, emerged from the relative darkness of the back part of the workshop, looking at her curiously.

'Gerry, this is Connor,' Ryan said unnecessarily. She nodded to Connor, but her attention was mostly on the bag Ryan was carrying. Couldn't either of the men feel the throbbing coming from it?

'I've got the stuff set up inside here,' Connor told them. He obviously thought this was something they were doing together. Ryan followed Connor to a workbench with Gerry only just behind him. There were a couple of clamps ready there with the torch beside them. Other bits of equipment had been pushed to the far end of the bench, out of harm's way.

'Let's see it, then,' Connor said cheerfully. He gestured at the clamps. 'I didn't know how big it would be so I got different sizes.'

Ryan put the bag on the bench and took out the chalice. It looked very small here, the jewels dimmed in the gloom. Connor went to a wall switch and the working area was suddenly flooded with light. It caught the gems and they blazed out as if under the midday sun. Connor looked surprised.

'Hey,' he said, 'you did say this was, like, an old theatre prop? It looks bloody real.'

'Sure,' Ryan said nonchalantly. 'I always carry jewels around at work. The gold's supposed to be real, though it's only

9 carat. If it turns out to be just gold plated, well, then someone's lied to me.'

Connor picked up the chalice and Gerry felt a jolt inside her ribs. No man was supposed to handle the Chalice of the Rainbow. Okay, Ryan had, but then Hedra had given him permission. More than that, she'd commanded him to. Connor turned the Kelegel over, still looking puzzled.

'It's a bit scratched, been knocked around, but the colour's good. These,' he tapped the amethyst and Gerry wanted to snatch it from him, but Ryan was holding her arm and she couldn't get loose. 'If these are glass,' Connor went on, 'they'll dissolve, but if you're taking the melted gunge to a jeweller I'm sure he'll be able to separate the two. You said you wanted a bracelet from this? I'd reckon you'd get a necklace and earrings as well.' He smiled at Gerry, a smile uncannily like his brother's. 'I could just keep the gold as payment for my hard work. Then if you get bored with him, come and see me and I'll give you the bracelet.'

'Hands off,' Ryan said equably. 'Can we get started?'

Ryan wasn't as calm as he sounded. Gerry could feel his agitation through the sleeve of his jacket.

'Let me go,' Gerry hissed to Ryan as Connor bent over the clamps, adjusting the smaller one to the upper part of the cup. The stem was too narrow and the base too flat for the supports to get a firm enough hold. Gerry felt as if it was her ribs they were gripping, as if it was she and not the Chalice about to be blasted into oblivion. She strained forward but Ryan caught her other arm too. Connor had pulled on a thick eye shield and was firing up the torch.

This was it. This was Gerry's moment. She felt the power of generations of former Guardians, all their combined strength, pulsing through her. Ryan must have sensed it too, for Gerry felt him startle. Then she shook him off as if he were a kitten.

Connor had just got the flame going to his satisfaction and was bending towards the Kelegel.

In the name of the Goddess!

With a vivid memory of Baranwen raising her double bladed axe, Gerry flung up her arms. White fire blazed from the cup and the blast threw Connor backwards. His head and shoulders slammed into the raised metal strut of one of the ramps, and he slid to the floor in a heap.

Ryan yelled 'Conn!', and raced to where his brother lay slumped on the ground. He knelt down beside him and laid a finger on Connor's wrist, feeling for a pulse. After a moment's silence he raised his head.

'He's alive,' he said, 'but he needs help.'

'Don't try to move him,' Gerry said, memories surfacing of advice about accidents. 'He might have broken something.'

'As if you'd care,' Ryan snapped. He pulled his phone out and jabbed buttons, put it to his ear, shook it then tried again. Gerry stood where she was, still charged with the force that had swept through her. The torch had gone out again and was lying beside the unharmed chalice.

'There's no sodding reception in here.' Ryan stood, looking anxiously at Connor. 'I'll try outside.'

He stood up, and a voice spoke from behind Gerry. A cool, amused voice.

'Your phone won't work,' said Justin. 'Not if it was caught in that power surge. You'll probably need a new one.'

He moved closer and laid his hand on Gerry's shoulder.

'I came here to support you,' he said, 'but you seem to be managing quite nicely without me.'

'Don't touch me,' Gerry said. The flare of power was still burning inside her. Justin had already taken his hand back, blowing on it as if the touch had scalded him. 'And don't go near the chalice,' Gerry added. 'Either of you.'

Of course Justin ignored that and went straight to the work bench. He put his hand out, and white fire flamed from the Kelegel again. Justin promptly retreated.

Ryan bent over Connor, his face anxious. 'Lend me your phone, Gerry, he needs an ambulance.'

'Soon,' Gerry said. Connor shouldn't have tried to melt the Kelegel. 'Let me have the Chalice and I'll call an ambulance myself.'

'No!' Ryan sprang up. 'I shouldn't have let him, it's my fault. You did say -' but he stopped. Gerry had said Connor might be in danger, but that was when she and Ryan were in collusion. She walked towards the bench but Justin was nearer to it and stopped her. Ryan removed Connor's eye shield, came to the other side of the bench and picked up the torch.

'I know how to use this,' he said. 'I'll have to do the job myself, like I should've in the first place. And don't try the same trick again,' he warned. 'It won't work on me. I'm protected.'

He meant, by the gold chain. And Gerry herself had given it to him. How stupid had that been.

'Stalemate,' said Justin. Unbelievably, he still sounded amused. 'If I come round to stop you, Gerralda will take the chalice. If I don't, you'll set up the flame thrower. I think the odds need adjusting. In my favour.'

Gerry felt Justin go still, and knew what he was doing. He was summoning the remaining Wasps, Elwyn and Cathno. One to keep each of them back while Justin helped himself to the Kelegel. Surely she could blast all of them, any of them who tried to take it. Justin looked at Gerry and gave her that smile which she hated.

'I think you'll find you've drained yourself,' Justin said. 'You're not used to this. By the time you've built up enough power again I'll be long gone. Ah, here they are.'

221

Gerry looked behind her to see the two men she had last seen on the back of a farm lorry. They must have had a good meal or two, or whatever else, since then; both were looking remarkably pleased with themselves. Justin only had to tell the two to keep both Ryan and Gerry out of the way and then nothing would stop him. Justin would take the Kelegel back to the past, for his private revenge on his brother. And if he altered anything that had already happened, it would put all the future in jeopardy. The whole of history, from whatever date he went back to, could be changed. Today's world might simply cease to exist.

Chapter Eighteen

Monday September 15th continued - Tuesday September 16th
Cathno and Elwyn looked around, confused.

'Where is she?' Elwyn asked. He couldn't mean Gerry. No, of course, he was expecting to see Baranwen. Baranwen was the one who had brought the Gohi to this time, had used, rewarded and then seemingly abandoned them.

Gerry moved so that she stood full in the glare of the lights, in her green dress, green tights and copper jewellery. As close to a Guardian's attire as she had ever been.

'I am the new Guardian,' she said, and could feel the pride in her voice. 'Baranwen has gone.'

Elwyn recognised her as he had in Debbie's house.

'You!' he said with unflattering disbelief.

'Yes,' Gerry told him. 'Me. I am Guardian of the Kelegel a'n gammneves.'

Elwyn looked at her, then spotted the chalice.

'It's here,' he cried, and Gerry remembered how the Gohi had looked when they had been close to the chalice before, in the fogou and at the museum. That yearning, passionate craving, as if they would give anything and everything for it. She could understand them; that was how she felt herself. But they were not having it. Baranwen had told her that those desiring the Kelegel would fight and kill each other in their longing for it, thereby reducing the threat they posed. Gerry felt a stir of hope.

Perhaps that would happen now, and the chalice would be safe. In any case Justin was not going to have things all his own way.

Elwyn moved fast, lunging at the bench where the Kelegel was still held by the restraining clamps. Gerry reacted without conscious thought, and once more the white flames shot up from the bowl of the chalice. Elwyn reeled back, and for the first time ever Gerry saw him shaken. He gave her a doubtful look.

'Don't even try to touch it,' Gerry warned, then realised what she'd done. Ryan, always on the alert, saw her reaction.

'Yup, you can still do it,' he said. 'Justin was lying. As usual. I'm surprised you fell for it.' He paused, looked hard at her then said, 'or no, perhaps I'm not.' And he turned away from all of them and went back to kneel beside Connor, checking his breathing again.

Of course Gerry had believed Justin, she always had. That made her feel a fool, but also made her angry. Justin moved out of the shadows to stand before the Kelegel, and addressed his henchmen.

'She is not the one who summoned you,' he declared. 'It was I who did that. Hold them back, both she and that man there. She is not full Guardian, you are committing no sacrilege.'

What happened next took everyone by surprise. Everyone except Ryan. Cathno, who up to this point had stood back, let out a bellow of rage and launched himself at Justin.

'It's you!' he roared, grabbing Justin by both shoulders and flinging him back against the bench. 'I swore I'd cut his balls off,' Cathno yelled, and drew out his knife.

Elwyn looked thunderstruck.

'Him? He's the one you meant? The one who –'

Justin didn't wait for him to finish, shouting to Elwyn to come and help him. He was physically strong enough in his own way, but Cathno was half again as big as he was, and he was

224

holding Justin down as he pummelled every bit of his body he could reach. Justin yelled with pain, while Elwyn seemed too stupefied to act. Cathno's knife had fallen onto the bench, but for the moment he seemed too busy using his fists to attempt to carry out his threat of castration, while his blows broke every rule of boxing. Gerry didn't try to intervene. Justin had intended to take the Kelegel by force. Let the Goddess's wrath be visited on him, even by so unlikely an agent.

Ryan was watching the rain of blows with a grim satisfaction.

'He asked for it,' he mouthed to Gerry, and she finally put the pieces together as Ryan had the day before. Gerry had told Ryan that Ysella had left Cathno for another man, and that Ysella behaved like Monica. Ryan had deduced that Justin had been screwing them both.

'So that's why you told him not to call on the Wasps,' she breathed, staring at Ryan. 'You guessed?'

'It was more than a guess,' he said, 'it was a dead cert. He just can't keep it in his trousers. Or his breeches or whatever.'

Gerry winced. Justin had kept it in when he was with her. He'd done just enough to keep her under his spell, and no more. He'd used her from start to finish.

Elwyn was standing beside the two struggling men, uncertain what to do. Justin twisted his head sideways to shout at Elwyn, and as he did so he caught sight of the knife on the bench where Cathno had dropped it in his initial fury. Justin began to pull his arm free to reach for the hilt, but Cathno spotted the movement and grabbed the knife instead. To do this he had to let go of Justin with one arm. His captive twisted, trying to free himself, but Cathno yelled something, then drove the knife down hard into Justin's groin.

The blade was long and viciously sharp. It sliced straight through the fabric of the stonewashed chinos Justin was wearing, and the pale cotton began to change colour as Gerry stared, mesmerised. It felt more like watching a tv drama than something that was actually happening in front of her, but it wasn't tomato ketchup making that dark stain which spread out from the crotch, up towards the waist and down to the knee, soaking the material. At that, Elwyn snapped out of his inertia. He lunged at Cathno, trying to catch his arm.

'That's enough, leave him!' he yelled, but he was too late. Cathno plunged the knife down again and this time it went straight into Justin's stomach.

Justin let out a terrible scream. Only the one. Gerry couldn't bear to look and shut her eyes, but even behind the scrunched up eyelids she seemed to see the welling blood. She heard swift footsteps and felt a hand on her arm. Gerry flinched, but it was Ryan who spoke.

'Cathno's had his revenge,' Ryan said gently. 'It's time they went home. Can you do that? You know the place. Didn't you say it was a village in the woods, near to where you took me?'

Gerry opened her eyes and looked at Ryan.

'You're saying we should send the Wasps back to their own village?' she asked. 'Back to their own time?'

'Uh-huh. And,' Ryan looked at the two men, who seemed to be arguing, 'I'd suggest we do it now, before they start trying to get hold of the chalice again.'

That broke through the numbing horror of what Gerry had just witnessed.

'If we send them back now, that'd be for good,' she said. 'They'll never come back here.'

'Right,' Ryan agreed. 'I reckon they'd be happy with that too. Might not be a good idea to hang around with bodies bleeding all over the place.'

226

He walked up to the Gohi and, with the chain still translating for him, explained succinctly what he intended to do. Then he beckoned to Gerry.

'I've told them to tell Talan and Kenver's families they won't be coming back,' he said. 'Now, can you concentrate hard on what their village looks like? Will you make a clear picture of it in your mind?'

Gerry looked at him, doubtful.

'Will that work?' she asked. 'You make it sound as if sending them there was as easy as, oh, sending a text.'

Ryan reached up and put the gold chain outside his t-shirt.

'Put your hand on this,' he told her. 'Don't you see, it's the chain and the ring that'll do it. They're far more powerful combined than either is on its own. You only need to give them the focus. Please, Gerry, come on, before anyone comes to see what all the shouting was about.'

'Okay, right.' Gerry closed her eyes again and remembered the first time she'd seen the Wasps. It had been at the edge of the woodland, outside the settlement. She could see the buildings round their courtyards, and the stone wall surrounding them all, smell the smoke, hear the sound of voices. She felt Ryan grip her hand hard, keeping it in place on the gold chain.

Send them back. She addressed the chain and ring together, and concentrated as hard as she could. After a minute or so she opened her eyes again. There was no sign of the Wasps.

'They've really gone?' she asked.

'Yep,' Ryan said. 'You did it.' But he didn't offer any praise or thanks. He had gone back to Connor's side, and was trying his phone again. So much had happened it was hard to realise it was only moments since Connor had gone flying against the metal strut, but Ryan looked anxious.

'Now there's just – him.' Ryan nodded at Justin. 'Then I can get the ambulance here.'

'Is he still alive?' Gerry asked. She didn't want to go close enough to Justin to see.

'Barely,' Ryan said. 'I wouldn't give it more than a few minutes, I'm surprised he lasted even this long.' He stood up and approached the bench where Justin was lying back, his hands clasped hard across the wound in his stomach. They couldn't do anything for him now even if they'd wanted to. If they'd tried to get medical help straight away, could they have saved Justin? Gerry would never know.

Ryan leaned over the dying man.

'Do you want to go home?' he asked. 'Back to your family?'

Justin gave him a filthy look and managed to croak a couple of words.

Ryan shook his head, then turned to Gerry. 'He said no. Well, he's not staying here.'

He looked Justin up and down. There wasn't a trace of sympathy in his face or his voice.

'I'd suggest,' Ryan said to Gerry, slowly and deliberately, 'that we send him to join his two friends. Let them deal with him. Take responsibility for burying him. Or they can leave his body in the woods for any passing animals. I don't suppose anyone's going to be charged with his murder. Like he wasn't for killing Talan and Baranwen. Nothing can make up for all the things he's done, but he's not going to cause any more trouble here. Just do what you did for the other two.'

Gerry glanced at Justin, and looked away at once. He looked dreadful, half sprawled across the bench, his face sunken and his clothes covered in blood. That wasn't what she'd wanted for her last sight of him. Hastily Gerry repeated her former actions, taking hold of Seona's chain again and closing her other fingers round the ring. Once more she shut her eyes and concentrated on the woods near the Wasps' village, and when

228

she reopened them Justin also had disappeared. There were only the bloodstains on the bench to show where he had been.

'Right,' Ryan said, returning to the workbench as Gerry released the gold chain. 'I'll just finish this then I can get Conn seen to. He's been concussed, he'll need to be checked over.'

He reached across the bench and, ignoring the blood staining the wood and the drops landing on the floor, he picked up the torch.

No, he couldn't be doing this, not now. After everything else Gerry had already been through, it was more than she could believe. As she tried to gather her wits, Ryan was already fastening on the eye shield and building up the flame on the welding arc. And she found she couldn't do anything to stop him.

Gerry tried to fill the chalice with flames as she had before, but now nothing happened. She tried to call for help to all the past Guardians but something was preventing her, blocking her powers. All she could feel was a rage and despair like Baranwen had when the Makers had taken the life from the Kelegel on the hilltop at midsummer. Gerry wanted to scream as the Guardian had done, fling herself at the man who was checking the torch to see if it was ready; but she couldn't move.

'Gerry, don't,' Ryan said, but without looking at her. 'You're forgetting everything you knew. Seona told you the chalice should be destroyed because it had acquired a life of its own. It's been taking you over since it made Baranwen give it to you. I told you that you don't understand what this –' he touched the chain '- and your ring can do together. I'd reckon the last powers Seona gave them was to make sure that this –' he nodded towards the Kelegel, '- was finished off once and for all. They're working with me, but it's to help you. I know you don't believe me, but you will. When it's all over.'

229

Gerry was speechless. She gripped the edge of the bench, willing Ryan's words not to be true. It was the ultimate betrayal, by the two gifts which Seona had laboured over for so long, giving them all the powers to help her great-niece. Gerry had worked with both artefacts so intensely that they knew everything about her mind, and it seemed they had somehow used that knowledge to shackle her as effectively as heavy chains would have done. She was forced to watch, immobilised and helpless, as Ryan gave the torch a final check then directed the jet of flame across the rim of the Kelegel.

It was agony. As the precious metal began to melt under the heat it was as if the flames were blazing through Gerry too. There was fire in her head, flowing down her veins, burning through her limbs. Her mouth and throat were too parched to even let her scream. She was forced to hold all that torment inside as she watched the chalice losing its shape. Bit by bit it dissolved into a golden-coloured puddle spreading over the heat proof surface that the clamp was fixed onto. The cup melted first, then the stem; last of all the base was absorbed into the pool of gold.

Gerry never knew if it took seconds, minutes or hours. Nothing existed, not even time, only the flame searing the existence from the living gold. The Jewels slipped in turn into the molten pool, first the rock crystals, then the four larger stones, the sapphire last of all. Gerry could feel the hopes and the gifts, worked into them by the women who had created the chalice, dying as each gemstone slipped into oblivion.

Once it was all over Gerry was released. She was still holding onto the edge of the bench or she would have collapsed. The fire within her body began to cool as the liquid gold swirled into an abstract shape, bright against the dark grey surface beneath it. Ryan cut off the torch and removed the protective shield from his face. Gerry saw him lean forward and lift something out of the coagulating metal. He put whatever it was in his front jeans pocket, then took out his phone, but it still didn't seem to be working. Ryan went to Connor and hunted through his pockets till he found his brother's mobile but that must have been damaged in the same surge as his own; it was dead too. He gave Gerry a quick look but decided not to ask if he could borrow hers. He went off to the workshop's office to use their landline instead but found the door was locked.

Ryan came back to Gerry. 'Okay,' he said, 'I'm going over to the cab firm, they're open all night, I can call from there. Please, Gerry, will you wait for me to come back? If Conn comes round, will you tell him I'll be back in a minute.'

Not a word about what he'd just done. But what, after all, was there to say? He didn't ask if she was all right; they both knew that would have been an insult. Gerry did think she saw pity in his eyes, but seconds later Ryan raced off on his errand, leaving her standing in front of the melted gold. He'd really done it. The Kelegel a'n gammneves had ceased to exist.

Gerry didn't seem to be able to think at all. The Chalice had taken over her life from the moment in the summer when she had first heard Kerenza describe it. She had believed she was to be Guardian, but her first and only act as Guardian had been to lose the Kelegel entrusted to her; and to lose it to its worst enemy. Gerry had betrayed the chalice, betrayed Baranwen who'd given it to her, and betrayed the Makers. It would have even been better if Justin or Elwyn had taken the Kelegel; then at least it would still be intact. Gerry expected to sense something, some final message from the remnants lying on the tray. She'd read that people who lose a limb still feel pain in the hand or foot that no longer exists. But it didn't happen. She was drained of all feeling, and as weary as if she'd been pushing rocks uphill.

There was a faint noise but Gerry couldn't identify it at first. None of her senses seemed to be functioning above the

231

barest minimum. Finally she tracked it to Connor who had groaned, then lifted his head. It looked like that had been a mistake; he put his hand to his head as if trying to keep it together. Gerry didn't go to him; she was too numb to move. But almost at once Ryan came bursting back through the door of the workshop. Seeing that his brother was coming round, he hurried to where Connor sat, propped against the metal strut which had done the damage. Connor was probing the back of his head with tentative fingers.

'Don't try to move,' Ryan told him. 'You were knocked out, but the ambulance is on its way and they'll take you to the hospital to have you checked over.'

Connor started to nod his head, then stopped and felt the top of his skull with his other hand gingerly.

'Hurts,' he muttered, then opened his eyes and looked around properly. 'What happened?' he asked.

'What do you remember?' Ryan asked, his voice gentle.

'Can't say.' Connor's forehead creased. As he came to his senses he would feel his headache in full, and his back must be badly bruised where he'd been slammed into the metal by the force Gerry had unleashed.

'I'd guess,' Ryan said, measuring each word, 'that there was something else mixed in with the gold, and whatever it was exploded under the heat. The cup seemed to blow up in front of you, and you went flying. You hit the back of your head and that knocked you out.'

Ryan looked at Gerry, the lift of his eyebrows asking her not to contradict him. Like she was going to tell Connor there was no foreign substance in the gold and actually she'd filled the chalice with magic flames?

Ryan, seeing that Connor was as comfortable as he could be, came up to Gerry, pausing to shove the now cool lump of melted gold into his jacket pocket. It was a very small lump.

Gerry glared at him, but didn't have the energy to tell him to get lost. She didn't want anyone feeling sorry for her, Ryan least of all. He just watched her at first, and from the look in his eyes he was having to use a lot of will power not to touch her hand or shoulder, or simply put his arms round her to offer comfort. That was the last thing she wanted. Ryan sighed.

'Gerry, I know you hate me right now,' he said quietly, 'but I'm not going to leave you alone here. You're in shock, and even if Claudia was at home that wouldn't be enough. I've got to wait till Conn's been checked out. I called Jez and told him to meet us at Penzance A & E. If they say Conn can go home, he'll need someone there. I got knocked out once, playing rugby at school, and I can still remember the fuss they made. There was a whole list of things that Mum had to watch out for for days afterwards.'

'What did you mean, meet "us" at A & E?' Gerry asked, finally taking in what he was saying. 'I'm not coming with you.'

'You have to,' Ryan said. 'You wouldn't be safe driving back to the house, and besides I don't want you locking me out. I'll drive, and we'll come back for your car in the morning. It'll be all right here.' He looked at Gerry critically. 'Have you had anything to eat today?'

What had that got to do with anything?

'I had breakfast,' she said, 'and I fell asleep this afternoon. Look, leave me alone. I was fine driving here. I'll just go home.'

This time Ryan did put his hand on her arm.

'No,' he said simply. 'You won't.'

Then they heard the ambulance pulling up outside, and through the open door caught a flash of the blue light whirling on its roof. Two paramedics came in, and Ryan directed them to Connor without letting go of Gerry's arm.

It was too much effort to fight him. Ryan kept Gerry beside him as the paramedics did some basic assessments on Connor, then helped him to get outside, while Ryan saw to securing the doors under his brother's direction. Then he walked Gerry to the Skoda, his other hand over the pocket where he had put the remains of the Kelegel.

'I hope Conn isn't given grief over this,' Ryan said as he drove off in the wake of the ambulance. 'It's not the first time he's stayed on to finish a job, but there's quite a bit of blood on that bench and on the floor. I'll tell Conn a couple of drunks wandered in and had a knife fight while he was out of it. It's close enough to what happened.'

Gerry just sat there in listless silence, letting him talk. When they got to the hospital, Jez was waiting, a tall, subdued figure in jeans and a dark jacket. Ryan told his housemate that seeing Connor's accident had upset Gerry. 'Conn just went flying,' he said, 'then cracked his head on this metal thing. Shook me a bit too.' Then he gave Jez some money and sent him to the vending machine, saying that neither he nor Gerry had eaten.

Jez came back with plastic cups of tea, packets of crisps and a couple of pieces of fruit. Ryan stayed close to Gerry, kept his arm round her shoulders, encouraged her to eat and drink. She knew that Jez and Connor assumed Ryan had moved in with her. It didn't matter. Nothing mattered. The two men talked softly and Gerry just sat, silent, till at last the doctor came back with Connor.

'He can go home,' the doctor said, 'as long as there's going to be someone with him.'

Jez said he would be, so the doctor gave him a print-out of things to be aware of, then said they could leave. Ryan said goodbye to his brother, but Gerry tuned out while they spoke. Then Ryan took her arm again.

'He'll do,' he said, and Gerry could hear the relief in his voice. 'Now, I can concentrate on you.' She tried to tug her arm away but didn't have the strength. Ryan led her out to the Skoda, opened the passenger door and helped her in.

'Like I said, I'm not going to leave you alone,' Ryan said as he started the car. 'I picked up a sleeping bag from the house this morning, so I can sleep on the floor in your room tonight. You shouldn't be on your own. Oh, you needn't worry,' he added, as he turned left into St. Clare, making for the bypass. 'I'm not going to try and push my way into your bed. You've made it clear enough you don't want that.'

He sounded bitter, and Gerry had a brief impulse to contradict him. A warm body beside her could be a shield against the aching emptiness. Then she thought of the welding torch and felt again the flames scorching through her body. They had burned everything out of her. She didn't see how she could ever feel happy, laugh or even smile again. Still less make love. Gerry heard Ryan give a deep sigh, but he drove on steadily and she sank back into brooding until they reached Windhaven.

The courtyard lights came on as Ryan opened the gate, and Gerry had a creepy notion that Justin would be there waiting for them. She shivered, and was suddenly glad that she wasn't alone. She was still wearing the imitation Guardian clothes and jewellery she had put on with such care in the morning. She wanted to rip them off and put every item in the bin.

Ryan took charge of everything. He took Gerry's key to unlock the door, cancelled the alarm and brought her inside. His first action was to search out Claudia's decanter of brandy, and sit Gerry down in the lounge with a glass in her hands. After that he went round the house, switching on lights and closing curtains. Outside it was dark and the temperature was dropping, but Gerry wouldn't have thought of doing any of these things. Lastly Ryan hunted through the fridge, found some Parma ham and made a sandwich for each of them with some of Claudia's bread and butter.

Gerry was still sitting, just looking at the brandy in her glass, when Ryan brought in the two plates, then two mugs of tea.

'Drink the brandy,' he urged. 'It will help. Or have some tea.'

Ryan spent what must have been a good half hour coaxing her into drinking most of her brandy and at least some of the tea, and eating the sandwich. Gerry didn't see at the time how patient he was, never pushing but getting results without her realising. Finally Ryan was satisfied. He left the plates and mugs on the coffee table and told Gerry she needed to sleep. She had to show him the way to her room. Even that took a major effort.

'I'll go round and switch most of the lights off while you get undressed,' he said. 'And I'll need to get the sleeping bag from my car, but I won't be far away.'

Like that was supposed to make her feel better? Yet Gerry had to admit it was easier to do what Ryan suggested than to try to think for herself, so she pulled off her clothes and dropped them on the floor, along with the earrings and necklace. She could ditch them in the morning. She went to the bathroom to get her dressing-gown, more out of habit than for modesty.

Ryan finally came back, dragging a brown sleeping bag that looked as if it had seen a lot of use.

'I've checked all the house,' he said, 'except Claudia's room, it doesn't seem right to go in there. I'll talk to her tomorrow, she needs to know about Justin.' He looked around. 'Is that your bathroom there? I'll go and brush my teeth.'

Gerry waved him towards the door. She hadn't actually spoken since they had left the workshop; the idea of putting words together was too hard. Ryan had done all the talking. By

236

the time he came back, wearing a t-shirt and boxer shorts, Gerry had managed to get into bed.

'I know it's much too early,' Ryan said, 'but you could do with sleeping the clock round if you're able to. Do you want to leave a light on?'

Gerry shook her head. Ryan switched off the overhead light and spread his sleeping bag out on the thick mat on the far side of the bed. Once he'd climbed into it Gerry switched off her bedside light. Curiously, it didn't seem odd to have Ryan lying on the floor in her room. She closed her eyes, and exhaustion claimed her.

Sleeping wasn't a problem. Gerry didn't even have any bad dreams. Perhaps the evening with its knives and blood and flames had been nightmare enough. What was unbearable was waking up and remembering. Gerry had thought her life was empty through the long, tedious weeks of the summer, with no chalice and no Justin. That was nothing against the tide of loss that swept over her now as she understood what she'd done, and what she'd lost. She'd been so proud at the idea of being Guardian, had been filled with wonder and excitement. Ryan's threat to destroy the Chalice had seemed unimportant; Gerry had been certain she could stop him, sweep aside his puny intentions. She recalled Baranwen's shout echoing through the galleries in Truro as the Guardian lifted the Rainbow Jewels in her hands. Then Gerry remembered the haunted face behind her in the car, moments before Justin had rammed into them.

For the first time a doubt, speaking in Ryan's voice, raised its head. "It was only using you, Gerry. Remember what happened to Delenyk, to Wylmet and Morvoren." Gerry didn't want to listen to that, but as she pushed it away she was overwhelmed with pure, unalloyed misery. She hadn't meant to, but found herself starting to cry. It began tentatively but built up, took her over and shook her till she was literally howling, helpless to stop the flow. She wept for the chalice, for her own hopes and pride. For Justin too, and what she'd felt for him, which had been real enough, although he'd made her fall for him just to serve his purposes. And Gerry wept for Seona who she'd never see again, and who had forgiven her even for her last terrible misjudgement.

Ryan had been holding Gerry for a long time before she realised. Although she'd always heard that men didn't like women crying, he was speaking quietly, even reassuring her.

'Let it all come out, you'll feel better.'

Gerry caught other words too, so soft that he must think she couldn't hear him. Words like 'darling' and 'my dearest love'. But if he really loved her, he wouldn't have destroyed the Kelegel. That thought stopped her crying, and she pulled away. Ryan's arms fell back. The shoulder of his t-shirt was soaking wet and had black marks on it. Gerry's pillow case was the same. She hadn't taken her mascara off before she went to bed. She did it automatically every night however tired or distracted she was, but hadn't done last night. Ryan had switched on the bedside light on the side where he'd been sleeping. Gerry reached under the pillow for a tissue, and realised she wasn't wearing anything; she hadn't put on pyjamas before going to bed. She made a grab for her dressing gown, which had slipped onto the floor, feeling her face go pink. Yet Ryan had only had his arms round her shoulders, supporting her like a brother might. Gerry flushed more deeply, and Ryan climbed off the bed and disappeared into the bathroom. By the time he came back wearing jeans and a clean t-shirt, Gerry had got her dressing-gown on and belted it tightly.

'It's not quite morning yet,' Ryan said, as easily as if nothing had happened. 'It's only just after six, but I'm going to make some coffee. Would you like me to bring it up here, or will you come down? It's still dark, and there's not a sound anywhere. I've never been in such a quiet place.'

'Oh, the birds'll start up when it gets light,' Gerry said, taking her tone from his. 'No, I'll come down in a minute. If you'll go and put the kettle on?'

As he went downstairs Gerry went into the bathroom and looked in the mirror. Her face was still flushed, her eyes were red and her eyelids swollen. Plus she'd got mascara streaks down her cheeks. She would never have let any other man see her like this, but somehow with Ryan it wasn't a problem. Gerry found him in the kitchen, and he handed her a steaming mug as soon as she reached him.

'Do you feel better now?' he asked.

Gerry thought about it. 'Yes, I do,' she admitted at last.

'Good,' was the reply, 'because there's something I need your help with.'

Gerry nearly choked on a mouthful of coffee as alarm bells began to ring. She put her mug down.

'What sort of something?' she asked. She could feel the familiar plummeting inside her stomach. Surely everything was finished now?

Ryan reached into his jeans pocket and pulled something out. Four somethings to be exact. Four squares of glowing colour. The Jewels of the Rainbow.

Gerry reached out and picked up the blue one. It was her sapphire.

'They're all right?' She couldn't believe it.

Ryan looked at her, and Gerry thought he looked unhappy, but she was too absorbed by the Jewels to wonder about that. She'd never had the chance to hold them all, examine them properly. The size, the cut, and the colours were all incredible, shining under the ceiling spotlights in the kitchen. Gerry picked each up in turn, revelling in their beauty, overjoyed just to have them in her hands. Ryan's voice brought her back to earth.

'Depends what you mean by "all right",' he said. 'They're not physically damaged. A short blast of heat, even intense heat, wouldn't hurt them. But if Hedra was right, there won't be any magic, or power, or whatever you call it, left in them. Not now the chalice itself has gone.' He took an irregular shape from the pocket of his jacket, which he'd left over the back of a chair when they'd got back from the hospital. Gerry gasped as she recognised it. It was the swirl of melted gold from the chalice.

'Didn't want to leave it around for Connor's boss to find,' Ryan said. 'It's going to be enough of a job explaining the blood.' His face hardened as he looked at Gerry, so that she was sure she must have imagined those tender words he'd murmured upstairs. She hadn't known Ryan could look so harsh. 'What you have to understand, Gerry, is that there's no way you are ever going to revive these. I know Baranwen brought the chalice back to life, but by all accounts the chalice itself was instructing her how to do it. They'd been linked for – how long was it?'

'Two hundred years,' Gerry said.

'Right. Well, even if you took this gold and these four,' Ryan picked the Tegennow out of her hand, 'to a craftsman along with a picture of the chalice, and got them to make you an identical-looking chalice, it's lost any power now. It's just gold.'

Gerry felt a glimmer of hope. Whatever Hedra, and Seona, had said, Ryan might be wrong. He sounded definite, but how could he possibly know? The jewellers on Causewayhead would be able to give her the name of someone who could do the work.

Ryan must have read her face. Now he looked exasperated. 'I mean it, Gerry,' he said. 'If you don't believe me, ask your ring, I'm sure that'll confirm it. Anyway, let's leave that aside for the moment. There's still one piece of unfinished business left, and

I was hoping you'd help me. It would mean going into the past one last time. This –' he touched the gold chain, '- and your ring should take us. I know you said you wouldn't go back again, but I think you can make an exception for this.'

"Leave that aside"? Ryan must be kidding. And he thought Gerry was going to help him with anything, after what he'd done? But she couldn't help being curious. What on earth could Ryan want to go back to the past for? And with her??

'Well?' he asked, 'are you up for it?'

Chapter Nineteen

Tuesday September 16th continued

'Am I up for what?' Gerry asked. She wasn't going to agree to anything blindly. She took a mouthful of coffee. At least Ryan hadn't put sugar in it. He'd seen her making coffee in the staff room often enough to know. 'And can I have my chain back?'

'Sorry,' Ryan said. 'I'll need it while we're there, for translating and stuff. You can have it when we get back here.'

Gerry's face must have fallen, because Ryan's tone softened. 'Gerry, I hate arguing with you. I'm on your side, you'll understand in the end. What I want to do now is to go and see those three women you told me about, the ones who made the chalice in the first place.'

Gerry hadn't given a thought to the Makers.

'Only, it was your idea in the first place,' Ryan went on, watching her. 'You said that the damage Baranwen caused wasn't physical, she did it just by using the chalice. You told that woman Hedra you thought you might be able to use your ring to heal them.'

Yes, she had said that. And if they did that, what might the Makers do in return, out of gratitude? If she took the gold and the four stones with her?

'Forget it,' Ryan said, following her thoughts, but he sounded more resigned than angry. 'They can't restore it.'

'You're as bad as Justin,' Gerry muttered, picking up her mug again and drinking some more coffee. 'Stop reading my mind.'

'It'll stop when I give you the chain back,' Ryan said. 'And I'll do that as soon as we get back here. But that was obvious just from your face. And I promise I'll never treat you like he did. Now, if you finish your coffee and get dressed, we could go. Unless you want breakfast first?'

Gerry shook her head, then drained the mug and went off to her room. When she came down again she was wearing jeans and a t-shirt, the only clean clothes she had left. She usually wore loose smocks, and it was silly to feel self-conscious about how closely these fitted. She never had with Justin, or with Martin in London. At that, she realised she'd not thought about Martin for weeks, apart from telling Ryan about what had happened, yet only three months ago she'd truly believed she'd never get over him. She had thought her heart was broken for ever. She'd been so innocent back then.

Ryan certainly did look twice at what she was wearing when she came back into the kitchen.

'I haven't got anything else that's clean,' Gerry said defensively.

'That sounds just like Conn, he's terrible,' Ryan said. 'Ends up wearing the same things for work three days in a row, not that it matters in that place.' His face clouded, and she didn't need to be a mind-reader to guess he was hoping his brother was feeling better. 'Well,' Ryan went on, 'I promised Claudia I'd talk you through the controls on her washing machine. I'll speak to her later, they're a few hours behind us there.'

243

'Speak to her about the washing machine?' Gerry asked, irritated. 'You don't need to rub it in, I know I'm rubbish with things like that.'

'No, of course not, I need to tell her about Justin,' Ryan said. 'How d'you think she'll take it?'

Gerry considered this, tapping her fingers on the glossy work surface.

'She was devastated last time,' she said at last. 'It might be different now, I really can't guess. But at least she'll know he can't do any more harm to me or her, so she doesn't need to worry about us.'

'Does that 'us' include me?' Ryan asked. He shook his head at Gerry's blank expression and dismissed the question. 'Let's get started. Are we going to that same place on the hilltop?'

Gerry tried to focus but found that for some reason it was more difficult than she'd expected. 'I can't think properly.' she complained.

Ryan looked at her with concern, but then almost at once became business-like.

'Okay, let's sit in there.' He moved towards the conservatory, and Gerry followed him. It was easier just to agree, like it had been the night before. Outside, the sky was rapidly growing lighter. On clear mornings the sun could be seen rising over the line of the hills to the east. It was rising a lot further round to the right now than it had when Gerry first moved in at midsummer. The room with its glass walls and ceiling was chilly, and she shivered. Ryan went to get his jacket and put it round her shoulders.

'You don't need to bother,' Gerry muttered, knowing she sounded ungracious. 'I'm not a child.'

'You've got to concentrate, and you can't do that if you're thinking about how cold you are,' Ryan said, taking a chair beside her. 'Now, tell me about the last time you saw the Makers.'

'I can't,' Gerry said. 'I don't remember.'

'Okay.' Ryan's mood had changed again, and he became as patient as he'd been the night before when he'd coaxed her into eating and drinking. Now he tried to take her step by step to what he needed.

'You gave me a very vivid description a couple of days ago, up at Lescudjack,' he said. 'Don't you remember?'

'No,' Gerry said, 'I can't remember that at all.'

This was getting seriously scary, like bits of her mind were disappearing. Gerry clutched the edge of the table and did her best to picture the Makers, but the harder she tried the more the memories streamed away from her.

'I'll try to help,' Ryan said. 'You said they were outdoors, and the Mother one was holding the youngest, the one who was blinded. Can you see her – is she tall? Dark? Are they wearing long dresses?'

'Robes,' Gerry corrected without thinking. A picture flashed into her mind, but it was gone again, and trying to keep it was like trying to hold onto a dream after you wake up. Perhaps Ryan had caught it. Gerry touched her ring, hoping that perhaps it could send the picture to Seona's chain and so to Ryan. Ryan had been so certain that the two had been made to work together. Now, she hoped he was right.

'They were outside,' Gerry told him. 'They didn't want anyone to come and ask them for help. They had this room inside the fogou, it was set up for seeing people. I suppose you'd call them clients. They had some really good stuff in there.' Then the memory had gone again, but Ryan didn't seem discouraged.

'Good,' he said, 'that's great. Can you give me an idea of when this was? Don't worry if you can't, I'm sure these two will remember.' He touched the chain at his neck, and put his hand over hers, covering the Rainbow Ring.

'I think,' Gerry said, feeling the knowledge slipping away again even as she spoke, 'it was about six or seven hundred years before the Wasps' time. But that's just a guess. Oh, there's one thing I do know.' It was something she'd looked up at Cornish Studies, not learned while using magic. 'At that time, the village was up nearer the top of the hill. The villagers moved down the hill later when they began to do farming, and they needed flatter land for crops and animals.'

Gerry looked at Ryan, expecting him to be pleased, but his eyes were anxious. Baffled, she asked 'Doesn't that help?'

Ryan put both his hands on hers. 'We'll just have to have a go,' he said. 'I'll try and get us as close as I can to when you last saw them. I was hoping you could give me a picture of – what's the oldest one called?'

'Colenso,' Gerry said, and as she spoke the name all at once she could see the Wise Woman, confronting Baranwen in the cave, radiating cold fury.

'Brilliant,' Ryan said, 'I've got her now. That should do it.' He looked at his watch. This was a chunky black and grey object with a big round face; it looked like it could do emails and Instagram as well as telling the time.

'Now, I'll try and get us back here afterwards as close to now as I can,' Ryan said. 'I mean within the next couple of hours. I know you've said it's not an exact science.'

Gerry remembered something else.

'Claudia's cleaner comes round on Tuesday and Friday afternoons. She'll be here later.'

So it looked like here and now things weren't sliding out of her mind. Only anything related to the Kelegel.

'Not a problem,' Ryan said calmly. 'Claudia's so efficient she's probably already let the woman know I'm staying here. Now, forget all about that. We're going to see the Makers.

246

Does it help if you close your eyes?'

It should have, but it didn't. Gerry could feel Ryan sitting very close beside her, his hand circling her wrist. A memory stirred and vanished.

'It's blank,' Gerry told him, 'it's like I'm blocked off.' This was creepy.

'Then we'll both have to do this on trust,' Ryan said, sounding grim now. 'There's one thing you should remember. The women we're going to, one can't see, one can't speak, and one can't hear. It was your precious chalice did that, and don't forget it.'

He stopped speaking, and the next moment they were in darkness. Gerry could still feel Ryan's hand, but nothing else. The minutes seemed to go on far too long. Had it always been like this? She couldn't recall. Then they were out in daylight, and it had come right. They were on Chapel Carn Brea. Ryan let go of her arm, and Gerry saw him go to check the landmarks for himself. No roads, no airport. Then he went to the other side of the hill to see where the village was. He came back and nodded.

'Got it,' he told her, 'but I can't see your Makers anywhere.'

It was raining, solid Cornish rain. Ryan's jacket was still over Gerry's shoulders and it was getting wet already. She slid her arms into the sleeves.

'Perhaps they've gone inside,' she suggested, 'to get away from the rain?'

'We'll try,' Ryan agreed. 'Where's the way in?'

Gerry led the way to the entrance without any trouble, though a nagging memory suggested this was a place she should be afraid of. She shook it off and followed Ryan as he ducked under the granite lintel to go into the passage. It was almost dark inside.

'There ought to be torches,' Gerry said, 'in the round room

at least, if not here. The light kind of came through into this bit. You'll crack your head on the ceiling if you try to walk blind in this passage.' So she still knew that much.

'Not a problem,' Ryan said. 'There's a torch on this.' He felt in his pocket and pulled out his phone. He pressed a button and a blue-white light appeared. It was enough to indicate the height and width of the stone around them. Ryan looked at the phone. 'No signal of course – that would be totally weird.' He turned the light in every direction.

'It looks like there's an opening in the wall on the right, further along,' he said. 'Would that be it?'

'I think so.' Gerry had a tantalising image of sloping walls of neatly graded stones, flickering yellow light from the torches in metal holders. 'Go find.'

Ryan took her hand.

'Stay with me,' he murmured, then set off along the passage towards the opening. 'It looks like there's a light in there, but not much of one,' he said as they got nearer. A few more steps took them to the opening that was the entrance to the fogou. Ryan looked inside cautiously, then yelled 'No!' He ducked inside, shouting, 'Gerry, help me!'

Gerry ran in after him, but was slower to catch on and for a moment she just stared at the scene before her. Colenso, Rosenwyn and Keyna were sitting round the table. A single candle burned low in front of them. The light was poor, but Gerry could see that each woman had a cup in front of her and they were just reaching to pick them up.

'No!' Ryan shouted again, 'don't do it!' As his words echoed round the walls he had dashed forwards and swept his hand across the table, knocking over all three cups. Dark liquid spilled over the embroidered cloth.

Rosenwyn, who had not been able to hear Ryan's shout, stared at him, confused. Keyna had heard but could not see who it was. She was bewildered too, but angry as well.

'Who's there?' she cried, then, 'How dare you come in here! We have forbidden all visitors.'

Seeing how helpless and frustrated the Maiden was, despite her challenging words, Gerry was filled with pity for her. Then she realised what the three had intended, and guessed that she and Ryan been brought here specifically to stop them. The ring and chain had cut the timing a bit fine, though.

'Gerralda,' Rosenwyn said, sounding oddly resigned. 'You time your visits carefully. What could bring you here now?'

Gerry found herself coming out with words that she had heard before, but had no idea where or when. 'To take, or deliberately risk, your own life, except to save another's, would be a sin against the Goddess who gives us life.'

Ryan looked at her, as startled to hear Gerry come out with such profound words as she was herself. He mouthed, indicating Rosenwyn, 'Which one's she?'

'Rosenwyn, the Mother,' Gerry said. 'She won't have heard that.'

Colenso could hear, but couldn't answer. She looked moved by Gerry's words, but Rosenwyn's hand was straying towards the spilled liquid. Ryan, who was watching for any such move, promptly got between her and the table.

'No you don't,' he said. 'You won't need that. We've come to heal you.'

Keyna gave a bitter laugh.

'And who are you to presume you can perform such a miracle? This is arrogance beyond belief!'

Rosenwyn put a restraining hand on Keyna's shoulder, sensing if not hearing her response, but the young woman shook her off.

'My name's Ryan Luscombe and I'm from Penzance,' Ryan

answered, 'but Penzance in Gerry's day. Gerralda's. She told me that your injuries were inflicted on you purely by the power of the Kelegel.'

There was a hiss from Keyna. Rosenwyn moved closer, as if to try to sense the meaning of the words she could not hear. Colenso, who'd been watching Ryan steadily, framed the word "How?" with her lips.

'With these.' Ryan unfastened the chain from his neck, placed it on the table and gestured for Gerry to put the Bysow a'n gammneves beside it. Rosenwyn explained to Keyna what was happening.

'The man with Gerralda has the gold chain that Gerralda showed us, the one she used to enable her to come here. She has a ring.' Rosenwyn picked it up to look at it, and cried 'Mother Goddess! These are the Jewels of the Rainbow! Small stones,' she added for Keyna's benefit, 'set onto a gold ring, but they are the same four gems.'

Gerry took the ring back from her, not knowing if it would work in here, but hating the scorn and disbelief surrounding her so much that she was determined to prove herself. She wanted to show them what the ring could do, but the light from what was left of the candle didn't look like enough to work with.

'Have you any more candles, or torches?' Gerry asked.

'No,' said Keyna, 'we have refused all supplies.'

'Then where did this come from?' Ryan asked, pointing to but not touching the damp cloth. 'How did you get hold of the poison?'

'We have always kept some,' was the unexpected reply, 'against the direst emergencies. A merciful end for those in extreme and incurable pain. Never did we dream we would one day need it ourselves.'

Well, if there was no more light, Gerry would have to

make do with what there was. She put her finger to the edge of the ring and breathed 'Show them!'

Gerry thought at first that it wouldn't work and that she and Ryan were there on a fool's errand, but then the colours began to move. Rising from the ring, they joined and began to spread, shining with a luminous radiance in the dim cave as if a rainbow had formed under a full moon rather than in broad sunlight. She'd only meant to give a small demonstration, perhaps a rainbow stretching across the table, to prove that the Bysow a'n gammneves was worthy of its name. The four who could see all watched, transfixed, as the glowing lines of colour lengthened, split into three and one moved towards each of the Makers. Gerry felt Ryan gripping her elbow. He was breathing fast.

'What's happening?' Keyna begged. 'Tell me!'

Quietly Ryan started to describe what they were looking at, but Keyna cried out that he must be lying. Colenso came to the Maiden and put both hands on the young woman's shoulders. Each of the three rainbows formed an arc about two feet long. The first streamed down to Keyna and wrapped itself around her eyes like a beautiful multi-coloured blindfold. Keyna let out a soft cry, and put her hands to her face as if she could feel the lines of light. The second covered Colenso's mouth, circling her jaw like a soft gag, while the third looped around Rosenwyn's ears. They looked at each other in wonder, except for Keyna, but no-one spoke. Gerry watched, amazed, her hand still on the ring, as the colours softened and then blazed, pressing where the healing was needed. She heard Rosenwyn breathe 'Merciful Mother of us all.'

Gerry staggered as if she were carrying an enormous weight, and Ryan put his arms round her shoulders. 'Hold on, Gerry,' he whispered. 'You must keep going, you're doing so well, you mustn't give up now.'

'It's – it's draining me,' Gerry murmured. She felt as limp

251

as wet paper. Ryan put his arm round her, not round her shoulders this time but under her armpits, holding her up.

'Just a little longer,' he breathed into her ear, 'then you can rest. You're so brave, don't let go till I say.'

Gerry closed her eyes and let him hold her. She felt sick, and colours were swirling behind her eyes. Not beautiful, clean rainbow colours but muddy browns and dirty reds. She sagged against Ryan. 'You're almost there,' he said softly. 'Open your eyes and look now.'

Gerry looked, though everything seemed faint. The rainbows were beginning to fade. The ring lay on the table, just a piece of jewellery, near the gold chain. Rosenwyn touched her ears with a tentative gesture. Colenso moved her lips experimentally. Keyna opened her eyes, and even in her weakened state Gerry could see two things. Keyna had her sight back, and she still looked angry.

Rosenwyn looked at Keyna, then at Gerry and Ryan, and smiled. She began 'We should -' but Keyna stood up and spoke across her.

'That was the least she could do,' she said. 'If Gerralda had never come here, first bringing Iestyn to us then leading us into Baranwen's hands, none of this would have happened. Nothing can restore the reputation we have lost. How will any see us as all-wise and all-powerful after we have been laid so low?'

Ryan muttered something inaudible and turned a look on her as cold and bleak as midwinter.

'No, I didn't expect thanks,' he said. 'Gerry told me what you were like, all of you.'

'I didn't -' Gerry began, but Ryan touched her hand, and shook his head.

'No, you didn't,' he said, 'but I can read between the lines. It was more what you didn't say.' He turned to face Colenso.

252

'I don't have time for this. I need your help, and quickly.'

'Of course,' the Wise Woman said, 'you did not heal us purely out of the goodness of your heart.'

'No, I didn't,' came the prompt answer, 'but Gerry would've. It was her idea, after you told her what Baranwen had done.' Gerry collapsed onto a seat as Ryan spoke, finding her legs wouldn't hold her up any more. 'Look at her, she's nearly finished. She's spent her last strength to help you.'

Rosenwyn took a step towards Gerry, but Colenso laid a hand on her shoulder.

'Wait,' she said. 'Nothing is ever straightforward where Gerralda is concerned. Explain yourself.'

Keyna stood up, interrupting her.

'I'm thirsty,' she said, and walked to the door. 'I'll fetch some water.' She stepped through the entrance to the chamber, then screamed. 'It's all dark, I cannot see anything. Has he blinded me again to make you agree?'

'No,' said Ryan scornfully, 'there's no torches out there. I'll light you.' He walked to where Keyna was standing and used the light from his phone again. 'I'll see her there and back,' he said, 'but get some lights up here, and fast.'

He disappeared after Keyna. Colenso's face went still, and Gerry was reminded of Justin calling up the Wasps. They waited in silence as the candle burned lower, but almost before Ryan and Keyna returned, the latter carrying a full ewer, half a dozen men and women from the village had arrived. They were carrying torches, lamps, food and drink. Gerry had seen such a summoning here before, when Colenso called for men to oppose the Wasps. Someone in the village possessed enough latent power to receive messages from the Wise Woman.

Ryan stood beside Gerry, his hands clenched, as the supplies were brought in. He kept muttering 'Just get on with it and go,' over and over, though only Gerry could hear him. Keyna need not have worried about their status. The villagers were more than reverent before their Wise Women, as if healing themselves of such injuries was the ultimate proof of their powers.

Gerry stayed on the seat, with barely enough energy to drink from the beaker Ryan held to her lips, or taste the bread he put into her hand. When at last the villagers had gone, Ryan addressed the three Makers.

'I'll let you lot take the credit for that little miracle,' he said. 'Now, since Gerry last came here a lot's happened. You know the Kelegel used Baranwen to bring back whatever potential you took from it. Then it dumped her. She was forced to give it to Gerry, or Gerralda if you prefer. No, stuff that, she's Gerry to me.' He shifted to stand close behind Gerry. 'Then it got Justin to slaughter Baranwen, but not before she had passed on the Chalice. Meanwhile we'd gone to the Bees but there were no Guardians left.' At the murmur this caused he added impatiently 'One of them drowned, might've been suicide, the other went off home. So we talked to the old teacher and agreed we must finish off the chalice.'

'Well, you have been busy,' Colenso said. Ryan ignored her. He was in full flow now.

'Where my brother works they have a tool that can melt metal. We were ready to go and do that,' he went on, disregarding the startled exclamations, 'then Gerry announced she was meant to be the next Guardian. It had got hold of her now.' He stroked Gerry's hair gently. 'I'd kept it, wouldn't let her touch it, but that wasn't enough.' He pulled out the lump of gold and the four gemstones, and put them down on the table. The Makers crowded round, examining them in the bright light of two lamps burning with strong clear flames. Gerry couldn't look

254

at the flames; they were too like the welding arc.

'I underestimated the Chalice,' Ryan said, as the three women picked up the stones in turn. 'I should have learned from everything I'd been told about it. As it began to dissolve under the heat, whatever was animating it passed out of the cup and the jewels directly into Gerry's mind. It had started on her as soon as Baranwen handed it over.'

Gerry looked up at him, puzzled, but Ryan went on, addressing the Makers. 'It's eating her up. I need you to stop it. You're supposed to be here to help anyone in need. You created the Kelegel for that purpose. There's no one else who can halt this,' he stopped, searching for the right word, 'this monster.'

'This monster that we ourselves created,' Colenso said gravely. She looked at Ryan as he stood silent after his outburst, his hands resting on Gerry's shoulders. 'For these,' she indicated the remains of the chalice, 'I can tell that they have no degree of life left in them. For the rest, we have only your word.'

Gerry thought Ryan would explode at that, but he kept his temper though she could feel his fingers digging into the flesh of her upper arms, and he drew a deep breath before answering.

'I'd've thought you could sense it for yourselves. Just try to put your hand on Gerry's bare wrist.'

Keyna had been sitting listening, sipping water and watching Ryan and Gerry. Now she reached over to touch Gerry as Ryan had suggested. The result was like the flash of sparks when water hits a live electric wire. She pulled back, and Gerry clutched the spot with her free hand. It burned.

'Well, there's one simple way to deal with this,' Keyna said. Her eyes went to the far side of the cave where the cloth lay on the floor. It was a beautiful piece, but now they ought to burn it for safety's sake. It had been wrapped carefully so that all the spilled poison was on the inside, while the outside was clean and

255

safe to pick up. Keyna's intention was plain enough.

'Don't even think about it,' Ryan warned her. 'If you so much as touch it I'll get the worst bit and ram it down your throat.'

'Poisoning Gerralda is not the answer,' Colenso told the younger woman. 'If what this man says is right, then whatever is inhabiting her could transfer itself to one of us, and what would happen then?'

Rosenwyn's hand went to her mouth, but she at least was looking at Gerry with sympathy. 'Then what can we do?' she asked. The question was not directed at anyone in particular.

'Use the chalice,' Ryan said impatiently. 'Your own one. And if you don't do it soon, I'll go and get it myself. I told you we're short on time. I can tell where it is.'

He picked up the Rainbow Ring and put it on. Ribbons of light began to weave round his fingers, as they had round Gerry's the first time she wore it. Watching them, Gerry felt her brain clear a little, and reached out towards it, but Ryan moved his hand away. That really hurt; didn't he trust her? No, of course he couldn't.

'There is a story I have heard,' Colenso said, 'of a man distraught with grief after his wife died. He loved her so much that he went down to brave the Guardian of the world of the dead in an attempt to win her back.'

'Yeah, I know that one,' Ryan said impatiently. 'Orpheus, we did it at school. So?'

'I may have a solution,' Colenso replied, looking Ryan straight in the eyes. 'Would you dare as much for Gerralda?'

'She's not dead, not yet,' Ryan said, 'and she's not my wife.' Did Gerry imagine an unspoken "not yet" there too? 'But yeah, I'll do anything I can to help her.'

Rosenwyn looked anxious, but Keyna appeared

triumphant. Ryan glared at her. *And would anyone do as much for love of you?* Keyna scowled back, and Gerry wondered if the Maiden had heard that.

'I've a pretty good idea what you're planning,' Ryan said. 'You're going to use your chalice to shift whatever's in there,' he laid his hand on Gerry's forehead, and she registered that when Ryan touched her there was no explosion of sparks, 'from Gerry to me. I'm stronger, and of course I'm a man. So I'm not as likely to be bewitched by it, and if I do get my brains scrambled you won't mind so much. You can burn it out inside my head and if I'm lucky I might even survive.'

'No!' Gerry cried, 'Ryan, you can't!'

'Yep, I can,' he told her and planted a kiss on the top of her head. 'I can and I'm going to. Now can we get started?'

Colenso gave him a measuring look, then nodded to Rosenwyn. She went round to the far wall and placed her hand against one of the stone slabs in the wall. It swung open and Gerry expected to see the Chalice resting on the casket of Delenyk's ashes. But no, of course that would be centuries in the future.

Rosenwyn took out the Kelegel. Even in the light of the lamps and torches it shimmered, the gold reflecting the flames, and the gems and the crystals sending out lines and points of colour. Now Gerry could understand what Colenso had meant when she brought Baranwen's chalice to them and the Wise Woman said that the stones had lost the joy and hope they had made them with. This Kelegel was pure and untainted. Just looking at it made Gerry feel dirty by contrast, as if some foul thing was crawling inside her. How could she have believed that the one she knew was so perfect? Gerry could hardly bear to look at the Chalice as Rosenwyn carried it to the table.

'We should go outside,' Rosenwyn said.

'But it's pouring with rain,' Gerry objected.

'No, there will be sunshine enough for our purpose,' Colenso said, and the certainty in her manner brooked no argument. Was she saying she could make the sun shine if she needed it? It sounded that way.

Gerry tried to stand up and Ryan was there at once, supporting her. Then his put his arms round her, gave her a fierce hug and kissed her hard.

'If I don't survive this,' he said, 'I want you to take those jewels and the gold and have them made into a bracelet. Wear it and remember.'

'Remember what?' Gerry asked bitterly. 'I've made a total mess of everything I've tried to do.' She knew that much, even if the details were lost to her. She had a brief but vivid flash of Seona's face as she realised Gerry had set a period to her life. Then another of Wylmet choking on the deadly cup of wine, Claudia watching the paintings burn in her gallery, Kenver running headlong into a moving van.

'No, my love,' Ryan said, so quietly that even in such close quarters only Gerry could hear him. 'Remember me.'

At that he gave her hand a final squeeze and turned to Colenso.

'I'm ready,' he said. *Do your worst.*

They all went outside, and Gerry saw that Colenso had been right. Beams of sunlight were breaking through between the clouds. Keyna, already taking her returned sight for granted, went to the barrel to fill the dipper with water. She used it to half fill the chalice, then returned the dipper to its hook and came to stand beside Gerry.

'You must keep absolutely still,' she said. 'It is essential for the working.'

Rosenwyn looked at Gerry, then her face became remote

258

as Colenso's had earlier. Colenso herself was totally focussed on the chalice. She rested it on the ground in a patch of sunlight. As Gerry watched, the drops of water began to move upwards. Lines like golden sunlight came next, pouring from the rock crystals towards the rising water. Then the four great gemstones began to glow, and the rays of red, yellow, blue and violet streamed into the beams of the sun. They overlapped to form a steady rainbow, the colours so clear and exquisite that Gerry wanted to weep at the beauty of it.

Colenso raised her arms, her lips moving in silent prayer, then sank her hands up to the wrists in the indigo/blue section of the radiant arc. Gerry had never taken tranquillisers but the feeling that engulfed her then was what she supposed they would do. She felt as if nothing could affect or worry her, that she was cushioned against anything and everything. Colenso did not even look in her direction, intent only on her hands, bathed in the coolest colours of the spectrum. She was chilling Gerry out, and as Gerry recognised this she became aware that bits of her memory were coming back, starting with the humiliation of all the mistakes she'd made since first seeing the blue stone on the market stall. Yet she could not agonise over her failings, filled as she was with the peace engendered by the sapphire blue light.

Gerry became aware of movement and sound nearby and turned to see what looked like everyone from the village gathering on the slope below. They all looked solemn, even the children, and kept still and quiet. Then Keyna beckoned to five of the men, who moved out of the small crowd and walked up to her.

'You,' she said to two of them, 'stay with this woman and keep her here. You others go to the man standing there and make sure he stays where he is. If she,' she nodded at Gerry, 'tries to go to him, you must prevent her by any means necessary.'

The two men assigned to Gerry nodded to Keyna, the

gesture deferential. The remaining three went to Ryan, not standing too close but forming a loose ring around him. All the others stayed as they were, watching intently. Gerry was too well shielded to know if they were emitting sympathy and support, or merely observers, though surely not hostile ones. Gerry could have believed that of anyone Keyna had summoned, but not Rosenwyn. Yet the Mother must have called them for a purpose.

Then everything changed. Gerry's brain felt clear again, and her normal energy was restored. Whatever had been in her head, blocking her, had left. The sedative effect had gone too and she became sharply aware of Ryan. He was standing with his back to Gerry, a few metres away, but she could feel as clearly as if they were touching that there was something else there, another presence within him. As if he felt her looking, Ryan turned slowly, and Gerry saw with horror that his face had become slack, his eyes unfocussed. He knew she was there but did not seem able to see her. Was this what she had been like since the Chalice took hold of her? Gerry took an involuntary step towards Ryan and at once strong hands gripped her arms so she couldn't move.

'Keep still,' Keyna hissed from nearby. 'Stay there and watch.'

Rosenwyn went to stand near to Ryan. Not touching him, not quite within the circle of his guards but close enough to convey the encouragement and understanding which were the core of her nature. As she was the one who had summoned the watching crowd, Gerry trusted that was what they were there for - to add strength to Rosenwyn.

Colenso took her hands out from the section of the rainbow where she had been holding them. The colours still shone steadily, as vivid as ever, but Gerry shivered as she watched. The beauty of the Chalice of the Rainbow could no longer move her. She was too afraid of what was going to happen next. Her hand was across her mouth and she bit into the fleshy pad on the inside of her finger to stop herself from crying out. Gerry wanted to wrench herself free, to shout to Colenso, 'No, you should do it to me, it was all my fault'. She was the one who had brought Baranwen's chalice here and events had led from there in a remorseless circle, ending with the Makers being called to Baranwen's time and destroying, as they believed, the powers which the Kelegel had so wrongly acquired.

Gerry's struggles were futile. She was gripped tightly by her guards, forced to stay put. She felt Keyna move to reprimand her again, but Rosenwyn motioned to Keyna and she stepped back. *Don't move.* Rosenwyn's words passed directly into Gerry's head. *The best way to help your friend is to leave him to hold onto his own being. If you distract him he may fail, and if you care for him you must understand this.*

Gerry did more than "care for" Ryan. She loved him, she knew that now, and she'd never told him. She might never get the chance to tell him. How could she not have understood? Why she had worried so much about him and Claudia, why she had wanted him to hold her every time things got too much. He had stayed with her despite all the terrible things he'd learned, adapted to the impossible, and done everything she didn't want him to in order to free her from the Kelegel. He was utterly true, trustworthy and straight; and she hadn't seen it. She'd been too wrapped up in herself. Now he was out of her reach, risking his sanity and his very life, and the only help she could give was to keep away. He'd done so much, and what had Gerry turned him into? The Ryan who had come here with her today was so different from the one she had laughed with in the summer. Even if he survived, that carefree man would be gone for ever.

Colenso plunged her hands into the orange rays, spreading

her fingers into the red and yellow on either side. These were the colours of flame. Ryan had said it; they would have to burn out the thing that the soul of the chalice had become. Burn it out of his living mind and brain. How could anyone survive that? How could the Makers do this to another human being? Gerry couldn't bear it but she had to watch, and if it was torture for her, she couldn't begin to imagine what it was like for Ryan. Unless he was distanced from himself as she had been, unable to remember or feel anything properly.

That hope vanished almost at once. While Ryan's own nature had been submerged, the spirit of the chalice, or whatever it was, knew that it was fighting now for its life, or for its continued existence. After all the decades of manipulating Baranwen, and the shifts of the past days, now it had truly met an equal opponent. Colenso was more powerful than Gerry had given her credit for. Because Gerry had been so deeply linked to the chalice she could follow the struggle between the two. The Wise Woman was trying to surround her adversary with the fire she held in her hands, while it took every twist and turn that it could to escape. What Rosenwyn was doing was containing it within Ryan's head. It was essential not to let any of that essence escape, as even the smallest portion could start the evil all over again. It had dominated the Guardians, dominated Gerry, and even Justin, powerful as he was, had been no match for it. Gerry was certain now that if Justin had been able to use the Kelegel, he too would have ended up doing its bidding, not his own.

Was Gerry seeing Justin as a victim now? Forget him, she should be thinking only about Ryan. But there was so little of him left in there now. If she could boost him just a bit?

No! This time it was Keyna's voice in Gerry's head, but she hardly recognised the harsh Maiden. Keyna too was within the circle of the flame and her role was to keep Ryan's mind protected from the burning as best she could. Keyna was the last person Gerry would have assigned to shield Ryan, yet she seemed to be throwing all her strength into her task. Reluctantly, Gerry had to give Keyna credit for that, but Ryan was slipping away. He had sunk to the ground, crouching with his arms around his head and although he was not crying aloud, the fire was running round the edge of his awareness and he was in agony. There must be some way Gerry could help him. She had survived through the melting of the gold, when the welding flames had seemed to run through her whole body, and if she had done that, surely he could too.

That's a good thought – hold on to it. This time Gerry couldn't tell whose voice it was, but she took the advice. She conjured the memory of how the fire had blazed through her then, as she stood at the bench in Connor's workshop. It had felt at the time as if it was burning everything out of her, yet afterwards there had been no trace. Not a burn or a scorch mark, not even a scar, like the shiny white ones left afterwards if you catch your hand on the edge of the iron or a shelf in the oven. Physically it was as if it had never happened.

With no conscious intention Gerry crouched down too, wrapping her arms round her own head as if to mirror what Ryan was doing, thinking over and over how she had come unscathed through that torment. An image of cool ice formed round the edge of her thoughts and she heard a shout in a voice charged with emotion. Gerry kept her eyes covered, unable to identify the voice, or whether it had been a shout of triumph or despair. Then she felt strong arms round her, lifting her up.

'You can stand up now, Gerralda,' someone told her. 'It's all over.'

Gerry stood there, swaying a little and keeping her hands across her face till she had a better idea of what she would see when she removed them. Like a child playing hide and seek she made a small gap between two of her fingers and peered through. The rainbow had gone. Two of the village women were supporting Colenso, one holding out a beaker to her. Gerry saw others turning to go back to their homes, the children running between them or pulling at their mothers' skirts, wanting attention now that the serious bit was over. The men who had restrained Gerry and Ryan had left with the rest. Rosenwyn joined Colenso, took a quick drink from the beaker, thanking her helpers and dismissing them graciously. The Makers wanted to be alone to recover from the immense struggle they had undergone. Gerry opened her eyes properly. It was Keyna who had just spoken to her. Her expression was neutral again, and Gerry couldn't connect this cool, distant young woman with the emotion the Maiden had thrown into her part in the fight.

Gerry made herself look away from Keyna and round to where Ryan had been crouching. He was lying on the ground, curled up and not moving. "It's all over". Did that mean he was – she couldn't even frame the thought. She moved towards him step by step, dragging her feet to delay the inevitable, though she knew she had to face it. The evil essence had gone completely. Gerry could tell that. It had been part of her and if there had been even a vestige left it would have spoken to her. Gerry didn't care. All that mattered was Ryan.

She knelt beside him, but his face was hidden. She laid her fingertips on the nearest part of him, his shoulder. What she really wanted was to gather him up in her arms, to cling to his body even if it was too late.

Then the fingers of Ryan's right hand began to uncurl. Gerry forgot caution and gripped every bit of him she could reach.

'Gently,' said the familiar voice. 'I'm a bit fragile.'

'Ryan?' Gerry whispered. 'I thought I'd lost you.'

264

He raised his head and looked at her. The steady brown eyes were his own again and he was smiling.

'I thought that about you too,' he said, 'and it was worth everything to see you looking at me like this.'

'Like what?' Gerry asked.

'Like you want to kiss me.'

Gerry didn't even bother answering. Not caring who might be watching, she reached for Ryan's shoulders, turned him to her and kissed him. Then she opened her eyes to find the three Makers standing in front of them.

Gerry and Ryan scrambled to their feet, but kept their arms round each other.

'Very touching,' said Colenso. Her voice was dry, and she looked weary but also satisfied.

'They both helped.' Rosenwyn was smiling at them, though she too looked weary.

'As they should,' Keyna said, back to her usual self. 'Given it was she who began it all.'

'No,' said Colenso, 'we began it. We drew on powers we did not know enough about.'

'With the best of intentions,' Gerry said.

'Does the end justify the means?' Ryan asked. 'You can talk about that all day if you like. I'm not hanging around. I've got better things to do. And I could remind you that we stopped you poisoning yourselves.'

The three women exchanged looks, but Gerry couldn't gauge their response.

'Please, Ryan, don't wind them up,' she said. 'We need them to send us back, and I don't know if our things are working any longer.'

Rosenwyn was holding a bronze platter. On it lay the lump of gold and the gems that had been the chalice, as well as the ring and the chain.

265

'These are yours,' she said, 'but they have no magic any longer, nor will they ever again.' She moved her hand towards the gold chain and the Bysow a'n gammneves, close to but not touching either. 'These two for now have used all the power that was in them. They have done what they were made for. I cannot tell if they will ever reawaken. Do you still wish to keep them? And to take these back?' She offered them the platter.

'I don't know,' Gerry said. If she did it might be for all the wrong reasons. She turned her head to look at Ryan, sliding her arm down from his back and taking his hand instead.

'Yeah,' he said, looking at the melted gold and the four jewels, then facing the Makers squarely. 'I think we should take them. That'd be fair payment for saving your lives and your precious prestige. We could hang onto them till we decide what to do with them. Wear them, sell them, make them into ornaments. I wouldn't say no to a bit of the gold. I might want a gold ring or two one day.' He looked at Gerry with a question in his eyes, then shook his head. 'Not yet though.' Ryan picked up the contents of the platter in his free hand, then slid them into his pocket. It was surprising what a small space they took up. 'There's only one thing I want now.' He kissed Gerry very lightly. 'I think it's time we went home.' He looked at Rosenwyn. 'Can you fix that?'

Rosenwyn nodded, then smiled at him.

'Yes, we can do that. We will send you back to the point when you left.'

Gerry gripped Ryan's hand tightly. "Home" sounded good. "Time we went home" sounded even better.

'Yes,' she agreed. An unfamiliar feeling had begun within her, and she realised with surprise that it was happiness. 'Let's go home.'

Words and phrases in Cornish used in the book

Bre/Brea	Hill
Bysow a'n gammneves	Ring of the Rainbow, Rainbow ring
Fogou	Underground passage and chamber, stone-lined pronounced 'Foogoo'
Gohi	Wasps
Gwenen	Bees
Kammneves	Rainbow
Kelegel	Chalice
Kelegel a'n gammneves	Chalice of the Rainbow
Tegennow	Jewels
Tegennow a'n gammneves	Jewels of the Rainbow

Character list

In the present:
West Cornwall

Gerry (Gerralda) Hamilton	Library worker and unwitting time traveller
Claudia Mainwaring	Gerry's landlady
Justin Chancellor also known as Iestyn	Claudia's former lover
Mr and Mrs Angove	B & B owners
Francis Trewartha	A jeweller
Alastair Fletcher	Another jeweller
Simon	Mr Fletcher's assistant
Ethan	Deputy in Claudia's gallery
Connor Luscombe	Ryan's brother
Jez	Connor's friend and housemate
Frances	W.P.C. in Penzance

Penzance library

Hilary	Library manager
Debbie	Gerry's friend
Monica Fraser	Not a friend
Ryan Luscombe	Gives computer lessons
Ernie	Agency staff member
Tasha	Works with children

Cornish Studies library

Lowenna	Assistant manager
Graham	A librarian
Mark	Doing work experience

Elsewhere:

Seona	Gerry's great-aunt in Scotland (deceased)
Bill Hamilton	One of Gerry's brothers in Scotland
Martin	Gerry's former boyfriend in London

In the past:
Bees/Gwenen:

Baranwen	Guardian
Morvoren	Guardian (deceased)
Ysella	Guardian
Delenyk	Guardian (deceased)
Hedra	Teacher
Meraud	Healer
Wylmet	Novice (deceased)
Nessa	Beekeeper

Wasps/Gohi:

Cathno	Villager
Elwyn	Villager
Kenver	Villager
Talan	Craftsman

Makers:

Colenso	Wise woman
Rosenwyn	Mother
Keyna	Maiden

Other:
Gregory Chancellor	Justin's brother

Author's note

In this book I have put a fogou (stone chamber) at the top of Chapel Carn Brea. The one described is actually at Carn Euny, a few miles away. I have also put a couple of fictional villages nearby. The courtyard houses depicted were only found in the west of Penwith at the far end of Cornwall, and on the Scilly Isles. They date from the Iron Age, continuing into the Romano-British period. Remains of the foundations of some of these can be seen at Chysauster, Carn Euny, and Mulfra.

The story is set in 2014, when smock tops and leggings or tights were a popular fashion. The Penzance public library was still a two storey building in Morrab Road before its move in 2016 to the lower ground floor in St John's Hall. The Cornish Studies library was in Alma Place in Redruth; it has now become part of Kresen Kernow. None of the fictional staff in either library are based on anyone I've met working there.

Acknowledgements:

I owe heartfelt thanks to Kate Mole, Laura Hodgson, Louise Toft and Liz Allmark for all their enthusiasm and encouragement, which gave me the confidence to get this book into print. Plus extra thanks to Laura for her wonderful cover designs.

I'm grateful to Daphne Chamberlain for support in the earliest days; and to Mark Leyland for useful advice about writing. Then to Inez de Miranda and Steve Blake for critiquing and support; and Teresa Benison for her creative writing classes. To Sarah Westcott for professional critiquing, then Sarah Ash, Deb Adams, and the late John Nash, for valuable practical suggestions. Plus Steph Haxton for recommending TJ Ink. Also Craig Weatherhill, as it was one of his books which introduced me to the courtyard houses of West Penwith.

Finally thanks are due to David, who thought he'd retired from the world of design and print but voluntarily returned to it to help with the technical stuff which is quite incomprehensible to me. Also to Magda and Andy at TJ Ink, then to Jamie at PH Media for dealing with everything so efficiently and cheerfully.

'Guardian of the Stones' is the second book in the Jewels of the Rainbow trilogy
The third one is 'The island outside the world'